Who was he to argue with a de___ __ ___ that?

Smooth, firm, creamy skin yiel___ ___h, molded to his palms as if her body had been made for him. She moaned as he ran the pads of his thumbs over her nipples, each one hardening under his caress, and he lowered his head to trace one pebbled tip with his tongue. The taste of h__ __in __ __ intoxicating . . .

He froze, the mu___ __ __ __ ___ __ re-sponse to her hands__

"You don't like ___ ___ __ __ __ly. She wrapped her je___ __ ___ ___ __ps, encouraging him d__

Oh, he liked it. "Like it. Too much," he panted. Still holding her wrists, he lifted them over her head and sank into her, kissing her breast, her arm, her elbow, her forehead, her neck, and finally, her beautiful, full lips.

"Mayhue's world is magical and great fun."
—*Romantic Times*

"A delightful world of the faerie."
—**Fresh Fiction**

"A lovely getaway to fantasyland and I can be ready to go again in a moment."
—**Fallen Angel Reviews**

"Melissa Mayhue rocks the Scottish Highlands."
—**A Romance Review**

DISCARD

Also by Melissa Mayhue

Thirty Nights with a Highland Husband

Highland Guardian

Soul of a Highlander

A Highlander of Her Own

MELISSA MAYHUE

A Highlander's Destiny

POCKET BOOKS

New York   London   Toronto   Sydney

Pocket Books
A Division of Simon & Schuster, Inc.
1230 Avenue of the Americas
New York, NY 10020

This book is a work of fiction. Names, characters, places, and incidents either are products of the author's imagination or are used fictitiously. Any resemblance to actual events or locales or persons, living or dead, is entirely coincidental.

Copyright © 2010 by Melissa Mayhue

First Pocket Books paperback edition January 2010

POCKET and colophon are registered trademarks of
Simon & Schuster, Inc.

For information about special discounts for bulk purchases,
please contact Simon & Schuster Special Sales at
1-866-506-1949 or business@simonandschuster.com.

The Simon & Schuster Speakers Bureau can bring authors to your
live event. For more information or to book an event contact
the Simon & Schuster Speakers Bureau at 1-866-248-3049
or visit our website at www.simonspeakers.com.

Cover art by Alan Ayers

Manufactured in the United States of America

10   9   8   7   6   5   4   3   2   1

ISBN 978-1-4391-4421-3
ISBN 978-1-4391-5601-8 (ebook)

To my wonderful family, for their support and love.
I don't know how I'd do this without you.
Frank, Marty, Bee, Chris, Nick, Megan and Chandra—
my life is enriched by each and every one of you.

And

To the Soapbox Divas, Rena Marks and Kirsten
Richard. Through their own unbelievable difficulties
and tragedies, these talented ladies have been there for
me, pushing me to make my stories the best
they can be. You guys are the best!

Acknowledgments

My sincere thanks to the following readers who won the contest to name Sarah and Ian's twins:

Laura L. Curtis
Tiffany George
Renee Jaramillo
Loes Molenkamp

Aislinn and Alexander McCullough thank you!

Thank you to Nick Mayhue for his computer expertise and very patient answers to all my technical questions.

Thank you to the security professionals at Denver International Airport for their technical input.

Many thanks for all the support and friendship at Colorado Romance Writers and especially to my favorite book-signing buddies: Lynda Hilburn, Tara Janzen, Elaine Levine, and Robin D. Owens.

Thank you to my wonderful agent, Elaine Spencer, for always having the answers to all my questions.

And, as always, a huge thank-you to the best editor anywhere, Megan McKeever. I am eternally grateful for the pleasure of working with you!

Prologue

~～～⌐

"Watch your step, Adira, there's another body here at the foot of the stairs."

For a moment, Adira Ré Alyn ignored the hand Flynn Dá Anan extended to assist her in her descent. But that moment was long enough to remind him of his place. That and the haughty look she sent his way.

"If you please, mistress." He continued to hold his hand out, but he'd lowered his eyes. As he should.

"Very well." With a nod of her head, she accepted his assistance.

It was important she maintain the distance between herself and her servants. It was bad enough she'd had to rely on Flynn and Dermond so heavily since Reynard's disappearance. Apparently that reliance had given Flynn the impression he was important to her. Indispensable.

He needed to be taught the fallacy of that particular assumption. Quickly.

Neither of Reynard's lapdogs were of any consequence when compared to her. Not in this world. Not any longer. They were all Faerie full-bloods, but she was also a Courtesan of Nuada and the acknowledged mate to Reynard Servans. As such, in his absence she ruled their sect in his stead. One day, they would all acknowledge her as their queen.

She had no doubt there were some who worked behind her back to grab that power from her. She could feel it. But she would deal with them all in good time.

Somehow.

What she needed was an edge. Something to consolidate the authority in her hands until Reynard returned.

If he returned.

No one had seen him since he'd gone on his last foray to find a female descendant of the Fae. A female who could lead them back home to the Realm of Faerie and end their exile on the Mortal Plain.

"This way, mistress." Flynn bowed his head, averting his eyes.

Good. He'd gotten the message. At least for now.

Pushing an errant lock of long red hair from her face, she followed carefully.

"You're certain your man saw to it that the Mortals were trapped before the explosion?"

"Absolutely, mistress."

Adira didn't miss Flynn's shifty sideways glance. His loyalty wasn't to be trusted. Not that it mattered anymore. Now that she knew how The Renewal was accomplished, she could handle all future arrangements for herself if necessary.

She had never suspected The Renewal was such a simple process. It only required bringing about the untimely death of a Mortal to release the life essence she so desperately needed. Without that essence, she would wither and age.

But not die. She would never die.

That was the fate that hateful bitch, the Earth Mother, and her High Council of the Realm of Faerie had decreed for the Nuadians when they'd been banished to the Mortal Plain. Banished from all contact with their magic and the Fountain of Souls.

The thought of living for untold centuries as a creature decrepit with age, weak and wrinkled, was beyond any horrors Adira could imagine. No, that was not a fate she would willingly accept.

Better to hasten the deaths of these pitiful Mortals. Force the life essence from their bodies before it was fated to leave and savor the rich flow of power and renewal.

"Are there none left alive?" Adira grew more irritable with each lifeless body they found, her suspicion growing that Flynn's puppet had completely botched the job.

Though he didn't answer her question, the stiffening of his back told her she'd touched on his own concern. He needed the life essence as much as she.

"Down this corridor, mistress. We must hurry. The police will be arriving any time now."

As if she cared about any Mortal authority figures. Thanks to the Earth Mother's decree, no full-blooded

Fae could be killed here on the Mortal Plain. Just as they could not harm anyone. Oh, they could reach out a hand to stroke, to play, to love. But let a single intent of harming another flit through their thoughts and their bodies became transparent as smoke. The Fae could neither commit nor experience violence in the Mortal World.

A fist sent out in anger would pass right through any person or object. Just as any weapon aimed at them would pass through their bodies as if through a shaft of light.

No, she didn't fear the police.

Still, the authorities could interfere unduly, so she picked up her pace. She nodded and followed Flynn's tall form through the darkened building, carefully stepping over the twisted metal and body parts, heading toward the room where the men were to have been detained.

"Shoddy work, Flynn. Wasteful."

His lack of response was wise. What excuse could he possibly give? He'd been sloppy with the compulsion he'd placed on the Mortal. Obviously the man had needed more specific instructions than he'd received.

Since violence was impossible for the Nuadian Fae, using Mortals to accomplish what they couldn't do themselves was an inconvenient necessity. So many Mortals possessed weak spirits and even weaker minds. The Nuadians only needed to find one of those and, with a simple mental push, replace the Mortal's will with their own in order to accomplish whatever they wanted.

Easy enough to do, but it required a great expenditure of energy, which was why she preferred to delegate that particular task to her subordinates.

That and the pain one could experience if the Mortal chosen had a stronger will and fought the compulsion.

Adira shuddered at the memory of such an experience far in the past.

No, she much preferred to delegate.

In this case, Flynn had directed one of the weaker Mortals to detonate an explosive in this research facility. The location was secluded enough that they should have had time to make their way through the building before anyone could arrive.

The only problem was that the Mortal Flynn had chosen had used too large an explosive and most people inside the building had died instantly or within minutes.

That did her no good at all.

Her only hope now lay in the men who had been locked in the outer room. Their injuries would be substantial enough that they likely wouldn't survive, either, but their distance from the center of the explosion should mean it would take a bit longer for them to die.

And that was key to Adira filling her needs.

If she wasn't there, physically present, when their souls unwillingly departed their bodies, she couldn't absorb the energy of the life essence that was given off by that process.

Ahead of her, Flynn punched a code into the electronic lock, pressed his shoulder to the door and, with a superhuman effort, shoved it open.

Adira stepped inside to the certain knowledge that even here the damage was greater that it should have been.

"It appears the instructions you gave your little pet

were unclear." How hard it was to control the disappointment, the desperation she couldn't allow to filter through her voice.

Flynn prodded at the rubble in the room, raising more of the fine, powdery dust that covered everything.

"Adira! Over here. One yet lives."

He'd found one! The news brought her such joy she chose to ignore even his familiar use of her name.

Nearing the Mortal, she could see it would be only a matter of moments. Not long to wait now. Quickly she crouched over him, eager to breathe in the essence that would erupt from his body as his life force was torn away.

But the uncooperative fool still struggled to hang on to his miserable life. He lifted one bloody hand to her leg, capturing the hem of her white designer pants in his weakening grip.

"Am I dying?" he asked through mangled lips.

"Yes, you are." She purred her response, her excitement growing.

His eyes flickered shut and she waited impatiently for signs of his end. Instead he stubbornly clung to his soul a little longer, his hand sliding up her leg, leaving a bloody trail on the expensive fabric.

"Are you an angel?"

His voice was weaker and the knowledge of what she would shortly receive from him emboldened her, excited her, drawing a sharp burst of laughter that surprised even her.

"You may think of me as the angel of death if you like." She lifted his hand from her leg, taking one long finger into her mouth, curling her tongue around the digit, sucking.

Adira barely noticed his eyes open wide in shock, remaining open even when the life behind them ebbed away.

Her vision faded as her attention centered on the intense physical sensations gripping her body. The tang of copper and salt permeated her senses, sending an electric jangle through her limbs. The feeling intensified, as if her veins inflated inside her body, growing larger and larger until she felt as though she might burst, filled to overflowing with an unfamiliar energy coursing through her.

It felt of power, pure and simple, so concentrated she almost missed the Mortal's last breath and the opportunity to capture the essence she had waited for so impatiently.

And then it was hers.

With one deep breath she could feel her skin smoothing, her vitality returning, even as the strange new energy swirled through her consciousness.

"Are you well, mistress?"

Adira glanced up to Flynn, surprised at the concern in his voice. Even in the dusty gloom of this room, the outline of his body fairly sparkled, as if she viewed him through foreign eyes. Eyes that saw so sharply, every strand of his long golden hair stood out individually.

"Of course I'm all right," she answered, accepting his hand to help her stand, her legs unexpectedly shaky. She couldn't remember anything like this happening before.

As she rose to her feet, the first sirens sounded.

Irritation raged through her mind. The Mortals couldn't harm her, but it meant an inconvenience she didn't wish to encounter.

The desire to vent her frustration was strong. She drew back her foot to kick the corpse of the aggravating Mortal whose pitiful, futile struggle to live had delayed her.

Her blow landed in the man's side with a solid *thwack*, throwing her off balance and shooting pain through her toe. She grabbed for the wall to steady herself, her mind reeling with the shock of what she'd just experienced.

It wasn't possible!

Her foot should have gone straight through the man. Where had this new ability come from?

Her mind raced, searching through recent memories for something, anything, to explain what was happening to her.

One action stood out in her mind.

Could it be the Mortal's blood? It was only after she'd tasted the blood that she'd felt the wave of power wash over her.

"I believe we can still make it out of here through the back unnoticed if we hurry, mistress." Flynn spoke from his position at the end of the hallway, his hand lifted to motion her forward.

He hadn't seen!

She hurried to him, following his lead mutely, her mind otherwise occupied.

This was it, the edge she'd prayed for. She wouldn't need to hunt weak-minded Mortals to do her bidding any longer. She could pick up a weapon, set her own explosives, do whatever she wanted. She could create an entire army of her own faithful Fae to do her bidding, each with the ability to battle on the Mortal Plain.

With power such as this, no other Nuadian would ever be able to challenge her. She wouldn't just be queen of their sect, she could demand the obeisance of all the Nuadians inhabiting the Mortal World.

And all thanks to the blood of one obstinate Mortal.

She wanted to laugh out loud at the pure, blind luck of the situation. She had thought only to taunt the dying man and look what she'd discovered. What wonderful fortune smiled on her this day!

Possibilities and plans crowded her mind, each more brilliant and compelling than the one before until at last she and Flynn reached the back of the building. She slipped through the door and a new idea pushed aside everything else.

If a pitifully weak Mortal's blood could give her this kind of power, what might she receive from the blood of a Fae?

Chapter 1

❧

"Is Rosie still having those awful dreams?"

Cate MacKiernan looked up from piping a sugary border onto the big birthday cake in front of her. She nodded her head in response to her sister-in-law's question, gathering her thoughts and steeling her emotions. The memory of the fear she'd seen in her seven-year-old's eyes brought a lump to her throat that she fought to force away.

"They've grown more frequent since we saw you last."

"Have you any ideas as to what's causing them?" Mairi MacKiernan Navarro ran her finger around the edge of the bowl on the table between the two women, scooping up frosting in the process.

"None at all." Cate tossed her pastry bag into the sink with more force than was necessary, spattering its contents up onto the surrounding marble.

They'd eliminated spicy foods, altered Rosie's bedtime, put a night-light in her room, and even limited her television time to only her most favorite feel-good, happy stories. Still, the child suffered through increasingly frequent night terrors.

"We've tried everything we can think of except taking her to a therapist."

"And?" Mairi's eyebrows rose and she shrugged her shoulders as she licked another gob of blue frosting from her finger.

"Are you kidding me? We can't take her to a therapist. Rosie starts sharing all her stories about Faerie ancestors and time travel and we'll all be living in padded rooms."

"No," Mairi scoffed. "I dinna mean a regular Mortal therapist. I was thinking more along the lines of one of those Faeries you were just talking about."

"I don't know if that's such a good—"

Mairi cut her off. "Think about it. Dallyn was able to help Ramos. And what of Pol? He adores Rosie. You ken he'd do anything in his power to help her."

"It's that whole *power* thing that worries me. Besides, I haven't seen any major improvement in Jesse's attitude since he got home, and he said he spent some time with Dallyn. Stop that!" Cate pulled the bowl from Mairi's hands and put it in the sink, running water into the leftover frosting. "You'll make yourself sick if you keep eating that stuff."

"I wondered about Jess. We've no seen him since we returned from our own trip to Scotland. I'd hoped his visit there would have helped him get over that hateful woman." Mairi leaned forward in her chair and flipped her long blond braid over her shoulder. "I never did understand what he saw in that awful Lara. To my way of thinking, their breakup was the best thing that ever happened to him."

Cate felt exactly the same way. "I totally agree. But it doesn't matter what we think. It's not even like it's the first time some woman has been after him because his last name is Coryell." Even she hadn't been immune to that problem back in her dating days.

"Is he in love with her, do you think?"

Cate sighed and leaned back against the sink. "I asked him that very question. He just shrugged it off with one of his typical Jesse lines about how easy it was to throw that word around, especially for people who didn't have any idea what love really meant. So, no, I don't think he was in love with Lara, but for some reason I can't see, he took her walking away particularly hard. He's really disillusioned this time."

"When you think on it, Cate, it's no really so hard to understand. Time is passing him by and his Fae blood is calling out for his Soulmate."

"I don't know. Maybe." Cate wiped the last traces of frosting from the countertop and rinsed out the dishcloth, hanging it over the faucet.

"Now that I think on it . . ." Mairi straightened in her seat, her blue eyes widening. "I've just had meself a wild idea. We've the Faerie gifts, you and I. Why can *we* no do something for Jess? Between the two of us, there should be a way we can help him find the one woman meant for him."

"Absolutely not!" Cate leaned back against the kitchen counter, staring at her sister-in-law. "After all we've been through with the Faerie magic, you, of all people, should know better than to even suggest such a thing."

"Perhaps yer right," Mairi conceded with a sigh.

"Perhaps?" Cate could only shake her head. The Faerie magic had sent both women on trips through time that had very nearly cost them their lives. Even now they weren't sure whether or not Mairi's adventures had somehow altered history. "There's no *perhaps* to it. The magic of the Fae is unpredictable and uncontrollable. It's way too dangerous to use for something like finding Jesse a girlfriend."

"Well, I wasn't thinking of just any girlfriend, but I suppose you've a point about the danger." Mairi tapped her fingernail against the shiny wooden tabletop. "So, what about some plain old matchmaking, then? We know lots of people. Surely we can come up with someone to take his mind off that little harlot he was dating. What's the harm in that?"

Cate sighed as she dropped into a chair across from Mairi. "You mean other than the grief we'll both take from our husbands if they find out what we're thinking of doing?" She felt a smile tugging at the corners of her mouth, mirroring Mairi's. "I don't suppose there's any harm in trying that. And you are absolutely right that Jesse needs a woman. Who knows? Maybe we'll even get lucky and find one who'll actually make him happy. It's about time his life settled down."

Rosie MacKiernan leaned her chin into her hands as she sat on the floor, her back against the wall, listening in on the conversation of the two women in the kitchen.

How could anyone as smart as her mommy and Auntie Mairi not realize they had it all wrong? The Faerie magic might be unpredictable, but it wasn't dangerous. Grandpapa Pol had told her it was like a living creature. Tell the magic what you want, and it finds a way.

You simply needed to be very, very careful of the words you said when you told it what you wanted.

Auntie Mairi was right about one thing, though. As a descendant of the Fae, Uncle Jesse didn't need to find just any old woman. He had to find his True Love, the other half of his soul. Only then would he be happy.

Rosie scrubbed at her eyes, trying to make up her mind about what she should do.

Grandpapa Pol had told her it was a very bad thing to use the magic on anyone against their will, so maybe she should try to find out what Uncle Jesse really wanted.

It would be easy enough to set him on the path to find the one meant for him, but she wasn't sure she should. That path was dark and scary, and if he wasn't ready for it, he could get hurt really bad.

She knew for a fact because it was what she saw in the awful dreams she had so often now. Dreams of something mean and terrible, a huge evil blackness creeping over the whole world, covering everything in blood. She'd told Mommy that much about her nightmares.

What she *hadn't* told Mommy was who she'd seen standing directly in the path of all the nasty evil.

Uncle Jesse.

But truly, she was getting so tired standing in between the two, holding back the evil until Uncle Jesse was ready to deal with it.

Grandpapa Pol had also told her she was very special

because even though she was a little girl, she had a powerful, ancient soul. Rosie just hoped that didn't mean she was supposed to know the answers to stuff because she certainly didn't.

It didn't make sense that the Faeries would expect her to have all the answers. Even Mortals understood it took time to learn, and until you did you went to the grown-ups and they told you what to do.

Her hand flew to her face, covering her open mouth when the obvious came to her.

Maybe she didn't need to know stuff! Maybe she only needed to ask the people who did know.

Leaning her head back against the wall, she smiled for the first time all day. She felt better already, just having made up her mind.

At the sound of Beast's first excited bark, she sat up straight, straining to listen for what the dog had already heard.

The roar of a motorcycle in the distance drew nearer.

Rosie jumped up and pushed her tousled golden curls behind her ears, joy racing through her little body.

"Oh, goody," she whispered as she raced for the door. Uncle Jesse had arrived.

Jesse Coryell slung a long leg over his brand-new Harley and hung his helmet on the handlebar. The gentle mountain breeze felt good blowing through his dark copper hair after the confinement of the stifling safety device.

His new Bertha didn't have the speed of his old Triumph Sprint RS, but he'd take care of that as soon as he had a chance to do a few modifications of his own.

With one last appreciative glance, he turned his back on his shiny new baby just in time to catch the full weight of his favorite real-life baby, his precocious little niece, Rosie.

With her halo of blond curls blowing in the breeze, she hurtled full speed into his arms, clasping her little hands behind his neck as he stood and lifted her into the air.

Her grin of welcome alone was worth the trip up here. The loud smack of her kiss on his cheek simply served to seal the deal.

"I missed you, Uncle Jesse," she squealed, squeezing her little arms around him. "You've been gone so long."

"I missed you, too, Tinker Bell." He hefted her over to one arm as he made his way up the curving stone path toward the big front porch, wary of stumbling over the massive wolfhound bounding up, demanding his attention. "Where are the boys?" His two nephews should be around here somewhere.

"They're out at the horses with Da and Uncle Ramos." Rosie tilted her head and gave him a flirty little grin before squashing his head in another bear hug. "You're all mine for right now!"

If she'd already mastered a look like that at seven, he pitied his poor sister and her husband when this kid turned sixteen. Of course, with him for an uncle and Connor MacKiernan as a dad, it wasn't exactly like the local boys stood much of a chance in getting to first base. It would, however, be entertaining to be around to watch the overprotective Highlander try to manage his daughter as a teen. Just the idea brought a smile to his lips.

"Come on, let's get this show on the road." He grabbed her arms and twirled her up on his shoulders, enjoying her carefree giggles, losing himself for a moment in her happiness.

If only he could stay lost there.

But he knew it wouldn't last. The gloomy depression, the lost feeling of having nothing waiting for him at the end of the day would overtake him again. The anxiety of some disaster looming on his horizon would eat away at his happiness soon enough. It was only a matter of time.

Mairi and Cate waited on the steps to greet him, twin looks of concern masking both their faces.

Just exactly what he'd been afraid of and the very reason he almost hadn't come up here today. A whole day of family pity was more than he could stomach.

But he knew Cate had put so much work into organizing this birthday bash for him. All his family would be here. He simply couldn't bring himself to disappoint his sister.

"It's okay," Rosie whispered in his ear, one little hand patting his shoulder as if she read his thoughts.

Jesse made a conscious effort to relax his shoulders in preparation for playing the part his family expected of him.

"How's my favorite witchy woman?" he teased as he leaned down to kiss his sister's cheek.

"Concerned about how you are," she returned, not fooled by his act in the least.

"Happy birthday, Jess." Mairi held her arms out, her expression telling him she wasn't taken in either.

His best bet with these two perceptive women was to forge ahead as if everything was fine. One show of weakness and they'd be all over him, mothering him half to death.

He lifted Rosie off his shoulders and stood her on her feet before giving Mairi the hug she waited for. "I heard you and Ramos were in Scotland. Sorry I missed you at Ian and Sarah's."

If he could distract her early, perhaps he wouldn't have to face any questions about where he'd been. Questions he didn't plan to answer. No one needed to know he'd spent the last four months in the Realm of Faerie, training with Dallyn's Elite Guard.

No more than they needed to know about the property he'd bought in the Scottish Highlands and his plans to move there. Not yet, at least. There would be plenty of time to discuss that in the coming weeks.

No, diverting her attention seemed a much better idea for now.

"Did you get to see the twins?" He grinned, hoping to disarm any prying she might attempt.

"Yes," Mairi answered slowly, pausing as if she had wanted the conversation to go elsewhere. Her blue gaze bore into him a moment longer before she continued. "They're adorable babies. Sarah and Ian are planning on bringing them over for a visit next month."

"Did you get to see them, Uncle Jesse? Alexander and Aislinn, I mean?" Rosie tugged at his leg. "We have pictures of them on Mommy's computer if you want to come see them with me."

"Okay, Tink, give me just a minute and then you

can show me the photos. Are the guys still down at the barn?"

Cate nodded, holding open the screen door for them all to enter. "Robert got here about half an hour ago. They're all down admiring the new colts. Dad and Cody picked Cass up at the airport this morning. They should be here any time now. You can either go on down there or hang with Rosie while we finish up in the kitchen."

His sister had gone out all out to make sure the whole family would be at his birthday party. Since he hadn't seen his dad and brothers for months, he was pleased they'd be here. And Robert, Connor's friend they'd brought forward from the thirteenth century in order to save his life, happened to be one of Jesse's closest friends now.

Still, whether to go outside or remain with his little niece was an easy choice. He was much less likely to run into any uncomfortable questions about how he'd spent his last few months from Rosie.

He allowed his niece to take his hand and lead him into Cate's office. As soon as he sat, Rosie perched on his knee and opened up the files with the photos she wanted to show him. Not for the first time, he marveled at how quickly she learned to do things he'd expect of an older child. Seven going on seventeen.

"Here." She pushed the mouse over to him as she hopped off his lap. "You can look through them by just rolling that thing on the mouse."

Barely a minute passed before he became aware of the child staring at him.

"What?" he asked without taking his eyes from the screen.

"You okay, Uncle Jesse? You look sad."

Rosie leaned onto the desk a couple of feet away, her elbows propped up, her chin cradled in her palms. Her penetrating blue eyes bore into him, making him feel as if she could see to the depths of his soul.

As if she knew the turmoil living there, the uncertainty that had driven him to Scotland and beyond, all the way to the Realm of Faerie, searching for answers.

"I'm fine, baby girl."

The disbelief clear in her arched eyebrows reminded him so much of Cate, he had to bite back the urge to laugh. Instead he continued to page through the photos of the adorable babies on the screen in front of him.

"You save people, don't you, Uncle Jesse? Like the heroes in stories."

He turned his attention to her fully, finding her gaze just as piercing as before.

"I don't know about any hero stuff. Saving people is what your granddad's company is all about. We all do our best. Your daddy, the uncles, me, all of us. One day, maybe you and Dougie and even little Cory will work there, too."

"Yeah." She lifted a hand and waved her little fingers as if to brush away all the words she didn't find important. "But you? If there was some lady in big trouble and only you could help save her, would you do it?"

He smiled at her earnest expression now. Cate must be drowning the kid in romantic fairy tales. "That's what I do, Tink."

He reached out to tweak her on the end of her turned-up nose, but she pulled away, her head tilted, her brows drawn together in seriousness.

"Even if it was really dangerous and scary and you could get hurt bad?"

"Even then."

Her frown melted and she crawled back up into his lap, snagging an arm around his neck. "Do you like what you do, Uncle Jesse?"

"I wouldn't give it up for anything." A truth none of the women he'd dated ever seemed to understand. Except the ones who didn't care and only wanted their name on the insurance papers so they'd have a steady supply of his money should anything happen to him. Like Lara. "My work means everything to me. It's more important to me than anything in the world. Well, anything except you and the boys, that is."

He ran his finger down the slope of her nose and poked the tip into the middle of her belly, holding on to her as she flopped over backward, giggling.

After a moment, she snuggled back into his lap, her hands on either side of his face, her expression once again serious. "You need to go after your destiny. It's time."

"Time for what? What are you talking about?"

Rosie's blue gaze bore into him, almost unnerving in its intensity.

"You just got to find your destiny, Uncle Jesse. Believe in your destiny and fight real hard and then everything will be okay."

"My destiny, huh?"

She nodded her little head, the curls bouncing around, reminding him more of a Christmas angel than the New Age guru she'd sounded like a moment before. He'd have to remember to give Cate grief about letting her kids spend way too much unsupervised time playing those RPG fantasy world video games.

Sliding out of his lap, Rosie tugged on his hand. "Let's go to the barn and I'll show you the baby horses. One of them has spots on his legs and looks just like he's wearing socks."

Once again he allowed the little girl to drag him along, this time out the back door and across the lawn toward the barns.

Destiny.

Maybe that was what he needed. To search for what meant the most to him rather than simply allowing life to toss him around like a leaf floating in water.

He'd always known he wanted to help those who couldn't help themselves. It was why he'd fallen so easily into working for his father's company. It was why he was so good at what he did.

The last few months had shown him a variation on how he could help. A new path he could walk. A path that could lead to a safer world. Maybe that was the whole key.

Figure out who he was, what his destiny was, and that lonely hole in his soul would be filled at last.

Out of the mouths of babes, as the saying went.

Chapter 2

"This whole thing's a con, Carol. I told you it was a waste of twenty bucks. Fortune-teller, my ass."

Destiny Noble kept any retort to herself. Even though the man's attitude and words stung, she couldn't afford to say anything that might make the big jerk any angrier than he already was. She needed this job.

So she bit her tongue to stay silent as he pulled on his wife's arm, dragging her from the tent where Destiny did business.

Still, she couldn't let Carol walk away without adding one more thing.

"You're right to be concerned about that spot under your arm. You should get it checked out right away."

The woman's head snapped around, her eyes large. And though she didn't answer, she nodded her head in understanding.

"Just ignore her, honey. They only say that kind of crap to scare you." The husband's voice rang with protective defiance as the tent flap fell shut.

Destiny let out a deep breath and stood, stretching her spine after a half hour of nonstop hunching on that uncomfortable little wooden stool. In spite of the ache in her back, in spite of the irritating jangle of the fake coins attached to her cheap gypsy costume, even in spite of the man's attitude, she felt good about what she'd just done. That woman would go see her doctor, and that visit would save her life.

After all, Carol had never once mentioned any spot under her arm. Destiny had seen it in her vision.

She rarely spoke the whole truth to the people who came into her tent to have their fortunes told. She'd learned right away, when she began doing this, that for the most part people didn't really want the truth. They wanted a fairy-tale happy-ever-after version of life. For twenty bucks, she gave it to them. But sometimes—like now—the truth was so important, she couldn't resist.

She'd been able to see things from the time she was a child. Her mother had always claimed it was a gift inherited from her father because he was an enchanted Faerie.

Destiny shook her head in disgust at the memory.

Her mother, Rainbow, had been a true hippie, a child of the Generation of Love, raised in a commune by parents who'd worshipped nature. The experience had left her with some unusual ideas and practices. And then, of course, there was that little drinking problem she'd developed after the *Faerie* had up and left just before she'd learned she was pregnant with their third child.

Maybe thinking he was a magical being forced to leave her to protect his family had somehow eased her pain in those last years.

Destiny remembered her father, a tall blond man with serious almond-shaped green eyes identical to her own, striding out to the field with her younger brother, determined to teach the boy archery and swordplay.

"Bastard," she whispered, slamming shut the door on her memories.

How any decent man could just walk away after twelve years of marriage and two kids was beyond her.

Even from her deathbed, Rainbow Noble had clung to the Faerie story. "Be thankful for the gifts of your heritage," she'd told her kids.

Gifts? Seeing what was going to happen to other people had always seemed way more curse than gift to Destiny. Besides, it was a fluke that it even worked sometimes.

Like now, when she really needed to see what would happen? Her *gift* was absolutely no help at all.

If only she could see her own future as well as she could see that of others. But that wasn't the case. For her, or anyone of importance to her, the future was hidden in heavy curtains of dark mist. Only in her dreams was anything personal revealed to her.

It was one of those dreams that had brought her here, to this tiny tent tucked away in a far corner of the grounds of this Renaissance Faire. She'd seen herself working here, in this very tent, when the man who would lead her to her sister walked into her life.

She'd do anything that could help her find Leah, even put her faith in those stupid visions. She'd pay any price. Her time, her money, her pride—none of it meant anything compared to her younger sister's safety.

She tapped her foot impatiently, snatching a quick glance at the small clock she kept under the draping cloth of her table next to her purse and laptop shoulder bag. Only one more hour until she could leave here and get back into town to her little motel room. One more hour until she could check her email to see if she'd had any response to her plea for help.

Of course, it was silly to think a big organization like Coryell Enterprises would pay the least bit of attention to one lone woman seeking a missing teenager. But she'd seen the company's name in her dream, three nights in a row.

That was always how it worked. The dreams would return, over and over, until she either acted on them or what she had dreamed came to pass. Then, and only then, a new dream would come, like the next episode in a television series.

And as much as she hated to admit it, her dreams had never been wrong.

It had been as if she were standing on the sidewalk in front of their offices. People jostled all around her, bumping into her, until she looked up and read the large black metal lettering printed on the brown concrete building. The company's name and address were clearly displayed.

She'd written asking for help the very next morning, giving them her email address as contact. When she'd gotten no answer, she'd written again.

After that second letter, she'd had the next dream. The dream about *him*.

Big and tall, dressed all in black, *he* would come to help her. She hoped he'd show up before it was too late for her younger sister.

The emotions slammed into her at the thought of Leah, forcing her to drop back down heavily to the hard wooden stool. The memories flooded her mind as she fought against the fear and depsression threatening to overwhelm her.

She had been twelve when Leah was born. From the moment Rainbow brought the new baby home from the hospital, Destiny had felt a strong connection to her sister. That connection had intensified over the years, and when Rainbow's drinking had taken over their lives, Destiny had slid naturally into the role of mother to her younger sister.

After Rainbow's death, Destiny had come to feel as if Leah was her only reason to go on. They'd managed just fine for the past six years. Leah was such an innocent, her nose always buried in one of her books. Never any trouble, she did well in school, even if she didn't make friends easily.

That was how Destiny had known from the moment she'd come home to find their apartment empty that someone had taken her sister. The authorities refused to see anything but a teenage runaway.

From the first, Destiny had known they were wrong.

Then came the dreams, at first only bits and pieces too shattered to be truly helpful. Leah's voice calling her name. Dark, shadowy figures. When she'd realized there were hints to locations in those dreams, she'd sold all their belongings and started hunting Leah herself.

That had been over a month ago, and sometimes she wondered if she'd ever see . . .

Destiny forced out her breath in a deep, shuddering sigh, wiping her damp cheeks.

No. She wouldn't allow herself to even consider that possibility. She'd contacted the company in her dream. She'd seen the shadowed figure of the man who would come to help her. It was only a matter of time. For now, she had to be strong. For Leah.

Outside her tent, she heard hushed voices and the rustle of feet a moment before the flap whipped open and two elderly women peeked inside.

Pasting a patient smile on her face, she lifted her hand in greeting.

"Please, come in. Welcome to the House of Destiny."

Chapter 3

❦

"What do you think you're doing? We don't throw anything away here." Lovey Hamilton peered disapprovingly over the top rim of her blue plastic readers at the younger woman occupying the desk next to her.

"Well, this one we do. It's another one of those 'please help me' letters from that wacko."

Jesse halted his steps outside the stairway exit, very much aware of the fact that neither of the women behind the reception desks knew he was there. He could easily turn and disappear unnoticed down the hallway to his own office.

But something in what he saw called to him. Perhaps it was only Lovey's irritation and her younger counterpart's arrogance that pulled him forward. Whatever the impetus, he made his way in their direction.

"Morning, gorgeous." He strode behind the older

woman's desk to drop a friendly kiss on the top of her white curls, his standard greeting for as long as he had worked at his father's company.

Lovey had been Clint Coryell's original office girl way back when he'd first started the company, and in spite of her seniority, she chose to remain at a desk out here in the main lobby for all these years.

"About time you got back." Her no-nonsense attitude might fool some, but the color in her cheeks gave her away. "He's in, but he's on the phone. You want to wait?"

"No, ma'am." Jesse sauntered over to lean against the filing cabinet behind the desks. He'd just seen his dad up at Cate's this past weekend. There was no reason to bother him now. "I'm not really back for another week. Just thought I'd stop by the office to check in and see what's waiting for me. Couldn't resist coming in to steal a kiss from my favorite girl."

Lovey rolled her eyes as she always did. "Cut the crap, junior. I left my hip waders at home."

He smiled in spite of himself. No one could cross verbal swords like Lovey. Of course, she was thirty years his senior and as much mother some days as friend. "You wound me, Lovey."

She snorted a reply, but he'd seen her smile as she'd turned back around to her paperwork, actively ignoring him.

A casual glance over at the new girl's trash showed the crumpled letter that had been the topic of discussion as he'd arrived.

Not that he was really interested.

The majority of Coryell Enterprises' work originated from government contracts, both U.S. and foreign. They were contractors, pure and simple. Their missions to rescue captives were covert, under the radar and rarely publicized. They operated alongside or in lieu of various military entities and government agencies. Taking on a personal client was rare.

More important, all of it was negotiated and arranged by someone else. Not his job. He didn't get involved until it was time to plan the mission and carry it out. The paperwork, the back-office dealings, all that bored him to death.

So the letter in the trash didn't concern him in the least. Not his problem.

He had straightened, with the intent of making his way to his office to do just what he'd said, when one last glance at the ivory-colored stationery in the wire basket stopped him in his tracks.

A word on the bottom of the page leaped out at him, a part of the signature. Without thought, he reached for it, accidentally shoving the new girl's chair in the process of snagging the missive from the trash.

"Hey!" she yelped, her chair rolling across the plastic floor protector, stopping with a little bump as its wheels hit the carpet.

"What's this?" He found himself smoothing the paper, eyes fastened to the plain type, not waiting for her answer.

The new girl's head swiveled back and forth between him and Lovey, as if she were trying to decide what to do.

"Susan, this is Jesse Coryell. Since his name's on the front of the building, you might want to answer."

Not even the lure of the letter in his hands could keep him from looking up at the sarcasm in Lovey's voice. His dad always did say the woman could cut to the chase better than some of their overpaid negotiators.

"It's just a letter from some nut job whose teenage sister ran away from home. Coryell Enterprises doesn't handle problems like that."

"What makes you so sure she's a . . . nut job, as you call it?" He chose not to even consider how he knew the author of the letter was a woman, but he did know it. He felt it.

"Well, go ahead and read it for yourself. She says she was supposed to contact us. No reference as to who or why. Just a *supposed to*. There's . . . there's not even a return address or a phone number or anything. Just some fakey-looking email address."

He scanned the letter in his hands. Susan was probably right. Typewritten, no personal contact information of any sort. Only the email address that had snagged his attention: destiny@universalmail.com.

Jesse stared at the blank television screen, absently swirling the crystalline green liquid in his glass as he leaned back in his favorite recliner.

Just as he'd told his friend Robbie earlier this evening, it was a weird coincidence and nothing more, right? A fluke. So what if the woman's name was Destiny? It didn't mean anything.

So why couldn't he get the crumpled letter out of his mind?

He rose and drained the last of the heady ambrosia in his cup, reminding himself that this stuff wasn't normal alcohol. This was Faerie Nectar, a special birthday gift from Dallyn Al Lyre, High General of the Realm of Faerie. His new part-time boss.

Whoa.

Jesse stood very still, one hand grasping the back of the large leather recliner to steady his step. He'd felt just fine until he'd stood up. *He* still felt fine. It was the world that had suddenly gone tilting off-kilter, his brain and his body on total disconnect.

He should have remembered this. While alcohol had almost no effect on him at all, this stuff had put him on his ass for the first time in his life not three months ago. It had also given him his first experience with worshipping the porcelain gods, as Robbie liked to say.

He looked down at the odd metallic decanter holding the remaining liquid and felt a ridiculous grin creep over his face.

Enough of that stuff for tonight. The dizzy, happy early effects were fine. But if he had any more, the morning after would suck. One go-around with that experience was one too many for his taste.

"Should I take that silly grin to mean yer in yer cups?"

Jesse slowly turned his head, the world flowing around him as his eyes searched for a body to go with the voice. At length he located the source in the doorway to the hall: his houseguest, Robert MacQuarrie.

"Never mind. You've no a need to confirm or deny what I can see with my own two eyes."

Shaking his head seemed to help bring the big Scot into better focus. "It's that damn Faerie Nectar. Sneaks up on my body faster than it does my brain, I guess. Did you need something?"

Robbie leaned against the doorjamb, his mouth curled in a friendly smile. "It does my heart good to see you Children of the Fae fall prey to Mortal sins now and again. I only came out to see if you'd drunk yer way beyond fashin' yerself over that wee letter you rescued from the trash bin today."

"Yeah," Jesse lied. "Forgot all about it already."

"Aye? Is that so? Then why might you be holding it in yer hand?"

Jesse looked down at the paper he held, all the while shaking his head in denial. "I was just gonna throw it away." Instead he shoved it in his back pocket.

"Well, my friend, you'll do as you want, but I still say you could satisfy yer curiosity by getting yerself online and sending a message to this Destiny woman."

Jesse snorted his answer. He had no intention of doing anything of the sort. That would be like giving in. Utterly ridiculous.

Robbie shrugged. "Verra well. Then I'm off to a good night's sleep. I'm due at the office early in the morning. My thanks again for the hospitality of yer home. Driving up and down the mountain every day for two weeks would be a royal pain in the arse."

Jesse nodded his agreement as Robbie left. His dad's policy of having each of their field operatives spend two weeks training in the different departments within the company had been good for team morale, but it wasn't very convenient for those like Robert who didn't live in town.

He supposed his own turn at the training would be

scheduled as soon as he officially returned from his vacation next week. Of course, once he broke the news to his father of his plans to live in Scotland, that would probably change things.

It was the right thing to do, though. He was sure of it. Being a Guardian, now that was something worthy of devoting his life to. He only hoped that once he made the move, he'd find the fulfillment he so desperately sought. Or did the Fates intend him to be miserable for the rest of his life?

"Fuck it," he muttered, shaking his head.

He didn't believe in Fates any more than he believed in destiny.

There it was. That word again.

Destiny.

For something he didn't believe in, he sure seemed to be obsessed with it.

Letting go of the back of his recliner, he made his way across the room to his desk. Somewhere under all those stacks of papers was a perfectly good computer.

With one hand he pushed the ON button of the CPU while he shoved everything aside with his other. Papers fluttered to the floor around him as he hooked a bare foot under the leg of his rolling desk chair, pulling it forward. The computer screen flickered to life as he sank into the seat.

Before leaning back, he pulled the crumpled ivory-colored sheet from his pocket. He barely noticed the cold leather against his skin. His attention was fully focused on the letter in his hand, his eyes drawn to the signature at the bottom of the page.

Destiny.

Only a coincidence—a weird fluke and nothing more. So what if it matched the advice his niece had given him. She may be part Faerie, but she was still just a kid.

So why was it driving him crazy?

His fingers played over the keyboard, punching up screens as if they had a will of their own. Before he knew it, he'd filled in the form to email the author of the letter in question, this Destiny woman, demanding to know her location and contact information.

He wouldn't actually send the email. That wasn't the way Coryell Enterprises operated. Those things were handled through the office, by people who got paid to screen out things like this from the requests they would actually consider.

As Susan had said, the letter probably wasn't even legitimate. Who would ask for help and yet give nothing more than an email address for contact? An email address that was likely a fake at that.

Matter of fact, he had half a mind to hit the SEND key and prove that the case, all doubt being eliminated when his message came back as a mailer daemon.

His index finger hovered over the keyboard for an instant longer before jamming down.

Jesse stared at the screen, the little message YOUR MAIL HAS BEEN SENT flashing before him.

He leaned back in his chair, feeling relaxed for the first time all day.

It was done. Whatever happened now, so be it.

Chapter 4

"You do offer a money-back guarantee on these readings, don't you?"

"Pardon me?" Destiny stared into the elderly woman's huge eyes, made larger than life by her thick prescription lenses.

"Money-back guarantee, missy. You said you didn't see any plane crashes in my future. If I end up on an airliner that goes down in flames, I want my twenty dollars back." As the woman spoke, deep lines of irritation formed on her forehead, right between her unblinking owl eyes.

The fake coins on Destiny's gypsy costume tinkled merrily as her hand flew to her chest. Damn. Her necklace wasn't there. Instead her mother's heirloom lay in pieces, wrapped in a tissue at the bottom of her purse, where she'd placed it this afternoon. One wrong tug and it had broken, beads flying all around the small tent.

She could certainly use that little hematite heart about now to reflect some of this negativity.

These people never failed to astound her.

"Well, sure," she replied hesitantly. "If that's what you want."

After all, if this old lady survived a plane crash that Destiny didn't see happening, then the promise to pay back twenty dollars seemed a small price to avoid the aggravation she *did* see coming if she refused to agree to the request—and it certainly didn't take any magical visions to predict that one.

"All right!" The lines disappeared and the big eyes finally blinked. "If you guarantee it, then you *must* be legit. I don't care what my son said about you fortune-tellers. I feel so much better now." The old woman rose unsteadily to her feet and pawed through her enormous purse, dragging out another five-dollar bill. "This is for you. Extra. For being so sweet." She beamed her happiness as she started for the exit, stopping at the tent flap and turning the full glare of her owl eyes back on Destiny. "But if my plane goes down, I want that back, too."

Destiny nodded her agreement mutely and the woman disappeared through the opening.

"Another satisfied customer," she muttered to herself as she pulled the cloth from the table and began to neatly fold it, tidying up in preparation to end her long day. As late as it was, most of the nearby workers would already have closed up. She hoped she hadn't missed the last shuttle to the buses that would take her into town. Of course, she shouldn't have agreed to the reading for that last woman, but she needed the money, even though all she really wanted tonight was to get back to her motel to see if there was any additional word from Jesse.

Her hand stilled in the act of smoothing the fold in the cloth as his name floated through her consciousness. She caressed the name with her mind. *Jesse*. The man who would help her locate her missing sister.

Four nights ago, she'd opened her email to find a message from him. He'd read her plea for help and he wanted more details. Immediately she'd responded, telling him everything, her sister's disappearance, her job at this little Ren Faire in Virginia, everything.

Well, almost everything. She suspected the part about her having dreamed she should ask Coryell Enterprises to help her might be a bit much for someone to accept in an email. Sometimes her *gifts* were the sort of thing she had to work her way up to telling someone about.

She'd sent her response, expecting another long wait before she heard the company's decision on whether or not they would help her.

Instead she'd gotten an immediate response back.

I'm on my way.

That was it. And not another word since.

But one thing she was sure of—this Jesse would be the man she had seen in her dream vision. He'd been big and strong, and when he'd reached out his hand and touched her, a sense of peace came over her, as if finally there was someone to share her burden. In that dream, she'd felt safe for the first time in well over a month. Here was someone to end this awful nightmare that began the day she came home from work to find Leah gone.

Then she'd awakened, standing beside her bed, reaching out, grappling for a hand that wasn't there.

No matter. He had a name now. Jesse. And one day very soon, she'd look up and there he'd be, dressed all in black, holding out his hand, offering his help, just like in her dream. Only this time, she'd get to see a face to go with the rest of him.

A rustling of the tent flap jerked her from her reverie, sending a jolt of fear-induced adrenaline surging through her body. The fair had closed its gates over an hour past.

"Hello, Destiny."

The owner of the deep baritone ducked his head to enter, straightening to his full height only after he passed through the tent opening.

Somehow his voice wasn't quite what she'd expected. *He* wasn't quite what she'd expected, though he was certainly big and dressed all in black.

"Jesse?" Her voice arched up in a plaintive question mark, cracking at the end in a way she hated. It always happened when she was nervous.

A frown fleeted across his handsome face, chased away by a smile that didn't quite reach his hard green eyes.

"You weren't easy to find." Blond shoulder-length hair, gathered up and fastened at the nape of his neck, danced along the top of his back as he looked around the small tent.

"Sorry." Why the hell was she apologizing to him? This wasn't the way their meeting was supposed to go. "Anyway, I thought we'd agreed to meet in town. You were going to call me when you got here."

"Whatever." He shrugged and then motioned toward the tent opening with his head. "Let's go."

"Go? Go where?" Something didn't feel right. *He* didn't feel right. "Don't you even want to hear what I know about Leah's disappearance?"

Instead of answering, he crossed the distance between them and grabbed Destiny's wrist, jerking her up against his chest. The glitter in his eyes alone would have been enough to have her adrenaline flowing again, but the feeling that enveloped Destiny at his touch was the clincher.

Fear. Pure, unadulterated terror filled her mind as she tried to pull her arm from his grasp.

"You want to talk about your sister, or you want me to take you to her?"

His words stilled Destiny. "You . . . you know where Leah is?" How could that be possible? It couldn't be if he was the man she expected. "You're not Jesse. Who are you?"

He leaned in closer, his breath fanning across her face. "I don't have time to waste on this. You'll come with me. Now."

His voice rumbled over her, through her, carrying a chill that tingled along her skin as if every hair on her body stood on end.

When she again pulled against his hold, he laughed, but there was no humor in the sound.

"I should have guessed," he sneered. "No wonder Adira wants you found and brought to her. Well, little kinswoman, you may have the power to resist my compulsion, but you're still coming with me." He reinforced his words by tightening his grip around her wrist, dragging her through the opening in the tent and out into the dark Virginia night.

Destiny grabbed the material of the flap with her free hand, holding on tightly, hoping to slow the maniac down while she grappled for some way out of this situation. Damn the organizers of this place for having stuck her tent so far back in the trees. That's what came of hunting out some backwoods, off-the-grid carnival. If she got out of this in one piece, she was going to raise holy hell with the manager.

"Let go," the maniac growled. He jerked her arm, ripping the cloth from her grasp and slamming her up against his chest once again. With his free hand, he clinched his fingers around her upper arm and lifted, pulling her painfully up onto her toes as he glared into her eyes. "No more games. Just come along nicely and don't make any noise or I'll have to hurt you."

His expression told her that he wouldn't hesitate to do just as he said, and that doing it wouldn't bother him in the least.

Surely there was still someone around. Her thoughts raced in circles, clouded by the panic she felt. The food stalls would still be cleaning up if nothing else. When they walked through the main fairground area ahead, she'd call out for help.

Having something remotely resembling a plan in mind now, she slowly nodded her agreement, and he let go of her upper arm, allowing her to settle onto her feet again, though he still held her wrist clamped like a steel manacle.

She followed along quietly until she realized he wasn't heading toward the main gates. Instead he pulled her deeper into the wooded area. Once again, she tried to pull away from him.

"This isn't the way to the exit." She could hear the fear in the rising pitch of her voice but there was no controlling it.

He laughed again, a sharp, sarcastic bark of sound. "Employee parking lot exit. It's much quieter back there than out front. You don't pay much attention to your surroundings, do you?"

No, she hadn't, but she vowed she wouldn't make that mistake again.

Assuming she got a next time.

She stumbled along behind him as he pulled her through the trees until at last they reached the edge of the grounds and a tall wooden gate. He pushed through, dragging her after him.

Two ancient light poles cast their eerie glow over either end of a nearly deserted dirt parking lot, almost obscuring a dark sedan parked off to one side, all by itself.

This wasn't good. She'd be totally freakin' screwed if she let this psycho get her into his car.

Panic clouded her mind as her eyes darted from one end of the lot to the other, taking in the few cars sparsely scattered around. Directly across from them, a lone figure sat on a big motorcycle. He seemed to be looking in their direction, but it was hard to tell for sure in the shadows.

If she made her stand here, at least there'd be one witness, assuming Biker Guy was actually watching.

"No. I'm not going anywhere with you." Bracing her legs, she clawed at the grip on her wrist with her free fingers as she pulled against his hold.

"Stop it." Her efforts hardly seemed to faze him as he pulled keys from his pocket and with an electronic *beep-beep* unlocked the car and pulled open the door.

Please let Biker Guy be paying attention.

"Let go of me or I'm screaming my lungs out. You won't get away with this."

The words had barely crossed her lips before she found herself pinned, her right arm lifted, her body pressed against the car as his intertwined fists applied pressure to the side of her neck, sending streaks of pain radiating out from the spot.

"I told you, no noise. You scream and I snap your neck. You got that?"

As if to prove his point, he tightened his hold, causing little blue streaks of light to flicker in the corners of Destiny's vision as the pain in her neck and shoulder intensified so much she hardly noticed his forearms crushing her rib cage, preventing her from catching her breath.

"Where I come from, women aren't real impressed with that macho bullshit, friend. I think maybe you should let the lady go like she asked."

Biker Guy had apparently chosen to be more than just a witness.

"This doesn't concern you, *friend*," the maniac holding her snarled. "So do us both a favor and head back to wherever it is you came from."

As he spoke, his hands pressed into Destiny's neck, sending pain shooting down her upper torso and arm, blackening her vision.

She blinked, feeling like the world closing in around her moved in slow motion. The other man's response seemed to reach her as if from a great distance through a long tunnel.

"I'm afraid that isn't going to work for me. The way I see it, you need to take your hands off the lady and step away. Now."

With one last press of his fists into her neck, Destiny's attacker let go of her to turn his attentions to the big biker. Slowly, she slid down the side of the car, landing on her butt in the dirt, her mind desperately playing catch-up through the pain to try to process what had just happened to her.

"Aw, see, now . . . I really don't care for the way you did that," Biker Guy said.

Destiny looked up in time to see the pretend Jesse take a swing at her unlikely rescuer, who dodged away, putting distance between them while pulling what looked like a small gun from his pocket. Fire crackled from the end of his weapon too fast for her to even react.

The man who had held her captive moments before lay on the ground, frozen in the act of lunging.

"On your feet. We have to get out of here before your friend there recovers. I figure we have about a thirty-second head start." He still held the weapon, with what looked like strings hanging out the barrel.

Over her attacker's screams for them to stop, a clicking noise hit her ears as Biker Guy reached out and grabbed her hand, hoisting her up to stand.

When their hands met, one thing became immediately clear. She didn't understand how she knew, but she did. This was the man she had been waiting for. This was Jesse. In spite of everything happening around her, in his touch she felt the same peace and safety she'd felt in her dream.

Another series of clicks sounded as he pulled her along behind him, and when she stumbled, he scooped her up in his arms and ran the rest of the way across the lot to his enormous black bike.

Destiny took a deep breath. The pain, from whatever it was that guy had done to her, still consumed her upper body.

She stared at the motorcycle fearfully, knowing they had to get away, but on that? She was almost as terrified of riding on a motorcycle as she was of the big, blond psycho who was even now struggling to his feet behind them.

Surely Jesse didn't think she was getting on that thing!

Obviously he did.

In fact, he plopped her on the back of it, shoved a helmet on her head, and with a quick "Hold on!" from him, gravel sprayed around them as they sped through the dirt lot and out onto the dark highway.

She leaned her head against his back, her arms clenched around his chest, her fingers knotted into his jacket. Closing her eyes against the dark that sped by them, she concentrated on pushing back her fears.

Jesse seemed to know what he was doing with this machine, so she'd simply have to put her trust in him. How he'd found her or been there when she needed him didn't matter right now. And wherever he was taking her, at least it was away from that horrible man.

Though the wind rushed past, biting into her exposed skin, she found that by pressing herself closer into Jesse's back as he leaned forward, she was shielded by his big body from most of it. The large helmet gave her a sense of being sheltered. She could hear the dull roar of the wind they passed through, but inside her dark cocoon, she breathed in the smell of Jesse. It surrounded her, permeating her senses. His aftershave or the essence of the man?

Whatever it was, it reassured her. Soothed her, in spite of the terror rolling around inside her gut.

With his arrival, another dream vision had come to pass, and now she would be able to find the next clue she needed to locate her sister.

Chapter 5

What in the holy hell did a Nuadian Fae want with his new client?

Jesse glanced over into his rearview mirror to reassure himself that no one followed them yet. Logic and experience told him it would be a while before that asshole they'd left in the parking lot would manage to get his muscles to cooperate enough to be on their trail. The Taser jolts he'd given the guy would leave him exhausted.

Even with the extra strength he had as a result of being Fae.

Which brought Jesse right back to the beginning of this circular train of thought, because that asshole they'd left in the parking lot, the asshole who had been abducting Destiny, was definitely a Nuadian Fae.

A full Fae, which made all of this even more difficult to understand.

One of the first things Jesse had learned while training with Dallyn's Elite Guard in the Realm of Faerie was how to identify a full-blooded Fae. They gave off a signature vibe that any trained Guardian could feel.

A vibe that made the Mark of the Guardian tattoo on his upper arm fairly tingle even now when he thought back to his meeting with the man.

Setting aside for the moment the question of what the Fae had wanted with Destiny, an equally intriguing riddle was how he'd been able to hurt her and, even more important, how Jesse had been able to hurt him.

A full-blooded Fae shouldn't have any such abilities or weaknesses in the Mortal Plain. A swing at one should go right through him, just as his fist swung in anger would be like a wisp of smoke passing by.

Yet the Fae Jesse had just encountered had been solid enough to take down with a Taser, even though it had required repeated jolts to keep him down. He'd been solid enough to scream in pain when those jolts had passed into his body, too.

None of it made any sense to Jesse right now, but maybe Dallyn would be able to explain once he had a chance to talk to him about this.

The Fae wasn't the only surprise on his mind.

Ms. Noble hadn't turned out to be at all what he'd pictured when he'd read her email. She was short and frumpy from what he could tell. The way she disappeared in that lumpy, layered dark pile of clothing, he couldn't really say for sure. From what little he'd seen, he wasn't even sure how old she might be.

What he could see was that her hair was an impossibly curly, synthetic-looking black mess that hung halfway down her back, most of it was held away from her face by some scarf thing with annoying jangly coins hanging all over it.

She'd told him she was working at a fair of some sort; he just hadn't realized she'd be dressed up like some exaggerated fairy-tale version of a gypsy.

So she wasn't what he expected from her correspondence. Her initial letter and her email had both been so professional. So what? So she liked to play dress-up. When had he ever wasted time worrying about what a client looked like? That was the least of his problems.

He had a shitload of questions and no answers to go with any of them.

One thing seemed pretty clear, though. Destiny Noble hadn't exercised full disclosure in her email as she'd claimed. Otherwise he'd have known this wasn't just about her sister's disappearance. He'd have known she was in danger as well.

Of all the things he didn't like in a client, keeping secrets from him ranked right up there at the top of his list. Especially when the secrets were as important as having a Nuadian Fae hot on her tail.

Obviously he and Destiny needed to have a little chat. She needed to understand that keeping salient facts from him wasn't a smart thing to do if she wanted his help.

All he needed to do now was figure out exactly where they could have that kind of chat.

Her motel was out of the question now. If the Fae had been able to track her down where she worked, they'd almost certainly know where she was staying.

He took the next turn and headed for the interstate. If he remembered correctly—and he always did—there'd been a truck stop several miles before the turnoff to her motel. Well lit, very public, and with lots of dark places to tuck his bike that wouldn't immediately give away their location.

Ten minutes later he pulled into the parking lot, easing his bike to a stop behind a large semi. He peeled Destiny's fingers from their death grip on his jacket before stepping off his bike.

Damn. Her fingers felt like ice. He should have considered she might get cold, but at the time, getting her away from their Nuadian friend had been his only thought.

She sat on the bike like she couldn't quite figure out how to dismount so he reached down and lifted her off, placing her on her feet. She sure felt a hell of a lot lighter than she looked.

"How about we go in here, find a nice quiet booth, and get you something warm to drink. Sound like a plan?"

She nodded her agreement and the big helmet he'd shoved on her earlier wobbled back and forth, making him think of one of those bobblehead characters his niece had in her doll collection.

Reaching over, he pulled the helmet from Destiny's head and was immediately greeted with the annoying jangle of her coin-encrusted scarf.

That piece of crap had to go.

He didn't like the idea of anything that made them stand out in a crowd. The last thing he wanted was for people to remember having seen them if anyone came looking for her and asking questions.

"You know . . . your little Halloween costume makes it hard enough to avoid drawing people's attention without all that racket."

"Not a problem," she answered in a quiet, sweet southern drawl completely at odds with her appearance.

Reaching up, she dragged the scarf from her head, pulling with it the masses of tangled hair.

Jesse fought the urge to smack himself in the forehead. He should have realized that fake-looking mass of curls was just exactly that—fake. Her real hair was equally dark but short, with soft, tousled curls that framed her face while barely brushing her shoulders.

She leaned over and tugged at the massive skirt, pulling it down and stepping out of it. Its removal left her wearing a clingy belted top, long enough to be a regular minidress on its own, with her legs covered in tights.

Legs *outlined* in tights was a more accurate description. And what legs they were.

"Better?" Destiny wadded her clothing into a bundle and looked up at him.

He forced his gaze up to her face but maybe not fast enough if her skeptically raised eyebrow was any indicator.

"Apparently it is," she muttered, handing the bundle to him when he reached to take it from her. Shaking her head, she walked away across the parking lot toward the entrance of the little café.

Damn. He felt like he'd just witnessed a miracle akin to a butterfly climbing out of its cocoon. Considering the way she looked now, she probably would have drawn less attention in the costume.

"Wait up!" He shoved her unbecoming disguise into

one of the saddlebags on his bike and ran to catch up with her.

Those shapely legs might be short, but they could move.

Reaching the entrance at the same time as Destiny, he held the door open for her, then followed her inside. The inviting smell of fried food wafted to him as they slid into a corner booth, and he could almost swear he heard a cheeseburger and fries calling his name.

"What'll you have, sugar?"

The forty-something waitress smiled at him as she leaned closer, giving him a clear view down the front of her low-cut uniform.

He seemed to get a lot of that.

"Cheeseburger and fries." Destiny ordered without looking up from the menu that had been lying on the table when they sat down. "Well done, please. And sweet tea."

"We only have regular tea." The waitress—Pam, according to her plastic name tag—didn't bother to look in Destiny's direction.

"Fine. Regular." Destiny sighed and closed the menu.

"And for you, sugar?"

"I'll have the same." Jesse mirrored Pam's smile and she turned on her heel, headed for the kitchen.

"I guess I should say thank you. For what you did back there." Destiny spoke quietly, hesitantly, raising her eyes to meet his only when he didn't respond. "With that man out at the Ren Faire, I mean. I felt like he was using some kind of Vulcan neck pinch or something. It hurt so bad, my arms wouldn't even work."

The vibrant green of her slightly tilted eyes surprised him. Faerie eyes. Damn. Considering the twists of fate so far, he should have expected as much. As Dallyn had drilled into him during his training, there was likely as much Fae blood in this world as in the Faerie Realm.

He allowed himself only a moment of distraction before he got back to business.

"I'm guessing he was using pressure on nerve points, as well as cutting off your air with that hold around your chest. You'll probably want to avoid that sort of thing in the future."

"Yeah. Like I encouraged it tonight? In case you didn't notice, he was quite a bit bigger than me."

He'd noticed.

"Lift your foot up here." He reached his hand under the table.

The green Faerie eyes rounded in confusion. "What?"

"I'm not speaking a foreign language. Just do it. Lift your foot up here."

He grasped her ankle as she lifted her foot and traced his finger along the smooth stocking on the front of her ankle, up to her shin.

Soft. Warm. Firm. He liked the feel of her in his palm.

Focus. Back to business.

"There's a nerve in here. Since you're too short to do much else to a big guy like that, you might try stomping this spot."

He had to force himself to let her ankle go and return his hand to the tabletop.

"Would that have disabled him? Long enough for me to get away?"

Jesse shrugged. "Maybe. Depends on where you hit and how hard. But it gives you a better chance than you would have had if he'd gotten you in that car."

She sucked in a deep shaky breath, as if the potential outcome of the evening's events was just settling in.

"Again, thank you. I don't know what I would have done if you hadn't been there."

That was obvious. The thought didn't sit too well with him, either.

"Who was he?"

She shook her head. "I don't know. I thought at first he was you."

"Me? Why would you think that?"

"There's no one else I was expecting. Your last email said you were on your way. And then he showed up and he was big and he was wearing black. It only made sense." She stopped talking as Pam arrived with their tea.

Though his curiosity was piqued by her last comment, Jesse waited as well until the waitress left their table.

"What made you think I'd be dressed in black?"

She didn't answer immediately, her attention suddenly fixed on the straw she fumbled with as a deep pink stained her cheeks.

"Well, you *are*, aren't you?" She looked up at him then, a glint of defiance shining in her eyes. "And what were you doing out there in that parking lot anyway? Spying on me? We were supposed to meet in town."

Nice try. Going straight for the old "best defense is a good offense" play. Not that he was falling for it.

"I was merely getting my bearings, babe. I hadn't planned to approach you until you got to town. Your friend changed my mind." He didn't believe in walking into any situation blind. His intention in being out there tonight was exactly as he'd said, simply a recon visit.

Again she didn't respond right away, taking her time to meticulously tear the ends off two sugar packets, pour their contents into her tea, and stir. He'd begun to think her fascination with the swirling tornado in her glass was all-consuming.

"I think he knows where Leah is." Her voice was barely more than a whisper.

"Your sister?" What wasn't she telling him?

She nodded, finally looking up at him, her eyes glistening with the threat of tears. "He asked if I wanted to talk about Leah or if I wanted him to take me to her. What if I've screwed up my only chance to find my sister?"

The threat became a reality as one tear slid down her cheek, quickly followed by others.

Shit. Not crying. He didn't do crying.

"You did the right thing." He hastily pulled a wad of napkins out of the dispenser sitting on the table and offered them to her. "You wouldn't have been any help to your sister if they'd had you, too. Besides, I thought you said you know where she is."

In her email she'd mentioned that when Coryell Enterprises sent someone to help her, she'd be able to tell them where to go to find her sister.

She swiped at her face with the napkins, turning her head away as the waitress delivered their food.

Jesse placed the limp lettuce and pickle on top of his burger and covered them with a greasy bun, watching as Destiny seemed to search the booth where she sat.

"Oh no." She stilled, dropping the crumpled napkins next to her plate. "I have to go back out to the fair-grounds."

Like hell she did.

"No." There was no way he was letting her go any-where the Nuadians could be watching.

"No?" she squeaked, her hand flying to her neckline as if she searched for something. "You don't understand. I left my purse in that tent. And—oh my God!—my laptop! All the information I have on Leah's disap-pearance, the copies of the police reports, her photos, everything is there. I kept it with me all the time. I have to go get it."

"No." He had a better way to deal with this. "It's not safe. That big guy we left in the parking lot could still be waiting for you. And he might not be alone next time. We'll have someone collect your things and bring them to us. Will that work for you?"

Her warring emotions showed in her expression as he waited for her answer.

"Okay. But who?"

"Don't worry about it. I'll make a call and everything will be taken care of." He rose from his seat. "And when I get back, we'll talk about where it is we need to go to get your sister."

He headed out of the restaurant and into the relative privacy of the night, glancing back through the window as he pulled his cell phone from his pocket.

She sat where he'd left her, staring at her plate, chewing on her finger. He didn't get the impression of a woman consumed by worry so much as by sheer panic.

Now what?

How was she going to deal with answering Jesse's question? How could she possibly explain that she didn't know where to go next but by this time tomorrow she would? Now that he'd arrived, all she needed was to sleep, to slip into the altered state that allowed her to see what was to come in her life. His arrival had fulfilled the last vision, so now her unconscious mind would reveal the next piece of the puzzle.

If she told him the truth, he'd likely climb right back on that monster motorcycle of his and ride away, leaving her here to deal with all her problems on her own.

Alone. A familiar panic started to build low in her stomach, and she glanced out the window, scanning to find Jesse. To reassure herself he hadn't already decided to leave her behind.

No, he was still there.

A sharp sting brought home the realization she'd pulled the cuticle around her pinkie finger into the quick. Such a bad habit—chewing on her fingers. One she thought she'd outgrown at sixteen but that still haunted her in times of stress.

Stress? She was so far beyond stress right now, she'd have to invent a new word to even begin to describe how she felt. Her stomach knotted as she thought again of that psycho back at the fair and what might have happened if Jesse hadn't been there to save her.

Was this how Leah had felt when they'd taken her? Had he been the one who'd gone to their apartment that day? The one who'd kidnapped her sister? The image of Leah, helpless, scared half to death, trying to fight off that huge man stabbed at her heart, and her next breath escaped on a pitiful-sounding sob.

She bit down on her lips and placed her hands flat on the table on either side of her plate, spreading her fingers as she pressed against the cool Formica surface. Blood oozed from the small tear in her cuticle, slowly filling in around the outline of her fingernail.

I can't go on like this.

The fear and dread had to end. She turned, searching through the windows for the most recent cause of her anxiety.

His cell phone to his ear, Jesse stood at the edge of a circle of light, his handsome profile in sharp contrast to the pool of shadow behind him.

Though she couldn't make out his features from this distance, she had no need to. She'd memorized them as he sat across from her.

Rich copper-brown hair that shone with glints of red under the harsh fluorescent lights, framing the most unusual eyes she'd ever seen. Eyes that seemed to shift from brown to green and back depending on the moment. Whether it was a trick of the lighting or simply her imagination, when he looked at her, she felt as if he saw inside her with those beautiful eyes.

Which only made what was to come all that much more uncomfortable. There was simply no avoiding what she needed to do when Jesse returned to their table.

She would have to come clean about her gift.

If he didn't believe her, so be it. Since Coryell Enterprises had obviously agreed to take on her case it meant that she was the client. The company and its employee Jesse worked for her. It didn't matter what he believed.

Destiny took a deep breath, squared her shoulders, and picked up her cheeseburger, taking a large, deliberate bite, followed by a drink of the bitter tea.

She'd spent more than a month consumed by fear. But tonight was the end of all that. She was in charge. In control at last. She called the shots from here on out. She wouldn't be afraid any longer.

"Sorry that took so long."

She jumped, sloshing her tea down her chin and onto her front as Jesse slid into his seat on the opposite side of the booth.

Maybe she'd have to work her way up to the whole not-being-afraid thing.

"You okay?"

She nodded, embarrassment singing through her as she dabbed her napkin at the wet spot on her blouse.

Great. What a classy chick he must think I am.

Jesse bit into his cheeseburger and washed it down with the tea before fixing her with a no-nonsense stare.

"So where is your sister?"

Here it was—the moment she'd dreaded. Her stomach knotted and she knew before she said the words, she'd chickened out.

"I can't tell you yet."

"What?"

His questions sounded as much like a growl as a word and she could almost swear his eyes had glowed for a moment there.

"In the morning. I'll have the location for you in the

morning." The words tumbled out of her mouth as if each was in a bigger rush than the one that preceded it. "I promise I can talk about it then. It's been an awful day and I just need a good night's sleep first. I . . . I can't deal with any of it now. I'm exhausted. Please don't force me to think about any of this tonight."

Miserable sissy-girl.

She feigned a yawn, totally disgusted with her own cowardice. Even though she couldn't quite meet his eyes, she tried to rationalize her actions. It hadn't really been a lie. Maybe not the full truth, but tomorrow she'd face up to it. Tomorrow, when she was rested and had some actual information to dull the blow of *how* she got that information, then she'd come clean with him.

Chapter 6

*H*e was, by God, getting some answers tomorrow morning or there'd be hell to pay.

Jesse leaned against the doorjamb, staring into the darkened room beyond, to the bed where Destiny slept. A long, thin rectangle of light from the parking lot slipped through the crack in the drawn shades, illuminating her face. Sleep had relaxed the lines of worry etched there during her waking hours and her pink pouty lips were parted as if waiting for a lover's touch.

Where the hell did that come from?

He shook his head and turned back into his own room, stopping at his bed, where he sat down, propping his back against the headboard. He didn't get involved with clients. No exceptions. Not ever. Destiny Noble was a client, just like any other, even if Coryell Enterprises didn't know she existed. The fact that he was doing this on his own time, without company sanction didn't change anything.

In truth, she wasn't exactly like any other client. Most of them were so anxious for help they spilled their guts the moment he met them, sharing every scrap of information they had to help him do whatever it was they wanted done.

She had been absolutely unwilling to answer any of his questions tonight. Even when he gave her his "it's not good to keep secrets from me" speech.

No doubt about it, there were secrets Destiny was keeping. Secrets he needed to know to keep her safe and to find her sister.

Maybe when he heard back from Peter he'd get some of the answers he sought.

He rolled his head from side to side, the resulting crack of his neck the only outward show of his tension. For now he'd have to be patient. And he hated it like hell.

If the door between their rooms wasn't open, he'd flip on the TV to distract himself while he waited for Peter's call.

But the door was open, and, oh man, had Destiny ever been pissed about that.

Leaning his head back against the thinly padded wood that passed for a headboard, he smiled at the memory as he reached for the glass of water next to his bed.

When he'd pulled into the motel parking lot, she'd had her helmet off before he'd even dismounted, scrambling off the back of the bike to follow him into the office.

"We need a room for the night," he'd told the sleepy-eyed woman at the counter.

"What do you think you're doing?" Destiny had demanded. "Two rooms. We need two rooms."

"How about a double?" He'd attempted to bargain, knowing the longer the discussion continued the bigger the impression they'd make on the clerk. Something he wanted to avoid at all costs. The Nuadians might not pick up Destiny's trail, but he didn't want to bet her safety on that.

"No. No, that's not happening." She'd crossed her arms and her perky little mouth had gone all hard line. "Two rooms."

"Fine, you win," he'd said, relenting, and she had walked away, taking a seat in the lobby. "Two *connecting* rooms."

The opening he glanced toward now had been the second argument of the evening.

"What do you mean we're leaving the door open?" she'd squeaked. "I don't know you from Adam. How am I supposed to sleep with a strange man able to just walk in my room any time he wants to?"

"Better me than that guy in the parking lot, don't you think?" He'd seen the fear dance through her eyes and momentarily felt guilt at his words. Still, it was for her own good. "I can't protect you if I don't know what's going on. You still have your privacy, but I need to know if someone tries to get to you. Understand?"

She'd nodded mutely and taken the T-shirt he held out for her, disappearing behind the door to her bathroom.

The same T-shirt she slept in right now. His T-shirt, wrapped around those naked creamy curves . . .

Only the rattling of his cell phone vibrating along the surface of the wooden bedside table kept his thoughts from following that dangerous path. He grabbed it and pushed the TALK button.

"Yeah?"

"Hey, it's Peter. I have the info you wanted, but . . ."

"But what?"

Peter Hale was the best researcher on the payroll at Coryell Enterprises and even better, Jesse liked him personally. They'd frequently gone out for a beer or two after a long workout at the gym. And although he could be a stickler for detail, once you got Peter on a trail, he didn't give up.

"I can't find any active file on this Noble woman. What's up with that?"

"Let's just say we're flying under the radar on this one."

"Okeydokey, boss man. Whatever you say." Peter's skepticism rang through loud and clear. "I have someone on the way to pick up the items you requested and I'm sending the text on what I found through to your phone now. Anything else off the grid you want?"

"Yeah. Patch me through to Ian McCullough."

"You got it."

The line hummed with music as Jesse waited for his call to transfer over. Ian was a Guardian like him, only Ian had been at this for centuries. He was also a good friend of the family and the quickest way for Jesse to get word to Dallyn about tonight's strange encounter with the Nuadian Fae.

He hoped Dallyn would be able to give him some input as to what the hell was going on.

Because something told him, the way things felt, he was going to need all the input he could get.

A thick curtain of mist surrounded the car she rode in, but far from being frightening, it reassured Destiny she was back in the vision. Up ahead, the swirling gray tendrils cleared just enough for her to read the road sign they approached. ARIZONA, printed in block letters above a big yellow star and below that the words THE GRAND CANYON STATE WELCOMES YOU.

The sign whipped past and Destiny became aware of a growing feeling of claustrophobia, as if she'd over-stayed her welcome in this part of the vision.

As always, her body felt heavy, like she tried to move through thick mud. *Think!* What had she learned?

Leah was somewhere in Arizona, but that alone wasn't enough information to find her sister. Arizona was a big place. There had to be more.

"Go on." It was her own voice pressing for the vision to continue.

The mist roiled around her and suddenly she wasn't in the car any longer, instead an enormous computer screen filled her mind. A computer screen showing a list of her incoming email. The words were jumbled, unreadable, as if they'd been typed at random with fingers on all the wrong keys. All but one message. That heading was clear, the words sharp and distinct, catching her attention and riveting her to it.

If you want to see your sister alive . . .

A hand, her hand, floated toward a keyboard and pressed the ENTER button. The screen flickered and the text of the message shimmered into view, only to be instantly obscured by a vividly bright light flashing over the screen.

"No!"

The word was torn from her as she tried to sweep the light away, one hand shading her eyes, the other fluttering in front of the monitor. She grabbed onto its sides as the light engulfed the screen. It covered her hands and burned its way up her arms, a hot sting sent as an unfriendly warning to leave now.

The solid form of the monitor slipped from her fingers. Gone. Panic overcame her as she flailed her arms around the brilliant white void in a desperate attempt the find the machine.

An exercise in futility, she knew. Once the light closed in, nothing she did would make the slightest difference until she'd fulfilled that part of the vision.

So close. She'd been so close to finding Leah this time.

Tears of frustration burned her eyes and trickled out the corners, slithering down into her hair as she lay on her back, trying to force the sleep to return and with it the vision.

But the vision was gone, leaving her helpless, frustrated, and alone, as always.

Destiny's eyes flew open and she confronted a dark almost equal to that of her vision. Except that this dark quickly faded, pierced by a sliver of light. A tiny slice of illumination, as if curtains hadn't been fully drawn.

Not alone. Jesse was here, no farther away than the opening in the dark that separated their rooms. The opening she'd complained so heartily about earlier tonight. The opening that now seemed her only connection to safety.

She lay still, straining to hear his breathing, but no sound reached her ears over the pounding of her own heart.

He wouldn't have left her, would he? Surely not. Just her constant paranoia. After all, she'd dreamed he would help her. He couldn't leave. Not yet.

She heard footsteps outside, a lone person walking along the sidewalk. She held her breath, terror overtaking her as the steps drew nearer. By the time the figure passed by her window, blocking the narrow strip of light for an instant, she felt as if she might scream.

Was it him? Had that awful man found her so soon?

The steps continued without a pause, moving farther away until at last she heard a door slam shut.

Someone in one of the other rooms. Nothing more.

She lay unmoving, sweat beading on her forehead until all was silence once again. Slipping from her bed, she stared into the dark hole separating her room from Jesse's, indecision holding her captive. It would be so easy to run to him now. To stroke his hand just to feel the blanket of reassurance that came with his touch.

"No," she whispered, instead forcing her feet to move in the direction of her bathroom.

She wouldn't be dependent on any man, not even the one from her visions. Because vision or no, one day he'd leave. Everyone always did.

Once inside, she quietly closed the door and leaned against it, only then daring to flip the switch next to her. Harsh light flooded the room, bouncing off the mirror that reflected exactly what she had known it would. Her eyes were puffy and her cheeks blotched from having cried through the end of the dream-vision and from the terror she'd just experienced.

A splash of cold water to her face brought her fully awake. She dried off, burying her head in the scratchy cloth of the nearest towel. By the time she looked back into the mirror she'd come to her first decision.

The clue to her sister's whereabouts was to be found in her email. Since Leah's disappearance, Destiny hadn't let her laptop out of her sight for more than a few minutes. Every scrap of information, every tiny clue, was in that machine's memory.

She felt lost without it, as if her lifeline had been severed. She needed that laptop, and first thing tomorrow she was going back for it, no matter how angry it meant making the man sleeping in that dark room next door.

Chapter 7

⟨⁓⟩

"*T*he pain was excruciating."

Adira Ré Alyn tightened her fingers around the telephone receiver in her hand, fighting to rein in her temper and moderate what she wanted to say to the whining man on the other end of this call.

"Yes, Dermond, I'm sure you've suffered horribly."

She didn't doubt his sincerity for a moment. There had been a time, so very long ago, when their men had been fierce warriors. Before they'd been banished to the Mortal Plain. Before they'd been stripped of their magic.

It had been eons since any of her people had experienced physical pain. In those long years, they'd grown soft. Pathetic. Weak.

Dermond Aĺ Tyrn, for all his beauty and brawn, was no exception. Only his simpleminded devotion to her encouraged her to keep him around.

"You've found no trace of the girl? No clue to the identity of the one who interfered?"

The lack of anger in her voice was a true testament to her own strength of will. Dermond's incompetence had cost her the prize she sought.

"Only her belongings at the carnival grounds and here in her room. As to the Mortal who helped her, I don't think he was anything more than some armed biker who'd seen too many action movies."

He sounded like a petulant child, his feelings obviously hurt by her lack of concern for him.

Adira bit back an impatient sigh. The males of her species seemed to have developed such fragile egos, always requiring reassurance. Not so very long ago, a failure such as his would have met with certain punishment, not the coddling he seemed to expect from her now.

Still, times had changed. Dermond was beautiful to behold, and since the disappearance of her chosen mate, Reynard Servans, he was her favorite lover.

"Bring her things to me, my poor darling. And don't give those two another thought for now. We'll make them suffer for what they did to you. We'll find them, and when we do, we'll terminate the intruder for his interference. Does that make you feel better?"

"It does." His voice had changed with his pleasure, taking on the low, rumbling quality she so enjoyed. "Do you miss me . . . my queen?"

Ah, it took so little to make him happy, and once done, he was again eager to please her. Perhaps that more than anything else made him her favorite.

"I do, my darling. Hurry back to me."

Placing the telephone on her dressing table, she turned to stare at her reflection in the richly carved full-length mirror and realized with a start that she actually did miss Dermond.

Or more accurately, she missed what he did for her. To her. Just thinking of him, the hard planes of his body, the low rumble of his voice, the moist heat of his breath on her skin, filled her with an aching need.

Sex had been the focus of her entire adult life, but she'd never realized its pleasures until she'd come into her own. Having the power to control others was a heady aphrodisiac.

Lightly she ran her open palms across her stomach and up to her breasts, her nipples already hardened and sensitive beneath the sheer robe she wore.

Perhaps she'd consider inviting Flynn to her bed this night. He hadn't the skill or the breeding of Dermond, but he would do.

She loosened the sash of her robe, allowing the sides to flutter open, pleased with the sight of her own body. Still firm and unmarked after all these centuries.

Aided, of course, by the blood of her young captive.

She'd experimented with so many over the past year, and then, as much by accident as the initial discovery of what blood could do for her, she'd found this girl, Leah.

Leah, who was undoubtedly a half-breed Fae.

For centuries, Reynard had searched the world over for women of Fae descent, always hoping to use them to find his way back into their homeland, the Realm of Faerie.

He'd had it half right.

Adira had no desire to return home. She'd had nothing there save pain and sorrow. But here, with her new knowledge, she would one day soon rule all within her reach.

For some reason, all the Faerie powers that had been stripped from the world of man were returning. Not to the full-blooded Fae who'd been exiled to this world, but to the half-Mortal descendants of Fae.

What a joke. She almost wished she could see the Earth Mother's face when that impotent bitch learned how all her scheming had come to this. Her plans had failed.

Now, just as Reynard had, she would search out those gifted half-breeds, but unlike him, she had no desire to seek the portals that separated their worlds. She planned to soak up their gifts by taking their blood.

Only a little at a time, of course.

Thank the Fates, she'd learned on those others that it required only a few drops of blood to effect the changes in her own body. It would have been such a shame to lose something as valuable as Leah to those early experiments.

Worse even than failing to capture the girl's sister.

If one young woman had the gift to heal, what delightful gift might she be able to claim from the elusive sister?

Dermond's failure to hold on to Destiny was only a small setback. If they couldn't bring her here by force, perhaps they could lure her to them.

Face flushed with the excitement of her plans, Adira reached for a small ivory-handled feather brush, dabbing it into her perfumed powder before trailing it down her neck, across her breast, and around her hardened nipple.

"Oh!"

The intense pleasure of the light stroke tore the gasp from her lips.

There was no longer any question. She would definitely invite Flynn to her bed tonight.

Dropping the brush, she rolled the darkened nipple between her fingers, letting go to slide her hand down her flat stomach to the curve of her inner thigh.

The heat from within her body caressed her hand, beckoning her to continue.

With one foot propped on the mirror's raised leg, her slim fingers poised at her moist opening. Her reflection fascinated her, her building desire evident in her hooded eyes, her reddened cheeks, her skin so . . .

Damn.

Adira tossed back her long red curls and leaned closer to the mirror.

"Damn!" she hissed.

The age lines had returned to the corners of her eyes. This would never do.

Time for another visit with her little guest. A drop or two of the precious half-breed blood and the wrinkles would be long gone before she satisfied herself with Flynn later this evening.

Chapter 8

*E*ight o'clock. The woman slept like the dead.

Not that she was. Jesse knew because he'd checked earlier, prowling over to listen to her breathing, steady and regular.

He sipped his coffee as he leaned against the doorframe separating their two rooms, studying the unmoving figure huddled in the bed.

Destiny lay curled around a pillow, her arms clutching the bag of feathers like a drowning woman hanging on to the boat's last life preserver. Her covers had been flung to one side as if she'd fought a mighty battle, kicking them away into a heap.

And those curvy bared legs? They were the kind that had obviously inspired man to invent high heels and miniskirts.

Another sip of coffee, the dark liquid flowing down his throat, bringing a flush of heat to his skin. It was the coffee making him so warm, wasn't it?

Just his damned luck the first time he went off the grid to help someone behind the company's back, she'd turned out to be a sexy-as-hell Faerie descendant being chased by a mutant Nuadian. Then again, maybe it was more than luck. Dallyn had counseled the Guardians more than once about the rise of Faerie magic in the Mortal World. He'd also spoken about the numbers of Faerie descendants.

There lay his proof, curled up on the bed in front of him. All five feet, four glorious inches of her.

He'd heard her last night. At first he'd thought it might be the wind as it picked up, the leading edge of the hurricane Peter had warned him was headed their way.

But he'd been wrong. It had been Destiny, moaning in her sleep, the sounds followed a short while later by bare feet padding around the room and the click of her bathroom door. After the nightmares she'd apparently had, it wasn't any wonder she still slept.

No! No more Mr. Nice Guy.

The gloves were off today. He would not be sucked into feeling sorry for her again. He was getting his answers, and damn soon, too. They didn't have time to hang out here while she wasted the day sleeping. If she didn't wake soon, he'd be dragging her ass out of that bed and she'd be talking in short order.

He emptied the last gulp of coffee from his cup, but made no effort to move from his spot by the door.

Yep. That's exactly what he'd do. Any minute now.

Instead of crossing to the bed, he eased his phone

from his pocket, flipping it open with one hand, punching the necessary buttons to once again pull up the information Peter had sent him last night.

In addition to the missing sixteen-year-old sister, Destiny had a younger brother, born in between the two girls.

`Chase Noble. Whereabouts unknown.`

Jesse might be tempted to think that running away was a family trait if not for the encounter with that Nuadian Fae bent on nabbing Destiny last night. There was much more here than initially met the eye. First and foremost, the question was why the Fae would want Leah Noble. Or Destiny, for that matter.

He turned back to the scrolling information on the small screen in his hand.

`Mother, deceased. Father, deserted family sixteen years ago, whereabouts unknown.`

If the younger sister had been abducted, it sure couldn't have been for money. It appeared these people had lived hand to mouth for years, on whatever income Destiny could bring in.

"What do you think you're doing in my room?"

Jesse glanced up, snapping the phone shut and shoving it into his pocket.

"Technically I'm not in your room." He grinned as she grabbed at her covers, pulling them practically up to her chin. *Too late, babe. Assets already ogled.* "Why don't you climb out of there and we'll have ourselves that little talk you mentioned last night."

She shook her head and silky black curls curved onto her rosy cheeks. "Coffee, first."

He turned into his room and poured another cup from the small pot. By the time he walked back through the door, Destiny was nowhere to be seen, the sound of running water coming from behind the closed bathroom door his only clue to her location.

Setting both cups on the small nightstand, he sat down on her bed and propped his legs out in front of him to wait.

When she came back into the room, she was once again dressed in those black tights and the blouse that masqueraded as a clingy little dress, carrying the T-shirt she'd slept in—his T-shirt—neatly folded. She accepted the cup of coffee from him but ignored his invitation to have a seat next to him, instead primly arranging herself in one of the hard chairs across the room from him.

"Where's your sister?"

"Arizona," she responded, averting her eyes as she lifted her cup for a quick drink.

That was almost too easy. He'd expected more of last night's evasion.

"Arizona, huh? It's a big state, you know." He watched her closely, noting her hands begin to shake at his comment. "So how about you be a touch more precise, babe. Where exactly are we heading?"

Her lips tightened into a stubborn line and she set down her cup before lifting her chin to meet his gaze.

Uh-oh. Here it comes.

"Right now, the exact spot we're heading is back to the fairgrounds to pick up my purse and my laptop like I asked for last night. And then we're going to my motel to get all my things. I've thought it over and here's what I've decided—*I'm* the client. You work for me. We'll do what I say from this point on. And don't call me 'babe.'"

If she was going for tough and in charge, that shaky exhale at the end of her speech pretty much ruined the whole effect.

"No point in our doing that." He took another drink, watching her over the rim of his cup. She wasn't going to like hearing the news he'd gotten this morning. "Nothing there to go back for. It's all gone."

"Gone?" Her façade crumbled. "Gone as in 'those people you sent already have it'?"

"Sorry, babe. Gone as in 'not there when my people arrived.'"

She stood and started to pace back and forth in front of the bed. "I don't understand. What could have happened to my things?"

"My guess is that once our friend from the parking lot picked himself up, he went looking for clues as to where he could find you."

Destiny stopped, crossing her arms in front of her. "You mean Psycho Blondie stole my stuff?"

Jesse shrugged his response. In spite of the ridiculous name she pinned on the mysterious Fae, that certainly seemed the most logical answer to him.

Her cheeks went a blotchy red and she turned her back to him. He'd seen that performance from enough women, including most recently his ex-girlfriend, Lara. He knew what to expect and readied himself for the coming waterworks. Damn but he hated it when women cried.

Destiny, however, surprised him. When she turned around, it wasn't tears in her eyes. It was fury.

"Dammit. Dammit all to hell!" Her pacing started again, rapid and agitated. "If I ever get my hands on that jerk, I swear I'll make him think what you did to him in that parking lot was playtime. I *need* that laptop to find my sister."

"I thought you said your sister was in Arizona. Why do you need the laptop?"

"Like you said before, Arizona's a big place. And I won't know *where* in that big place Leah is until I read the email telling me."

She was making absolutely no sense.

"Wait a minute. You mean to tell me you can't remember what you read in an email about your missing sister's location?"

Hands on her hips, she leaned toward him, eyes flashing. "I haven't read it yet. It wasn't there the last time I had my laptop."

"Then what makes you think it's there now?"

"Because I dreamed it, okay?" she yelled at him before throwing her hands in the air and turning to fall into her chair. "I dreamed it. Just like I dreamed Coryell Enterprises, and you, and the Arizona road sign. I have visions. Weird, freaky-assed, totally accurate visions, okay? There's going to be a message sitting in my email that will tell me exactly where to find Leah."

There. She'd told him. Not at all in the way she would have preferred. A temper fit probably wasn't the best means to convince somebody you weren't a total looney tune, but at least it was out in the open now and she'd deal with whatever came next.

Jesse sat quietly for a long moment, simply staring at her, his expression completely unreadable.

"Interesting," he said at last. Swinging his long legs off the bed to stand, he dragged his cell phone from his pocket and held it up to his face. "Smile pretty for me, babe."

"What do you think you're doing?" Destiny was beginning to suspect she might not be the only looney tune in the room.

"Taking your picture, of course. We need to get you some new ID, if we're going to be flying out to Arizona to find your sister. Airport security is a little testy about things like that."

Destiny was struck mute at his words. No questions. No doubt. He'd simply accepted what she'd told him without blinking an eye. Unbelievable.

A small flash and he was once again looking at the phone, pushing buttons.

He'd already taken the photo?

"Oh!" Her hand flew to her messy hair. "You could have given me some warning. It would have been nice to have had some makeup. Or at least a comb." Wonderful. She was going to be stuck with identification that made her look like she'd just crawled out of bed. Which she had.

He grinned, his face taking on a whole new level of attractiveness. "Makeup? You kidding? You don't need that stuff. You look great just like you are. Peter?" This last was directed into the phone he held. "Damn voice mail," he muttered.

A warm feeling curled through her stomach. He thought she looked great just as she was.

"It's Jess. I've just sent over a photo. Call me ASAP when you get this." He snapped the phone shut and slid it back into his pocket as he strode through the doorway into his room. "You want any more coffee before I dump it?"

"No. I'm fine." Amazingly she really did feel closer to fine than she had for over a month. She got up and walked to the doorway separating their rooms. Stepping across the threshold into his room felt too odd, too personal, so she waited at the opening, her hands fidgeting together behind her back. "What do we do now?"

He leaned out of his bathroom, drying his hands on a towel. "Well, one thing's for sure, we can't hang out here waiting to be found by Psycho Blondie." Another killer grin as he parroted her earlier words. "We'll stop somewhere and grab some things for you . . . a toothbrush, some jeans, whatever you—"

The tinny notes of "Play that Funky Music" blasted from his pocket and he hurriedly grabbed the phone, flipping it open in the process.

"Yeah?"

He caught her eye and winked as he turned his back. She couldn't seem to tear her gaze from him as that strange feeling of delight filled her again. She shouldn't be staring at that made-for-T-shirts chiseled body. Or the perfect jeans-filling butt.

Well, maybe just for a minute wouldn't hurt anything.

But it didn't take that long for her internal critic to

kick into overdrive, setting all her emotional alarms to blaring.

Destiny turned and headed back into her room, forcing herself to ignore Jesse and his telephone conversation. One foot after the other, she made her way over to the big picture window facing the parking lot. Opening the drapes, she closed her eyes and hoped for the warmth of the morning sun to soak into her body, willing it to fill the empty spot inside.

But the day was cloudy and gray, much like the message her common sense was bombarding her with even now.

It was ridiculous to let herself get all gooey-feeling over this guy. He was with her because his company had sent him here and for no other reason. For all his winks and grins, she was just another job to him, and unless she planned to end up like her mother, she'd do well to remember that. From watching what had happened to Rainbow, Destiny knew that the only thing worse than a handsome man was a rich handsome man.

She could resist handsome . . . and she knew better than to trust any of them. Men were all alike. Even this one.

"That's bullshit, Peter. I don't care if it is Saturday. You know we sure as hell can't stay here."

Jesse's raised voice broke into her thoughts, pulling her attention away from her spot at the window, back toward his room. Through the opening, she saw him jam his cell phone back in his pocket and look in her direction, the scowl on his face quickly erased as if he didn't want her to know he was upset.

"What's wrong?"

"Nothing I can't handle, babe. Now get away from that window and close the curtains. Damn." He was into her room and pulling on the cords, sliding the drapes together, before she could move.

"I like it open."

The man was awfully bossy for someone who was supposed to be working for her. And he still insisted on calling her that irritating pet name, in spite of her having told him not to. He made her think of those annoying Highlanders in the romances she loved to read.

The ones who turned out to be heroes in the end.

But, she reminded herself, those were just books. This was real life, and she'd long ago made up her mind that the bossy, take-charge man she might find attractive in a paperback novel held no interest for her at all in real life.

"I don't care if you like it. The guy who's looking for you would like it if you made it easy for him to find you, too. Easy like you standing on display in that open window."

Oh. That made sense. She hadn't even considered something like that. A shudder of fear rattled through her body as she stared at the now closed draperies.

Okay. He'd been right and she'd been wrong. This one time. She could admit that much. Flustered, she followed him back to his room, trying once more to probe him for information.

"Problem on the phone? You sounded angry."

He shrugged, continuing to pick up his things and stuff them into the black bag she recognized from the back of his motorcycle. "Let's just say bureaucratic delays aren't one of my favorite things in life. Come on."

He walked over and opened the door, holding it ajar for her after scanning the parking lot.

"Where are we going?"

He fastened the leather bag onto his bike before taking the helmet off the back bar and turning to answer. "Norfolk International Airport."

The airport?

"I thought you said we couldn't fly out until I have photo ID."

"That's right. We can't fly yet. Won't have your fancy new government-issued identification until Monday morning."

"Then why are we going all the way to the airport in Norfolk?"

The grin was back, and this close, she could see that it crinkled the corners of his eyes.

"We're going to park my bike and nab us a car, babe. And then we're going on a shopping spree and heading out of town on a road trip."

Any further questions she might have—and there were plenty—were put on hold as he once again shoved the big black helmet on her head and lifted her into the air and down onto the seat of his motorcycle.

He climbed on in front of her, and when she heard the muffled "Hold on!" she fastened her arms tightly around his chest and tried not to stress over what was to come.

What kind of crazy man had come to save her? It wasn't bad enough her sister was missing and she had some insane kidnapper on her trail. Now it appeared she was about to become a car thief!

Chapter 9

Damn if she didn't have the most expressive face he'd ever seen.

"Is this where we're going to . . . to nab a car?" Destiny faltered, her eyes huge when he pulled the helmet off her head after their arrival in the long-term parking lot.

"Sure is. You carry this." He handed her the helmet before tossing his saddlebags over his shoulder and catching up her hand. He took one last look at his shiny black baby. After all the work he'd put into getting the new Harley just the way he wanted her, she had better show up in Denver in the same condition he left her here in Norfolk. "Come on."

To Destiny's credit, she followed him dutifully into the terminal and down the long hallway to their destination.

"Oh, thank God," she murmured at his side as they approached the counter with the big green and black ENTERPRISE sign hanging over it. "You're *renting* a car."

It wasn't like he really had much choice. They couldn't get her through security onto the tarmac, let alone on a plane, without official photo identification. And he wasn't willing to sit around here waiting for the Nuadians to sniff them out. He felt safer on the move, headed to an airport where both his company plane and the necessary identification would be waiting.

Unfortunately, with this storm system approaching, the best-case scenario would have them facing rain today and tomorrow. While he wouldn't have stopped to consider that if it were just him, he couldn't very well subject Destiny to the wet ride his bike would offer.

Right now, a car was the only reasonable way to go.

The thought had certainly crossed his mind that he was going to miss having her warm body snuggled up against his as it had been on the bike, her arms snaked around his chest, her fingers clutching his shirt. From that scenario, his mind quickly wandered to a memory of how she'd looked in bed this morning, and a mental picture sprang to life of those bare, curvy legs wrapped around him. Naked.

He caught himself and dropped her hand, moving away from her to stand in the short line.

Client, he reminded himself, even if she qualified as a client only in the loosest sense. True, Coryell Enterprises had no official idea of what he was doing with his time off, but that didn't make it any less business. Being with Destiny was nothing more than being on the job, and thoughts like he'd just been having had no place on the job.

Besides, the last thing he needed in his life right now was another needy chick looking for a sugar daddy to pay her bills.

When the young woman behind the counter finished with her previous customer and smiled her welcome, he pulled out his wallet and showed her his license.

"I think you have a reservation waiting for me?"

A few keystrokes and she looked up from her computer, her smile more inviting than friendly. "Yes we do, Mr.—"

"Jesse. Please," he interrupted, glancing down at her name tag. "Amber. *Mister* is my father. Just call me Jesse."

"All right, Jesse. Thank you." Her face colored attractively and she fumbled with the paper in her printer.

Perhaps it was stupid of him to keep the clerk from saying his last name out loud. So what? Destiny obviously thought he was no more than an employee of Coryell Enterprises and he'd just as soon keep it that way for now.

He'd learned the hard way, too many times, that women heard his name and saw dollar signs. Especially women who had no money. Things were going to get complicated enough over the next few days without adding that extra ingredient into the mix.

Amber dropped the key into his open hand, her fingers lingering perhaps a bit longer than necessary against his palm before he gave her a smile and turned away. The next man in line pushed up to the counter, leaving his suitcases behind, demanding the lovely Amber's regard for himself.

Destiny had moved away, her attention focused back down the hallway toward the entrance to the terminal.

Jesse followed the direction of her gaze down the crowded hallway filled with hurrying passengers. He turned at her gasp, reaching out to grab her arm as she stumbled backward into a large suitcase.

"Whoa."

"Look! It's him," she whispered, pointing down the corridor. "And he's got my laptop."

Jesse didn't need to ask who the "he" in question was. If he hadn't figured it out from the look of anger on Destiny's face, he would have when he'd had to tighten his grip on her arm to keep her from heading out after the big Nuadian.

Scanning the corridor with intent, he spotted the man who had attempted to force Destiny into his car fewer than twenty-four hours earlier. This time he wasn't alone. A second man accompanied him, and though Jesse couldn't be sure from here, he, too, had the look of the Fae about him.

"Let's go."

Wrapping Destiny's hand tightly in his, he pulled her along, forcing her to stay behind him as he followed their mystery Fae. Once they reached the main level of the terminal, he knew he'd need to stash Destiny someplace safe. He couldn't afford to have her seen and targeted again.

At the same time the two men stepped on the escalators heading down, Jesse pulled his hand from Destiny's.

"Go into that restaurant." Out in the open, around a crowd of people, was the safest place for her. "Order lunch for us. I'll be right back."

"But . . ." She clasped his helmet to her chest, looking small and defenseless in spite of her anger. "That man has my shoulder bag."

"Go. And if anyone tries to do anything but take your order, you scream your head off. Got it?"

"Like I needed you to tell me that," she muttered, before disappearing into the seafood bar.

Quickening his steps, he made directly for the escalators. Before he reached the bottom, it became clear this was the ticketing area. Fortunately his prey stood out from those around them, Destiny's hot-pink bag an out-of-place beacon hanging from the shoulder of the big Nuadian. Jesse slowly made his way to the line where the two men waited, doing his best to blend in with the crowd.

When they approached the counter, Jesse hung behind a large family carrying a full complement of luggage two windows away.

The uniformed woman behind the desk scanned the identification Destiny's Psycho Blondie had handed her before keying information into her terminal. "Do you have any luggage to check for your flight to Phoenix today, Mr. Tyren?"

He nodded and placed a large suitcase on the scale, keeping Destiny's shoulder bag with him. Since only Mr. Tyren took a boarding pass from the ticket agent, it appeared only he would be flying.

Jesse followed as far as the escalators, where the two men paused. Merging with a large group of giggling teenagers and adults, he moved closer, before kneeling down to fidget with his shoe. As discreetly as possible, he pulled his cell phone from his pocket and snapped off two quick photos while he listened in on their parting words.

"You have someone posted here watching the ticketing area?" When Mr. Tyren's companion nodded, he continued. "Keep searching for her. Do not fail me in this. I need that woman apprehended."

"As you wish, Dermond. We search for her even now."

Fuck. Jesse's stomach rolled. Someone he didn't know and couldn't identify was hunting for Destiny this very minute, maybe even right here in the airport, and he'd left her all alone.

"More coffee while you wait, miss?"

Destiny jumped, her empty cup clinking noisily against the thick white saucer. The voice at her shoulder was only the waitress.

Willing herself to stop shaking, she nodded her agreement and watched as the waitress refilled her cup before bustling away to check on her other customers.

No reason to be nervous. She was safe here. There were too many people around for that awful man to try to drag her out of this restaurant. And so what if she'd just ordered a full meal for two and didn't have two cents in her purse. Correction . . . didn't even have a purse to put her imaginary two cents into.

That big blond creep probably had her purse. He certainly had her laptop case, no mistaking that. Not too many hot-pink leather shoulder bags with gold roses stitched on them running around the country. Especially not being carried by a guy who looked like him.

"Here you go, honey. Anything else I can get for you?" Destiny jumped again when the waitress leaned across her to place the plates on her table. "You sure you don't want me to wrap up your friend's lunch to go?"

"No. Thank you. He should be here any minute."

The waitress lay the dinner ticket facedown on the table, shrugging as if she'd seen it all before. Working as waitstaff in a restaurant at the airport, she probably had.

Destiny certainly *hoped* Jesse would be here any minute. She picked up the tab and fingered it nervously. That was twenty-two dollars more than she could cough up at the moment. What would they do to her if he didn't come back? How long could she linger over this meal, pretending to eat before she had to deal with the whole "not one red cent to her name" fiasco?

She dropped the check and stared at her plate. Pretending to eat was about all she could do with her stomach threatening to turn itself inside out at any moment.

Where the hell was he?

She scanned the restaurant once more in vain before squirting catsup on her plate. Picking up a french fry, she swirled the crispy potato stick in the thick red sauce, flashing back through the years to another meal very much like this one.

That day had been burgers and fries at a local greasy spoon. She and her little brother, Chase, had been so excited to have a rare lunch out with Mommy, and on a school day at that. The only thing missing was Daddy.

It was after their meal as she swirled her last french fry in catsup, exactly the way she did now, that she'd listened to her mother explain that her daddy wasn't coming home anymore. That was the same day her mother had come up with the story of the evil Faeries, the ones who were after their father, and that he had no choice but to leave them to keep them all safe.

On that day, Destiny had left their table, her mother comforting her crying eight-year-old brother, to make her way to the bathroom, where she'd locked herself in a stall and cried until she threw up.

When she'd washed her face off and walked out of that bathroom, she'd known her life would never be the same. And it certainly hadn't been.

Within months her new sister had been born, and at twelve, Destiny had been forced to grow up quickly. When her mother's illness had struck a few years later, followed by Rainbow's hopeless decline into alcoholism, Destiny had felt as if the world often rested on her own pitifully incompetent shoulders. Always she could trace her feelings of panic back to that moment in the restaurant when she'd left the bathroom headed to her seat.

Her father had left them to make their way on their own.

Alone.

All alone.

Destiny could taste the familiar fear and desperation rising in the back of her throat now as she fought the need to escape to yet another bathroom. That same old horrible, all-consuming panic was rearing its ugly head, building, growing.

Once it took over, her ability to reason would vanish

and she'd be that scared twelve-year-old again, reacting wildly, unable to see the logic that might be staring her in the face. There was no doubt in her mind. It had happened too many times before. Too many times she'd been left alone—when her mother had died, when her brother had left home, when she'd realized Leah was gone.

Even seemingly small events could trigger the panic, like being stood up for a date or having a boyfriend tell her he didn't want to see her anymore. And this—what she experienced now—was no small event. Jesse was her best hope to find Leah.

If he didn't come back, she was lost.

She fought it, tried to deny the icy tendrils of fear closing in on her.

I don't need him or anyone, she told herself fiercely. She wasn't twelve anymore. She'd manage somehow. She always had.

"Come on, we've got to get out of here."

Startled, she looked up, shocked to find Jesse at her side. He'd come back for her.

"But what about the food? Should we have them wrap—"

"No," he interrupted, pulling at her arm to rush her from her seat. "You okay?"

Embarrassed that he'd caught her crying, she snatched up the ticket, waving it in front of him. "I couldn't pay."

His jaw tightened in what looked like irritation as he pulled bills from his pocket, tossing two twenties next to her plate.

"That's way too much," she began, but stopped as he practically dragged her from the table.

"Forget it. No time to wait on these people. We have to go. Now."

His urgency frightened her, so she said no more, almost running to keep up with his long stride. He didn't slow down until they reached the rental car parking area and he opened the passenger door on a large white SUV.

She climbed in and fastened her seat belt, trying to catch her breath as he gunned the engine and screeched out of the parking lot.

"What happened in there? You didn't get my laptop? Didn't you find him?"

He didn't take his eyes off the road when he answered. "Psycho Blondie is headed to Phoenix."

Arizona. Just like the dream had told her. If Jesse had any doubts before, this should eliminate them.

"For the record, his name is Dermond Tyren and he has people looking for you right now."

"People? As in more than just him?" Somehow the knowledge that this Tyren man wasn't working alone was much, much scarier than the idea of his being an isolated psycho kidnapper.

"Exactly. And as soon as we get out of town and I can afford to concentrate on something other than the possibility of our being followed, you've got some explaining to do."

"Explaining? What are you talking about?"

Jesse spared only a quick glance in her direction as he merged into traffic, his expression dark. "It's time for you to tell me the truth about why Psycho Blondie and his Nuadian Fae friends are really after you."

Chapter 10

❧

This was exactly why he always left interactions with clients to the office staff. Lovey always did tell him he was too blunt to be allowed to open his mouth around the general public.

But it was difficult to have the office interfacing with a "client" they didn't know existed.

Jesse turned his head from the dark, wet ribbon of road to cast a brief look in Destiny's direction. She lay with her head at an odd angle against the SUV window, cushioned by the pink VIRGINIA IS FOR LOVERS emblazoned T-shirt he'd bought her today when they'd stopped for supplies at the big discount store.

From the sound of her slow, regular breathing, it appeared she'd stopped pretending to sleep in order to avoid conversation with him and had actually dozed off.

One thing for sure, she was going to wake with one

hell of a sore neck, and from what he knew of Destiny so far, she'd likely be grouchy as all get-out. The thought made him smile. She certainly didn't go out of her way to hide her feelings.

Which was why it bothered him all the more that he'd hurt those feelings earlier.

Ah well, better a little emotional pain than a whole lot of physical pain. She'd just have to deal with the fact that Faeries actually did roam the planet, and for some reason she either didn't know—or didn't want to share—they were after her. And likely already had her sister.

It was the "didn't want to share" possibility that gnawed at him still, even though they'd discussed it.

Discussed? Yeah, right. That was like saying the drenching rain outside was a gentle mist.

She'd been withdrawn through their entire shopping trip, surprisingly choosing only a few items. She wouldn't even have picked up a purse for herself if he hadn't grabbed one. A purse, for God's sake. He hadn't put in all these years surrounded by the women in his family not to recognize how a purse was a female essential. Even his little niece already had a play purse she carried her favorite things in.

When he'd tossed the little pink leather bag in the basket, she'd simply eyed him with the same look of distrust she'd worn since they left the airport, continuing on in silence to the checkout counter.

The silence lasted until they left the store and approached their vehicle.

"I can't stand it any longer," she'd said, stopping with her bags clutched to her chest. "You need to explain what you said back at the airport. What the heck is a Nuadian Fae?"

He'd opened the back passenger door and tossed his bag inside. "The bad guys, babe. Faeries who want to alter life as we know it."

She'd tilted her head, her eyes narrowing suspiciously. "Faeries? Faeries as in . . . what? Disneyland faeries?"

He wasn't prepared to let her slide. He expected honesty. Demanded it. One hundred percent. He gave no less. "I think you know what I'm talking about. Faeries, as in otherworld beings. Like us, only . . . not. It would appear they have your sister and they're damn well doing their best to get you, too."

"Faeries. Have you actually seen any of these vicious little creatures flying around, carrying people off?"

"Sure have, babe, and so have you. His name's Dermond Tyren. Psycho Blondie, remember him?" He'd reached for her bags but she'd backed up a step, still holding them to her chest.

They'd needed to get out of that parking lot and on the road. They did not need to be standing there in the open discussing the goddamned Fae, where anyone searching for her could easily spot them. Maybe he should have reasoned with her. Should have tried explaining how he knew what he knew. But he hadn't. He'd lost his patience and grabbed her arm, tugging her toward the SUV.

"Look. I'm tired of the bullshit. The longer you withhold important information from me, the longer it's going to take to find your little sister. You're making this harder for all of us."

Destiny had jerked her arm away, her mouth drawn into a thin, disapproving line. "You're tired of the . . ." She bit off her words and slammed the bag she held into his chest, poking the plastic he now held in front of him like a shield. "Look. You don't want to tell me what's really going on? Fine. Don't make up crap like I'm some simpleminded bimbo who'll swallow whatever BS you dish out. I don't appreciate being treated like I'm twelve." She'd pushed past him and climbed up into the seat, leaning out for one last onslaught before slamming the door behind her. "What is it with you? Do you do drugs? Does your employer have any idea what a total freak you are?"

As he'd climbed in the vehicle with her, she was still muttering. The last words he'd heard between then and now was something about her life having turned into a toilet, surrounded by psycho kidnappers and wannabe Highlanders.

In response, he'd pointed out that technically he was a Highlander, but she hadn't been impressed enough to do more than glare at him.

One more glance in her direction. Yeah, she was one fiery little bundle of spunk, all right.

He could have pursued the discussion, forced the issue right then and there, but he'd thought of his sister and the thousand times she'd advised him to bite his tongue and back away from situations best left for another time. Finally he'd decided there was no gain to be had in slugging it out now. There would surely be a better opportunity before they reached Arizona.

And if there wasn't?

He'd just have to make his own opportunity. The

only problem was, if it came to that, there'd be no backing down to spare her feelings. He wouldn't have that kind of luxury next time they had the Faerie discussion.

Rain pelted the car as they sped forward, but he could still see well enough. According to the road signs, there was an exit up ahead lined with hotels.

He passed it by without even slowing.

No real point in pulling off now. Destiny was already out and he wouldn't be able to sleep anyway. Without all the facts he needed, it was probably just as well. Better he should try to plan for any contingency, try to be ready for any possibility.

Unfortunately it was starting to look an awful lot like one of those possibilities just might be that she really didn't have a clue about the Fae.

Or even—assuming those visions of hers were the real thing—about being descended from Faeries herself.

A fine, light-reflecting mist clung to her, flowing around her waist high, hampering her passage. It took all her energy to make the slightest forward motion, her body feeling as if she weighed tons. When she finally forced a step, her movement sent the smokelike tendrils dancing in beautiful swirls and eddies, each sparkling with rainbow hues.

Destiny pushed against an unseen force, fighting uselessly to move forward.

This was all wrong. Different dream-visions never came so close together. They had always repeated, like reruns on television, until she'd actually lived through whatever she'd seen last.

But this was no repeat. It was very different from the last vision she'd had. Stifling, dark if not for the incandescent flickering of the fog around her.

Destiny dipped her hand into the opaque vapors, fascinated by their writhing motion and hypnotic patterns. She allowed the undercurrent of the mist to gently carry her hand backward until she was forced to turn her whole body. Only then did she reluctantly lift her hand, watching as the colored vapors snaked around her fingers. Tickling and tingling against her skin, they spiraled up into the air before diving down to rejoin the mass.

The smoky mist felt almost alive.

"It is alive."

Her father's voice. Destiny knew that when she awoke she'd be angry that she had dreamed so vividly of the man who had deserted her family, remembering so distinctly the sound of his voice after all these years. But for now, here in her dream-vision, his voice guided her, comforted her, as it sometimes did in this reality.

"It's the time flow of the All-Conscious, Desi. Don't fight it. Let yourself go with it and it will show you what you seek."

Go with it?

Though her body struggled in vain to move forward, her hand had floated effortlessly backward in the mist, turning her body around, pulling at her as if she were to follow it. Was that the key, moving backward? Had she missed something in the vision she'd had earlier?

Tentatively she took a step, and then another. It felt as if the mist urged her on, pushing her to hurry.

No wonder it wanted her to hurry. In the distance,

she could see the light that would soon flood this reality already gathering its strength, roiling in great heaving clouds of white and yellow, like eruptions on the sun gone wild.

Her time here would be ending soon.

She broke into a run and the mist evaporated. Ahead she could see the Arizona road sign, but she was moving much faster than if she were on foot, or even in a car, because the sign flew past her. Now, in the distance and closing, another sign. Large, weathered copper held aloft by massive poles like stripped tree trunks. As she passed it, more slowly than the first sign, she thought she saw the word FLAGSTAFF, but it was as if she viewed it through a dirty pane of glass.

A car window?

Then it, too, was gone, and she floated, suspended once again in the mist.

"Keep an eye out, babe, our turnoff should be just ahead."

Jesse's voice. Even in the dream reality he insisted on using that stupid endearment when he talked to her.

She swatted away the thought. It wasn't an endearment. More likely it was because he couldn't remember her name half the time. Besides, the term itself wasn't an important piece of the vision, unlike his being here. He sat beside her, driving the vehicle in which they rode.

Lifting her hand, she reached out to touch him, but he'd already melted away. The car was gone, too. Instead she stood in someone's living room, surrounded by dark, rich colors and heavy leather furniture.

In the corner she spotted a desk littered with paperwork. So much paper, it even lay scattered on the floor underneath. She sat down in the chair and reached out to the keyboard in front of her, looking up as she did. An odd painting hung on the wall above. Tiny footprints, like those of a baby, trailed a pastel path across a large canvas. Stenciled across the top were the words FAERIE TRACKS.

Even her dreams were now taunting her with Faeries.

An arm brushed past her and her senses flooded with warmth and the clean scent of soap, heady and masculine.

"You can check your email here."

Jesse pressed a button and the monitor came to life, its screen flickering with numbers and letters even as the edges of Destiny's vision blurred in the growing glare of the gathering light.

"Trust me," he whispered, and she looked up at him. He was shirtless, holding a thick green towel he'd apparently used in trying to dry his tousled wet hair. Markings, a tattoo of some sort, on his arm drew her eyes from the infectious grin that melted her heart.

She reached out, thinking to trace the markings on his muscled arm. Not for the sheer pleasure of running her finger across his bare skin. Not that at all, she tried to convince herself as she hesitated. She only wanted to study the tattoo, but she'd delayed too long. The light was so bright now, even Jesse's face so close to hers became blurred.

In the short time she had left, she wanted to apologize for having lost her temper in the real world. It was safe here in this place to confess the shortcomings she fought to hide. She understood that his only concern was to help her find Leah while keeping her safe, but there was so much fear in her heart. So much of the world spun out of her control.

She opened her mouth to admit her feelings, but once again, her attention was drawn away.

The brilliant glare that reduced Jesse to nothing more than a bright spot at her side highlighted a doorway behind him where a silhouetted figure stood. She had only a fleeting glance at the man before the light consumed everything, so his features were lost to her.

What she did see was that he was a large man with long blond hair, very much like Psycho Blondie and his friend at the airport in Norfolk. Worse, he was headed directly for Jesse's back with a shiny metal object in his hands.

"Jesse! Look out!"

When Destiny screamed, Jesse slammed his foot on the brake, sending the large Dakota skidding forward on the black rain-slicked highway.

The rear end of the vehicle fishtailed and vibrated wildly as the big SUV eventually came to a stop on the deserted strip of road.

Completely deserted.

"What the fuck?" Jesse snapped, glaring at the woman next to him as he switched off the engine. His heart pounded in his chest. Just the thought of what could have happened if there had been other cars on the road left his mouth dry.

Her face looked pale in the soft interior light of the vehicle, her fear evident. "I thought there was a man. . . ."

"What? Were you fucking dreaming?" He tightened his grip on the steering wheel, fighting for the emotional control he didn't feel at the moment. He could have flipped the car. Could have killed her. Could have killed them both.

"Yes!" she snapped back, anger replacing the earlier fright in her expression. "As a matter of fact, I was dreaming. But that doesn't give you the right to use that disrespectful language when you're speaking to me."

The rebuke drew him up short and he felt his temper spiking. Disrespectful language? Who the hell did she think she was, his grandmother or something?

Rather than yell again, he took a deep breath and locked his jaw shut. In a matter of moments, as his adrenaline levels returned to near normal, logic kicked back in and he could think more clearly.

No, she wasn't his grandmother. She was his client. And everyone over the age of thirteen knew you didn't drop the F-bomb on a client. Not even when they deserved it.

Rain pounded on the roof, a driving background to the tense silence inside the vehicle.

"Sorry." He managed the clipped word as he fumbled with the keys. Apologies weren't something he handed out casually, but then he rarely dealt with an emotion like the one he'd just experienced. He was never frightened, never lost his cool with a client, and why he did now was beyond him. No matter how it felt, this wasn't personal. It was business, and he needed to remember that.

He restarted the engine and pressed gently on the gas as their speed gradually increased, keeping his eyes focused ahead of him.

"Thank you for the apology," she responded at length, her words barely loud enough to be heard over the pelting rain. "But I don't have any claim to moral high ground in being angry with you. I shouldn't have reacted the way I did. I was just scared. You were right. I was having a dream . . . another vision of what's to come."

Jesse took a deep breath and expelled the last of his unwelcome emotions. Time to get back to business. "And?"

"And . . . someone was getting ready to attack you. Psycho Blondie, I think. I was only trying to warn you."

"Well, babe, I do appreciate your having my back, but next time, why don't you try to figure out whether it's real or not before you sound the alarm, okay?"

"Easier said than done," she muttered, turning to stare out into the dark whipping past her window.

"This attack, was it happening someplace specific? In Arizona, maybe?" It would certainly be nice to have a destination in mind a little less general than just Phoenix.

"I don't know. Maybe." She turned in her seat to stare at him. "I saw a sign that had the word *Flagstaff* written on it, and then everything changed and we were in someone's home, maybe a living room. There was dark leather furniture and I was sitting at a computer, trying to check my email. I don't know where that room is. All I do know for a fact is that it's where I have to go next."

"Can you remember any other details? Anything at all that could help us find this place?"

"Not really. Oh! A painting of some sort hanging above the computer. I can't imagine that would help us at all. In fact, it's probably nothing more than my sub-conscious trying to offload unimportant information."

"Yeah? Why don't you describe it for me." They couldn't afford to overlook any possible clues, even things that, as she said, might not have any bearing at all.

"Okay. It was maybe six feet long, two feet high. Not much to it. Just a canvas full of little footprints. But nothing else, really."

I'll be damned.

"Was there maybe a title on the painting? *Faerie Tracks* by any chance?"

"How do you know that?" She stared at him, her pouty lips invitingly ajar.

How? Because he'd been there the day Cate had dipped Rosie's pudgy little feet in paint and let her take those first giggling steps across the long strip of butcher paper. He'd taken it to the framer himself, adding the title he'd thought so clever at the time.

Instead of answering, he pulled out his cell phone and hit speed dial.

"Peter Hale," a sleepy voice answered on the fourth ring. "Do you have any idea what time it is here?"

"Sure do. That's why I called you at home. Looks like we have a slight change in our flight plan."

Chapter 11

"You'll want to fasten your seat belt now, Ms. Noble. We've got thunderstorms all around Denver this afternoon, so it could get a little bumpy before we land." The young woman who'd introduced herself as the co-pilot when they'd boarded this small plane in Nashville smiled at Destiny as she strode toward the cockpit. "Now all I have to do is kick Jesse out of my seat so we can get you guys safely on the ground."

Destiny returned the woman's smile and took one last moment to study her new identification card, a Colorado driver's license showing her with an address on Adams Street in Denver.

Pretty neat trick considering she'd never even been to Colorado before, or anywhere west of the Mississippi for that matter.

She slipped the card into the purse Jesse had insisted

on buying for her on their shopping trip, and then snapped her seat belt on before leaning her head back against the buttery soft leather of her seat.

What a crazy morning it had been. Thank goodness she'd actually slept last night with nothing more going through her head than regular people dreams. Because as exhausted as she felt at the moment, she was willing to bet she'd be out cold if she'd had to deal with the dream-visions all night long.

They'd arrived in Nashville late yesterday evening. Jesse and the people he worked with had thought it best to get away from Virginia and the people who were hunting for her.

People, she emphasized to herself, not some bizarre evil Faeries.

They'd gone straight to an information desk at the airport this morning and picked up an envelope waiting for Jesse. Inside had been the photo ID that allowed Destiny access to the boarding area and this private jet sent for them by Coryell Enterprises.

It had seemed an inopportune time to tell him she'd never flown before. Thankfully the pantry of the plane stocked Dramamine or she would have humiliated herself shortly after takeoff. Who knew she was prone to motion sickness?

They all did.

Now.

"You okay?"

Jesse dropped into the seat next to her and fastened his seat belt just as a loud thump sounded below her feet.

She grabbed his arm and he took her hand in his, his thumb massaging her palm. "Don't worry, babe. That's just the wheels extending for landing. It's supposed to feel like that. It'll feel a little like running over a cow when we touch down and then that's it. You'll be on the ground, safe and sound, in no time flat."

Destiny tightened her grip on his hand and tried to relax. People did this flying stuff all the time. She could do it, too.

In short order, they were on the ground and in the concourse, making their way to an underground train that whisked them to the terminal.

"They all look the same, don't they?" Destiny felt like something of an airport expert, having been inside three different terminals in the last three days. "Everybody rushing somewhere."

"Pretty much," Jesse agreed, leading her forward through the big glass doors and out into the bright sun, directly to the open door of a waiting car.

"I thought the copilot said it was storming here," she commented as he assisted her into the backseat.

"Destiny, this is Peter Hale. Peter, Destiny Noble." Jesse's introduction of the vehicle's driver was hurried as he folded his large frame in next to her. He scooted into the center of the seat, forcing her to move to the far window, then reached across her to grab her seat belt and latch it over her body before taking a file folder Peter handed him.

"The weather rolls in funny around here, Ms. Noble." Peter caught her eye in the rearview mirror. "It can creep up on you awful fast. Have a look over there."

She followed the direction of his head nod as the car gathered speed leaving the terminal.

In the distance, clouds hung heavy and dark over a

small circle of skyscrapers. Occasional streaks of lightning threaded from sky to ground, their brilliant light standing out against the darker backdrop of the majestic Rockies.

The city looked so far away, she wanted to ask the distance, but both men were quietly discussing whatever paperwork Jesse had taken from the man named Peter. She leaned her head back against the seat and closed her eyes, comforted by Jesse's nearness.

Surely he'd move back over to his side of the car soon.

"She okay?" Peter asked quietly, his voice barely above a whisper.

"Yeah, just tired. She popped a motion sickness pill when we got on the plane."

Did they think it was okay to just talk about her like that? Like she couldn't hear or something? Destiny had every intention of opening her eyes and speaking for herself, but Jesse put an arm around her, pulling her closer. Instead of complaining, she found herself snuggling into the solid warmth of his body, completely relaxed for the first time all day.

"Not a goddamned word out of you, Pete."

Though Jesse's words of warning were quiet, they rumbled under Destiny's ear and she fought the sleep trying to overtake her long enough to open her eyes.

"Didn't say a thing, boss man. Didn't even think it."

Peter Hale's wide grin reflected in the rearview mirror was the last thing she saw before she gave in to the need to doze.

Booming thunder rattled the car, so close Destiny was sure it must be directly overhead, jerking her wide awake.

"It's okay." Jesse momentarily tightened his arm around her in a gentle squeeze before withdrawing and allowing her to sit up on her own. "We're only a couple blocks from home now."

Destiny rubbed her hands over her face, willing the last dregs of sleep away. With a surge of embarrassment, she realized her cheek was damp where she'd lain against Jesse's chest.

Life just kept getting better and better. She'd started the morning threatening to hurl on the guy and now she was finishing up by drooling on him. What other ways could she find to humiliate herself?

Hastily she pushed the thought away. No sense tempting fate. After all, fate seemed to have it in for her lately as it was.

Rain pelted the windows in torrents, making it almost impossible for her to read the street signs until the car slowed at a four-way stop.

ADAMS.

Wasn't that the same street name as on her new driver's license?

She didn't have time to think about it as they pulled to a stop on the street in front of a two-story brick house with a huge black Hummer parked in the small driveway.

"Sorry about the walk. This is as close as I can get. Drive's full." Peter leaned away to rustle around in the glove box for a moment before handing back a small blue umbrella. "This might help a little."

"Very little," Jesse snorted as he exited the car, stepping out into the downpour.

In the short time it took him to get around to

Destiny's door, he was already drenched, but holding the umbrella up for her to walk under. He smiled down at her and held out his hand to help her out of the car.

At least he wouldn't notice the small wet spot she'd left on his chest now. Maybe her luck was changing.

The front door, itself a rich emerald green, opened as they reached the covered stoop. The man holding it open was every bit as handsome as Jesse, but even bigger, with shoulder-length brown hair.

"About time you got here. Interesting trip you had, or so I hear." He backed away, allowing them room to enter a tiled foyer.

Jesse nodded as he closed the dripping umbrella and propped it against the wall. "You could say that. Why the hell didn't you move that beast of yours into the street if you knew we were coming?"

The man laughed, his eyes twinkling. "Yer neighbors are no too fond of my wee toy blocking a lane of traffic. The elderly gent across the street was quick to point that out the day after you left."

Jesse wiped a hand across his face. "I'm sure he was. I need to grab a towel. Destiny, this is Robert. Don't believe half of what this big Scot says before I get back in here. Robbie, this is Destiny Noble. Why don't you show her into the living room. She needs to use the computer."

Robert walked a few steps away, pausing at a large double-door archway. Destiny took one last look at Jesse as he hurried down the hallway and disappeared behind a door, more than a little sorry he was going to dry off.

There wasn't a single doubt in her mind that the only thing she'd ever see that looked better than Jesse in the T-shirts she'd seen him wear was Jesse in the wet T-shirt he had on right now. It seemed to cling in all the right places and clearly accentuated just how many right places the man had.

At the sound of Robert's pointed throat clearing, she snapped her head around in his direction, a dull warmth flooding her face. It was just damned sloppy to have allowed herself to get caught staring like that.

Ducking her head to avoid the big Scot's grin, she hurried past him into the large room and froze, a gasp on her lips.

Lit only by one small lamp, the room was cast in shadows, but even that couldn't mask its already familiar furnishings.

This was the room from her vision, right down to the painting that hung on the wall over the computer desk.

Almost like being back in the dream, she felt herself drawn to the desk, her feet carrying her there as if they did so in spite of any effort she might make to stop. She pulled out the big office chair and sat, scooting forward to the computer and reaching for the power button.

She hesitated, moving her hand instead to the keyboard, her fingers hovering over the instrument.

This was it, her opportunity to push beyond the vision, but something stayed her hand.

She jumped as an arm brushed past her and her senses flooded with warmth and the clean scent of soap, heady and masculine.

"You can check your email here."

Exactly as in the vision, Jesse pressed a button and the monitor was alive, its screen flickering with numbers and letters, only this time, in the real world, each of them was crisp and sharp.

"It'll be okay. Trust me," he said quietly, his serious eyes softened by a reassuring smile.

He was shirtless, as he had been in the dream-vision, carrying a thick green towel he'd apparently used in drying his tousled wet hair. He'd obviously been in a hurry to get back since a dry T-shirt was slung carelessly over one shoulder.

This close to him, she knew within seconds she'd been wrong earlier.

There *was* something better than Jesse in a wet T-shirt and it was standing right in front of her. She'd seen plenty of magazine photos of guys with rock-hard six-packs, but she'd be the first to admit, those photos were nothing compared to the real thing standing within touching distance.

She fought the urge to trace her finger across the ripples of his chest and would have lost the battle had he not spoken to her again.

"Go ahead, babe. Sign on and pull up your mail."

"Right." She dragged her eyes from his chest and let out the breath she hadn't realized she'd been holding as she pulled up her mail server. What a doofus. At this point, she only hoped Jesse either wouldn't notice or would chalk up her bizarre behavior to nerves about her sister.

The list of incoming mail was short, but the one she knew would be waiting for her jumped out immediately.

If you want to see your sister alive . . .

"I'll be damned," Jesse whispered, his face so close to hers she could feel the heat of him on her cheek. "Go on. Let's see what the bastards have to say."

This is your only chance. Off Highway 89A in Sedona, Arizona, you'll find the Farmers' Market. Be there at 5:30 on Tuesday evening. Be prompt. We won't wait.

"Oh my God. That's tomorrow." Destiny fought the tears she felt burning her eyes as she ran her finger over the words on the screen. "There's no way we can get there in time. It's impossible."

"Impossible's just a word," Jesse reassured her as he straightened, pulling his cell phone from his pocket and punching buttons. "And one that we're not going to waste any time worrying over. Peter? You're at the office already? Good. I need you to trace in on my home computer. I have an email and I need the sender's location."

"You can do that? From an email?"

Jesse grinned. "You'd be amazed at the magic Peter can accomplish with his techie toys." His expression went from smiles to serious in a heartbeat and he was back to business. "Hold on."

He laid the phone down and leaned across her, slanting the keyboard toward him to type.

REPLY.

A blank email form popped up with a prefilled address, and Jesse typed in a message.

I'll be there.

He highlighted the SEND button and the message was gone, winging its way to the people who held Leah.

"It's done," he said after picking up the phone again. "We'll need to be in Sedona early tomorrow afternoon. You'll make the arrangements and have everything waiting?" A pause. "Great. No need to tell you I'd take it as a personal favor if you had some coordinates waiting for me when we land in Arizona. Later, man."

As Jesse slid the phone back into his front jeans pocket, Destiny released a shuddering breath and looked up at him.

"Come on now, don't cry." He slid the pad of his thumb across her cheek, wiping away the tears she couldn't stop. "We'll be there in time. I promise. We're going to get your sister back."

Without thought, she was on her feet, her arms around him, her face buried in the edge of the crumpled T-shirt that hung from his shoulder. It felt so good not to be alone in this battle any longer, to have found someone at last who knew what to do and was willing to do it. Someone who believed her. Accepted her.

His arms tightened around her, pulling her closer, while he stroked her hair. "It's okay, babe," he murmured, his breath warm where it feathered against her temple. "It's okay."

A small turn of her head and the soft cloth bunched away. The clean, spicy scent of him enveloped her senses as her lips rested on the bare, heated skin of his chest, where the hard planes jumped and twitched in response to her touch.

The relief she'd felt only seconds before fled, washed away by a much stronger emotion, a need for the man who held her, a need so intense, she couldn't imagine ignoring it.

Strong back muscles rippled under her hands as Jesse brought a finger to rest under her chin, lifting her face to meet his gaze.

His eyes, those beautifully shifting brown-green lenses, captured hers, and he lowered his head even as she felt herself reaching up to meet his full, sensual mouth, drawn to him as the proverbial moth to a flame.

Their lips touched and she was lost, sinking into him, wanting him.

His hands slid to her waist and up, pushing ahead of them the cover of the pink T-shirt, leaving a trail of tingling heat where he traced up her sides.

The kiss broke and he lowered his head to her neck, his tongue and lips working a magic all their own that within seconds of contact had her ready to rip her shirt off.

Destiny rose up on her toes, pressing into his body, closing her eyes to block out the world, all too aware of her racing heart and the accelerated sound of their breathing.

In this moment, she didn't care. Didn't want to think. Wanted only to feel. To feel him, his hands on her body, his mouth on her neck.

Down his back she explored, slipping her fingers just into the waistband of his jeans, sliding them forward and down. Down the rippling abs that disappeared beneath his beltline.

"Jesus, Des," he groaned, his body tensing under her touch.

"I know," she whispered in response, opening her eyes to look at his beautiful face. "I know. I can't believe . . ."

She would have said more, but movement over his shoulder caught her attention.

There in the doorway, backlit by the bright hallway lights stood a lone figure. A man. Just as in her vision, he paused for only a moment before starting forward, the light reflecting off the long, shiny object he carried in his hands.

"Jesse! Look out!"

Destiny's scream of warning broke the spell that had so firmly held him captive only seconds before. He shoved her behind him as he twisted around to face whatever danger had invaded his home.

"Pol?"

The shock of recognition lasted only an instant, followed as quickly by confusion as to why the Hereditary High Prince of the Realm of Faerie—and his own Faerie ancestor—stood in his living room in Denver.

"You sound surprised to see me, lad. Or is my arrival simply at an inopportune moment?"

"Not at all." Jesse avoided meeting the Fae's discerning gaze as he moved to switch on the large lamps at either end of the sofa, flooding the room with a soft welcoming light.

"What's that he's holding?" Destiny's trembling voice belied her uplifted chin.

"This?" Pol laughed as he lifted the long, thin metallic decanter. "This is naught but a gift from home. Dallyn told me you had developed quite an appreciation for our Nectar. This is a particularly fine vintage, if I do say so myself. From my own stock."

"Oh." The little noise escaped Destiny's lips on a

breath as she sank into the large leather recliner. "A gift. I don't understand. I was so sure what I'd seen was . . ." Her words died off.

"This was what frightened you before? The other night in the car?"

She nodded before lowering her head into her hands, scrubbing at her face as if attempting to physically erase her confusion.

"This is Destiny Noble. She saw your arrival in a vision," Jesse responded to the question evident in Pol's uplifted brow. "And thought you were someone else. Someone carrying a weapon."

"Ah." The Prince entered the room, taking a seat on the sofa across from Destiny. "In that case, Ms. Noble, I'm pleased to disappoint you, my dear. But how delightful to find a kinswoman here, so far from home. Dallyn made no mention of this."

Jesse swept the shirt from his shoulder and pulled it on over his head before dropping to perch on the arm of Destiny's chair. The hand he placed on her shoulder meant nothing. Her evident upset tugged at some long-ignored emotion, but he refused to give in to it.

Just as he refused to let his thoughts dwell on what had just happened between them.

There were more important matters to deal with right now.

Like Pol.

"How did you get here? For that matter, why are you here?" Jesse couldn't recall any mention of Pol ever having strayed so far from his Glen into the Mortal World.

"I took an a-ro-plane." He pronounced the word as if it were as foreign to him as the object it represented.

"It was actually rather pleasant, though burdensome in the time it required. I did not even suffer from the morning sickness Dallyn had cautioned against."

"Morning sickness?" Destiny's head snapped up with her question.

"He means motion sickness. Dallyn confuses words all the time." Or he pretended to. Jesse hadn't completely decided on that yet.

"And Dallyn would be . . . ?" Destiny dragged out the words, letting the question linger between them.

"A friend." Jesse held up his hand and turned away from her. He'd have to explain all of this sooner or later, but at the moment he was opting for later, hoping not to have that particular conversation with Pol present. "I'm glad you had a good flight. But you still haven't explained why you're here."

"Ah . . ." The Prince sat back against the sofa, all pretense of a jovial visit wiped away. "When Dallyn brought word of your disturbing conversation with our Guardian, Ian McCullough, I had no choice but to come here in person."

Jesse turned his full attention to his ancient guest. "You know something about what's going on with the Nuadians?"

How bad must that explanation be if Pol came himself rather than sending his General?

"Are you sure you want to discuss it . . . now?" Pol cast a pointed gaze in Destiny's direction.

"Yes sir. This concerns her, too. It's her they're after for some reason, and I suspect they already have her sister."

"Unfortunate." Pol tapped his steepled fingers together before sighing deeply. "Very well. As you say, it is best you both know what you are up against. May I?" He held up the decanter he'd brought with him.

"Oh, sorry." Jesse snagged three glasses from the sideboard and returned, placing them on the coffee table in front of the Prince.

Pol completely filled two glasses, but poured only a splash into the third, which he offered to Destiny.

When she shook her head in refusal, he returned the glass to the table and leaned back once again, his eyes taking on a faraway look as if, for the moment, he was lost in his private memories.

"It began long before I was born, in a time when the royal family still ruled Wyddecol, what you know as the Realm of Faerie."

Jesse leaned forward, returning his untouched glass to the table. "I knew the Nuadians were old, but I was under the impression they hadn't been living in my world for that long."

"The Bloodlust didn't begin with the Nuadians. They were hardly the first of our people to be banished to the Mortal World to live out their lives bereft of their magic. In the Long Ago, it was a common punishment for the worst of our kind."

"Well, isn't that just great," Jesse muttered. That the Fae had used the world of man as a penal dumping ground for their worst offenders shouldn't surprise him. "What's this *bloodlust* thing you mentioned?"

"A black scourge on the souls of the Fae. In the Long Ago, the Exiled Ones discovered a way to regain their stripped powers through the consumption of Mortal blood."

A strangled sound came from Destiny. "You're saying that those people drank human blood?"

The palpable disgust in her voice reflected Jesse's own feelings.

"Yes. The Exiled Ones drank blood." Pol shrugged and looked away, as if trying to distance himself from the memory. "It was, in fact, the horror of those dark times that led men to create legends of an undefeatable race of monsters who preyed on the blood of the innocent."

"Vampires? Are you talking about vampires?" Destiny shook her head, disbelief in her eyes. "But they're not real. They're just make-believe. Nothing more than fairy tales."

"Exactly," Pol agreed. "Tales of the Faerie. The darkest side of the Fae. Though the practice rejuvenated their bodies, restored and enhanced their strength, it ate away at their souls. The putrid traces of what they had been was no longer fit for the Fountain of Souls. The disruption they left behind was rivaled only by the destruction caused during the Great War with the Nuadians. It was that horrific destruction that led the Earth Mother to remove Faerie magic from the Mortal World."

"If they were undefeatable, does that mean they're still around? Did the Nuadians hook up with those guys? Is that how they can do what they're doing?" Jesse didn't have time for a history lesson. He wanted to understand what he was dealing with in the now.

"I have no idea how the Nuadians discovered the ancient evil. I was but a lad when the Exiled Ones were finally defeated, though I do remember whispers in the palace about the means of their defeat being as danger-ous as the evil had ever been."

Destiny's shoulder stiffened under Jesse's hand and she pulled away, rising from her chair.

"This is crazy. You guys are talking about some old legend like it's real. There are no vampires. There are no faeries. None of that stuff exists."

"You must be aware of one other thing, Guardian," Pol continued, as if Destiny had not spoken. "The Whole has entered a new phase. It is as if the strings of fate are being gathered up, leading us all to the place we need to be. The magic forbidden in the Mortal World is returning with an unknown strength. Only this time it is not in the hands of the Fae, but instead resides with the new race."

A tension zinged through Jesse's veins at Pol's use of his title and the markings on his arm felt as if they had come alive. "New race?"

"Yes. The race created when Fae mated with Mortal. Neither Fae nor man, but a combination of the two. For better or worse, these beings now hold the power of the magic in this world."

"You mean like me?" Though Jesse used himself as the example, it was the face of his little niece that danced through his thoughts.

"Yes. Like you."

"This isn't funny, okay? Why are you two carrying on like this? There. Are. No. Faeries. Period." Destiny had backed away from them as she punctuated her words, her arms crossed defiantly, protectively in front of her.

The look Pol cast in her direction as he gestured to-ward her could only be seen as sympathetic. "Like her."

"Stop it! Stop it right now!" Destiny's voice shook with her emotion. "You can't frighten me with these fantasies. It's not real. None of it."

"It is real, Destiny. Denying it won't make it go away." Jesse stood and headed across the room toward her, but Pol stopped him with a gentle hand to his arm.

"Show her." Pol straightened, his arms at his sides.

"Show her?"

"Can you not feel the fear inhabiting the rips in her soul where trust has been torn away? She will not believe without proof. She cannot." Pol lifted his chin and held his arms out to his sides. "Hit me."

"What? What do you think you're doing?" Destiny looked as if she were ready to jump between the two of them.

As if Pol needed her help!

Jesse shrugged. He would have preferred to do this differently, but maybe Pol was right. They didn't have time to ease her into what she needed to accept.

"Whatever." He pulled back his arm and threw himself into a wicked uppercut.

With one slight miscalculation.

Destiny screamed as his arm flew through the unsubstantial mist Pol's body became. With nothing solid to stop his forward momentum, Jesse's body pitched through the Fae and his shoulder hit the floor with a thud that rattled his bones.

"Oh my God." Destiny's words died off, sounding as if they'd been dragged from the depths of her soul, and she repeated them over and over in a breathless whisper until she turned her sticken gaze toward Pol. "What *are* you?"

"I am Fae," he answered simply.

Chapter 12

"*H*ereditary High Prince of the Faeries, to be more exact," Robert said from his spot in the doorway before he walked to Jesse and extended a hand to help him up. "Now, would someone like to tell ol' Robbie what the bloody hell's going on in here? That scream likely aged me five years."

Destiny's mind crowded with questions, the shock of what she'd just seen blocking them all. It couldn't be. None of it was possible.

And yet . . . she'd seen the proof with her own eyes.

She watched silently, trying to sort out her thoughts as, with Robert's assistance, Jesse rose to his feet, rubbing his shoulder. A sheepish grin lit his face when he spoke to his friend.

"Just got a little carried away with our demonstration." Jesse tilted his head in her direction. "She didn't believe in Faeries. We were trying to convince her."

"Aye, well, that one is quite the big bite to swallow, is it no?" Robbie nodded thoughtfully. "I had my own experience with the believing of it a long time ago. There's many a mystery in the world, lass. Yer life will be easier by far if you just accept and move on. That's my motto these days."

"How did you do that?" Destiny at last untangled the words in her head and found herself moving across the room without thought, as if pulled by some unknown force. She stopped in front of Pol and reached out tentatively to trail her fingers down his arm. "You're solid. I can feel you. And yet, I watched you evaporate. How did you do that? How did he go right through you?"

"I told you. I am Fae. As the Earth Mother decreed long ago, the Fae can neither commit nor experience violence in the Mortal World. We are as the mist of the time flow."

The mist in her visions! What had her father's voice called it? "The time flow of the All-Conscious," she murmured, remembering the words from her vision.

"Yes," he agreed, catching up her hand.

Robbie cleared his throat, as if embarrassed to interrupt. "I'm all packed and ready to go whenever you'd like to leave, yer grace."

"You're not staying the night?"

Jesse asked the question as he took Destiny's hand from Pol's, lacing his own larger fingers with her smaller ones, though she hadn't even noticed when he'd moved so close beside her.

"No. Robert has kindly offered to transport me to

Seun Fardach to see my little Rosie and her family while I am here. If my fortune holds, I may even have the opportunity to visit with my Mairi before I return home."

"In that case, I'll see you off." Jesse squeezed Destiny's hand before letting go. "You okay?"

She nodded, her thoughts still too jumbled to voice all the questions running through her mind.

When the men left the room, she dropped her head to her hands, her fingers covering her eyes. This was too much to accept. It felt as if someone had turned her entire world upside down and dumped her out into some alternate universe where evil Faeries kidnapped young girls and drank their blood.

"My poor Leah," she whispered as the horror of her sister's fate washed over her, freeing the tears she had tried to hold back.

How could her life have come to this? Hadn't she done everything she could to be normal? And still her life had raged away, always slipping through her fingers no matter how hard she struggled to maintain control.

Memories, like jagged puzzle pieces, tumbled behind her closed eyes, vying for her attention.

Her father's desertion had taken them overnight from a life of ease to a poverty-level subsistence. They'd had nothing but each other, and then even that had been taken away. Her mother's long illness followed by her escape into alcohol, her subsequent death, Chase running away—all these memories and the feelings of loss she'd struggled to deny for so long washed over her now, their assault as painful as physical blows.

She'd managed to push them back, to lock them away into neat little compartments in her mind, allowing her to avoid the inevitable confrontation for years. Her family *wasn't* like everyone else. *She* wasn't like everyone else.

When Leah had disappeared and the authorities declared it simply another teenage runaway case, she'd thought that was as bad as it could get, but she'd been wrong.

What was it Robert had said earlier? Life would be easier if she would just accept and move on. But he didn't understand that accepting the bizarre truth they'd forced on her tonight would strip away all her barriers, all her defenses, leaving her naked against the onslaught of her memories.

All the things her mother had told them, all the things she'd chalked up to the woman's fantastic alcohol-fueled rants—they were all true. Her father really was a Faerie who'd left his family to protect them.

God, but she hoped the coward was pleased with himself. If the lives they'd had after he'd left was his idea of protected, she couldn't begin to fathom how awful his staying might have been for them.

She didn't realize she was sobbing until Jesse's arms surrounded her, pulling her into his chest while he stroked her hair, making soft little shushing noises of comfort.

How long she stood there, wrapped in the safety of his arms, she had no idea. Finally the onslaught ebbed, and she pulled away, wiping at her face.

Wonderful. She'd managed to leave a big wet spot on another of his shirts.

With an arm around her shoulders, he guided her from the room and toward the stairs. "Why don't I show you to your room? You can wash up and I'll go throw a couple of steaks on the grill. How's that sound?"

She nodded, not trusting the tears to be fully gone, and they slowly made their way upstairs to a landing that looked down over the foyer. A long hallway stretched out ahead of them, apparently running the length of the house, closed doors dotting both sides. They passed by the first doorway, stopping at the second.

After opening the door, Jesses stepped back, allowing her to enter ahead of him.

The bedroom looked like something out of a magazine photo spread. Beautiful and impersonal. Unlived in, as if a decorator had designed the perfect guest room and then walked out, closing it away from everyone.

"You've got your own bathroom and you're safe here, so I won't even give you grief about leaving your door closed tonight. Plenty of privacy. I'm just down the hall if you need me. My room is the one by the stairs. The door will be open." He traced his thumb down her wet cheek, staring intently as if trying to read her thoughts. "You okay?"

"Yes."

He started down the hallway toward the stairs, but she couldn't let him go just yet.

"You're always asking me that, you know. If I'm okay."

He looked back and shrugged, a magnificent grin transforming his face into a thing of beauty. "Yeah. I'm not so good at the emotional stuff, babe. Sorry. But I am good at steaks. You come on down when you're ready." With that he disappeared down the stairs.

Destiny shut the bedroom door and leaned her forehead against it, her emotions spiraling again, but not with sorrow or despair this time.

That man was much better at the emotional stuff than he knew.

"Motherfu—!"

Jesse bit down on the expletive as he jerked his hand away from the hot grill and then looked around the dark patio guiltily. He was grateful that Destiny had carried their dirty plates back inside a few minutes earlier and had missed his outburst.

He gritted his teeth in irritation with himself. He'd promised her during dinner that he'd watch his language. Though what possessed him to make such a promise was beyond him. There was just something about this woman that allowed her to get under his skin in a way no one else ever had.

She'd shared some little family story about her mother not allowing them to use curse words growing up, and her eyes had gone all sad with unspoken memories. Next thing he knew, he was making wild-assed promises to clean up his mouth, as if he were compelled to wipe that sorrow away.

Whatever. The promise was made now and he meant to keep it. No matter what.

He grabbed the platter and wineglasses left on the table and headed inside.

She was loading the dishwasher when he entered the kitchen. The sight of her there, all domestic and busy, so much like she belonged in that spot, stopped him in his tracks.

It had been the same all through dinner. They'd

talked nonstop, as if they'd known each other all their lives, sharing things he'd never shared with anyone else.

Watching her now, he fought the urge to go to her, to wrap his arms around her and run his hands over her enticing curves, to bury his nose in her soft black hair. To turn her around and lose himself in those soft full lips. To rip that tight little T-shirt off and wrap his hands around . . .

What was he thinking? He was losing it. *Client*, he reminded himself. He had to get over this.

"Is that everything?" she asked without turning from her task.

"Yeah." He crossed to the sink and turned on the faucet, holding his hand under the cold water to lessen the sting of the bright red welt.

Didn't matter. Small wounds always healed quickly. Thanks to his Faerie bloodline, the burn would be gone by tomorrow afternoon. Sure hurt like a son of a bitch right now, though.

"What did you do?" One second she was elbow deep in dirty dishes and the next she was at his side, fussing over his hand like a mother hen with one chick.

He was tempted to let her, but then reason kicked in and he pulled his hand away from her touch.

"It's nothing. Why don't you go on into the living room and make yourself comfortable. I'll be there in a minute."

"You sure?" Her expression was as doubtful as her tone.

Oh, he was sure, all right.

"Yeah, go on. Go put your feet up. You've got a big day ahead of you tomorrow."

She shrugged and turned her back, leaving him with his raging hormones and private thoughts.

For some reason this woman threw him off his game and he couldn't afford that right now. He had to stay sharp or people would get hurt. Destiny wasn't the only one expecting a big day tomorrow.

He would have preferred to fly out to Sedona tonight, leaving her here where he knew she'd be safe. On the off chance that Peter didn't manage to track the location of the computer that sent the email, he'd still need her to make the meeting at the Farmers' Market. And there was no way in hell he was taking her out there, closer to those monsters, any sooner than he had to.

So, tomorrow it was.

Robbie would meet them at the airstrip in the morning and accompany them as his backup. He couldn't ask for better.

They'd fly into Flagstaff and drive to Sedona. Not his first preference, but the safest choice. He'd bet money that whoever Dermond Tyren worked for would have people watching the Phoenix airport and possibly even the small Sedona airstrip.

But Flagstaff? Not the normal route for the casual traveler. No big airliners landed there. He might not even have thought of it if not for her vision of the Flagstaff signpost.

If all went as planned, they'd have the coordinates to locate the origin of the email by the time they landed tomorrow and he could find a spot to leave Destiny. Safely out of harm's way.

Under the circumstances, he'd tried to cover all his bases.

Jesse slammed the dishwasher door and latched it, Pol's parting words still eating away at the back of his mind.

Be vigilant, Guardian. Though the evil of the Bloodlust has returned, it's more dangerous now than in the Long Ago. The Nuadians aren't taking blood from Mortals. They're feeding off the new race, those half Mortal, half Fae creatures in whom the magic of the old Fae now resides. We've no way of knowing what powers this might give them.

And here he was, getting ready to drag Destiny directly into that viper's nest. He was, to borrow one of his father's favorite sayings, dancing on a thin blade.

In the archway to the living room he paused, absorbing the scene before him.

Destiny sat on the sofa, her head back against the cushion, eyes closed, her bare feet tucked up under her. He was once again struck with the overwhelming familiarity of her presence, as if she belonged there in his home.

Bizarre, really. He'd never brought his "work" home before. He'd always kept his personal life and his professional life entirely separate.

Believing her asleep, he quietly entered and flipped off the nearest lamp, leaving the room bathed in the soft, dim glow of only one light.

"Sit with me."

She patted the sofa and he turned to find her smiling up at him.

"I thought you'd dozed off." Maybe he'd even hoped she had.

She shook her head. "No. I know I should, but my nerves are too raw for sleep." She smiled and held up an empty glass. "I hope you don't mind. I decided to finish off the drink you didn't touch earlier. Thought it might help take the edge off."

A full glass of Faerie Nectar? Yeah, if it affected her like it did him, the next time she tried to stand up she wouldn't even remember she had edges.

"I don't mind. I hope it helps. There's wine left from dinner if you'd like more."

"No. I'm not really much of a wine drinker. But this"—she wiggled the empty glass—"this was good. It tasted like pineapple."

He always thought so, too, though his sister and her husband swore it tasted of chocolate.

Sitting down next to her, he piled a couple of small pillows in between them. Not as barrier, really. More to rest his arm on.

When he stretched out his legs, propping his feet on the coffee table, she leaned forward to set down the glass before shifting in her seat to face him.

"How's your hand?"

"It's okay." Still stung like hell, but she didn't need to know that.

"Looks like it hurts."

She wrapped her fingers around his wrist and he pulled it back to escape her grasp, but surprisingly she held on, the resulting tug jarring his still sensitive shoulder. His reaction was too slow to mask the wince of pain.

"And that . . ." Her eyes narrowed as she nodded her head toward his shoulder. "That happened when you and Pol performed your little demonstration for my benefit, didn't it?"

"It's nothing."

"Right. Show me, then, if it's nothing."

Irritating woman. "I told you, I'm fine."

She was on her knees now, legs under her, bending forward. "If it were me that had happened to, it would be altogether different, wouldn't it? But you're Mr. Macho. Oooooo, Big Boss Man. Too tough to admit to being human." She clicked her tongue in disgust. "Typical male double standard."

His temper flared. "You want to see it?"

It wasn't bad enough that all he could think about sitting this close to her was how good she smelled. How inviting she looked. How she'd feel stretched out under him.

Now, on top of all that, she wanted him to remove his shirt, feeding into the hunger he already battled.

A hunger to take her right here, right now, on the sofa where she kneeled beside him, her eyes sparkling with her challenge. But he was stronger than that.

At least he hoped he was.

"You want to see it?" he asked again, fighting to control his voice this time. He lifted the bottom of his shirt, pulling it up as he slid his arm out, baring his injured shoulder. "There it is. I don't do double standards, lady."

Immediately he regretted his impulsiveness. He should have gotten up and walked away. Left the room.

The control he'd always prided himself on was nowhere to be found.

Her eyes widened and she made a little noise, like air rushing from her lungs. She leaned closer, shoving the pillow barrier out of her way in the process.

"What is that?" She reached out to him, tracing her fingertip over the tattoo covering his arm.

The Guardian mark came alive under her touch, his skin tingling and burning.

"Just a tat." He covered her hand, reluctantly pulling it from its track.

"Where did you get it done?" She couldn't seem to tear her eyes away from it, stretching out her free hand to run her fingers over his skin again.

He captured that one, too, holding them together as she finally looked directly at him.

"I know that symbol, Jesse. That snake with the line through it. That same thing is engraved on the necklace my mother always wore."

He shrugged and pushed her away, unwilling to go into an explanation of how all Dallyn's Elite Guardians bore the ancient mark. He'd have to see later what he could find out about where the necklace had come from.

Right now all he could think about was the sensations left behind where she'd touched him.

She seemed to recover herself, and reached out again, this time for his injury, resting her hand lightly over the bruise that covered his shoulder. The heat of her palm burned his skin, as if imprinting the feel of her touch into his memory.

"You should probably have that looked at," she murmured.

"No need for that." It would be gone tomorrow. They always were. What he did need right now was to get her hand off him. To get some distance between them before he forgot things he shouldn't.

Things like her being no different from the long string of needy women he'd had pass through his life, all looking for some man to support them.

The instant the thought passed through his mind he recognized it as unfair to Destiny. He tried to dismiss it, struggled to rein in his cascading emotions, reaching instead for the safety of logic. It wasn't her fault he couldn't keep his mind off having her. She hadn't stalked him in bars, pressing his friends for an introduction, as Lara had. Destiny was different. She'd been up front in what she wanted from the first. She'd come to him needing his help to find her sister.

In her case, it was better he concentrate on things like her being emotionally vulnerable right now. Things like her being his client.

He pulled back from her, reaching up to shove his arm back into his shirt as an excuse to move away, but she stopped his movement with a cool hand to his cheek. With the barest pressure of her palm, she guided his face to turn toward hers, and he found himself allowing her to do it.

"You're all about protecting people, aren't you? Taking care of them." She slid her hand along the side of his face and down around his neck, her fingers tangling in his hair as she swayed closer. "But I wonder, my Jesse. Do you ever allow anyone to take care of you?"

"I don't need . . ."

His words stopped as her hands skimmed down and across his chest, pushing his shirt up and over his head, tugging it down his other arm and tossing it to the floor.

Why he didn't stop her, he couldn't say. Perhaps because he didn't want her to stop.

The next thing he knew, she was in his lap, straddling him, pulling her T-shirt off over her head and tossing it away, much as she had thrown his to the floor moments earlier.

"Des."

It was the only warning he could voice as her arms snaked around him, her fingers tracing the muscles he felt tensing in his back at her touch.

This couldn't be anything but bad news and still he made no move to stop her.

She pressed against him, the warmth of her melting into his chest, the contact of their skin separated only by the thin cloth of her bra.

"Shhh," she whispered.

And then she smiled. Softly. Slowly.

He found himself unable to resist the sparkle of invitation in her eyes or the siren call of those soft pink, pouty lips.

Good, bad, didn't matter anymore. Just words in the dictionary, and right now, reading was not on his To Do list.

Crushing her to him, he captured those lips, thrusting his tongue into the heat of her mouth, finding it welcomed, the thrust returned in kind.

By the time he reached behind her to unhook the delicate piece of lace covering her breasts, she'd already unbuttoned his jeans.

He laid her back on the sofa, looming over her as she lifted her arms for him to pull the bra away, and then her breasts were free, bared for his view, as if they demanded his attention.

And who was he to argue with a demand like that?

Smooth, firm, creamy skin yielded to his touch. Her breasts molded to his palms as if her body had been created just for his pleasure.

She moaned as he ran the pads of his thumbs over her nipples, each one hardening under his caress, and he lowered his head to trace one pebbled tip with his tongue.

The taste of her skin was intoxicating, as much like pineapple as the Faerie Nectar she'd drunk.

He froze, the muscles of his abdomen jerking in response to her hands pushing into his open jeans. Skimming relentlessly on until her fingers tightened around his straining erection. Gliding up and down until, with a ragged breath, he was forced to grab her hands and pull them away.

"You don't like that?" she murmured breathlessly. She wrapped her jeans-clad legs up and around his hips, encouraging him down onto her.

Oh, he liked it. "Like it. Too much," he panted. Still holding her wrists, he lifted them over her head and sank into her, kissing her breast, her arm, her elbow, her forehead, her neck, and finally, her beautiful, full lips.

Beautiful, full, completely unresponsive lips.

As he fought to slow his heart, he took in her closed eyes, the delicate part of her mouth, the tiny snore that escaped her lips.

"Holy shit," he muttered. Dropping his forehead to her soft breast, he inhaled the sweet, delicate scent of her silky skin, trying to breathe through the painful throb of his need. "Holy fucking shit."

He didn't even care if she heard him, though another quiet little snore assured him she wouldn't.

One last kiss to the supple mound beneath his lips and he rose, lifting her in his arms to carry her up to her bed, unsure whether he was grateful for her passing out or not.

Not seemed to be winning at the moment.

Tomorrow he'd have to face the aftereffects of what they'd nearly done and his serious lapse in judgment allowing it.

Maybe he'd get lucky and she wouldn't remember any of tonight.

He, on the other hand, knew there was no way in hell he'd forget even the smallest detail anytime soon.

Chapter 13

❦

"How can you deny me this, my pet? I ask so little of you." Adira stared at the teenager, forcing her expression to remain pleasant, innocent. Well, as innocent as she could manage. She would be the first to admit the ruse was quite a stretch for her.

"So little?" The young woman's strangled voice broke on her words, her eyes flashing as she strained at the binding connecting her wrist to the bedpost. "You people broke into my home and dragged me here. You keep me locked in this room. Your goons hold me down while you stick needles in my fingers and you . . . you suck my blood, for God's sake! You call that asking so little? You're a freak of nature! A sick, demented freak!"

"It could be worse for you, you know. I could make it much, much worse. And frankly, I'm tired of trying to be nice about this. I want you to tell me what gifts of power your sister possesses and I want you to tell me now. No more games, Leah. I'm done with those."

Adira's patience with the blonde waif had come to an end. She reached out and pinched the sides of the girl's chin between her thumb and forefinger, gradually increasing the pressure of her hold. "Tell me what I want to know or I'll see to it that both you and your sister are very, very sorry."

Her life would be ever so much easier if she could simply place the girl under a compulsion and direct her actions. But both Leah and her sister seemed immune to the power.

Not that she could have done it, even if it would have worked. She seemed to have lost that power since she'd been taking the girl's blood. No great loss, really. Placing a Mortal under a compulsion had always required more of her than she was willing to give anyway. That's what her minions were for.

Taking advantage of Adira's momentary lapse in attention, Leah twisted her head and jerked her chin from Adira's grasp. Two bright red marks stained her fair white skin.

"There's nothing you can do to Destiny. You don't know where she is and you'll never find her. She's too smart for you." She pulled herself up to her full height, straightening her shoulders defiantly. "And there's nothing you can do to me worse that what you've already done. I'd die before I tell you anything about my sister."

Adira stepped away, turning her back only when she'd put distance between herself and the young woman. She'd made the mistake of turning her back too early once before and didn't care to experience again the pain associated with having the little bitch pull her hair.

The memory brought with it a wash of anger.

"Oh really? Such a dramatic performance, foolish child. You should realize you're too valuable to me for death. Where would I get my beauty treatments if I allowed something to happen to you? No, my dear, I'll never allow you to die, not until you're so old your soul deserts you of its own will, despite my best efforts. You're mine. Now and forever."

The girl had the audacity to spit at her in response!

"Temper, temper, my little pet," Adira cautioned. "Your sister, on the other hand—I have no such attachments to her. No need to spare her life. Not unless you can give me some reason to keep her alive, that is."

Leah's head snapped up, her dark eyes large.

Wonderful! Now they were getting somewhere. Suddenly the girl was listening and not nearly so sure of herself anymore.

"But you don't have Destiny." Her words were slow, doubting.

"Don't I?"

Adira reached into her pocket and pulled out the broken necklace she'd found carefully wrapped in a tissue at the bottom of Destiny's purse. She was gambling on her guess that the woman wouldn't use such care unless the jewelry was special to her.

And if it were special to her, surely her sister would recognize the piece.

She tossed the shiny black stones to the floor, where they scattered at Leah's feet.

Recognition was instantaneous. The girl was on her knees, stretching, pulling at the strap that bound her one hand to the bed. She scrambled to scoop up all the stones and clutched them to her breast.

"How did you get this? What have you done with my sister?"

Adira wanted to laugh at the terror in the girl's eyes, but she used restraint, allowing herself only a small satisfied smile. Leah's reaction was all she could have hoped for and more.

"So you recognize it, then? Good. I'll give you two hours to think things over. When I return, you'll tell me all about your sister's powers and try to convince me why I should keep her alive."

She stepped out the door, locking it behind her. Satisfaction flooded her veins.

The young woman in that room had the power to heal. From ingesting her blood, Adira's youth and vitality had sprung anew, to a degree she'd never experienced before. For that reason alone she would never let the girl go.

Never.

But recently, quite by accident, she'd discovered a strange new side effect of taking Leah's blood.

If she concentrated on someone's injury, lay her hands upon it, she, too, bore the power to heal, even though it manifested itself for only a short time after taking the blood.

Not that she wanted that particular gift. In fact, after her experience in touching the cut on Flynn's arm, she'd made sure she kept her distance from everyone once she'd had her "beauty treatments." At least until the healing ability had worn off.

There was no one whose pain she'd readily accept in order that they might be free of it. No one.

No one had ever shouldered her pain.

The experience had opened her eyes to a world of possibilities. Magic had returned to this world, in spite of the Earth Mother. There were powers out there for the taking. She had only to find those half-Fae bastard offspring. Gather them like a harvest and, along with them, all the power she had ever wanted.

They were, unfortunately, very difficult to identify. Finding Leah and her sister had been pure luck. They were all she had for now.

Or would have, once they snatched Destiny Noble from the Farmers' Market tomorrow evening. Then she'd take both young women far away from here.

She might not yet know what gift flowed through Destiny's blood, but it didn't matter. Whatever it was, it would be hers.

Soon.

Chapter 14

Destiny wrapped her arms tighter around her midsection as she wandered through the relentless dark, shivering as much from fear as from the cold.

The dreams were changing, their pattern completely altered from anything she'd experienced before, and that deviation terrified her. Was there a reason the visions had changed so drastically? The only thing worse than knowing what she faced in the future was dealing with this uncertainty.

Was that how it felt for everyone? Everyone not Faerie, that is.

She paused, trying to gain her bearings as she peered into the inky blackness.

Here in this sleep-world, she'd always known, hadn't she? Known the Fae existed. Even if she'd denied it in her waking world.

Denied it before tonight, that is. But tonight the truth had smacked her upside the head, as her mother used to say, and she had no choice but to pay attention.

"I'm sorry, Mama," she whispered into the dark, regret piercing through her heart. Regret and guilt. If only her mother were still alive to hear her say those words.

A spark of silver shot past, leaving a ragged streak of phosphorescent light in its wake.

"That which is her essence hears."

Her father's voice?

"Where are you?" Destiny turned in a circle, but found nothing in the empty black around her. "I need to see you!" she wailed.

"No, what you need to see is this."

She stumbled forward as if someone had shoved her, straight through the jagged glowing rip and into a dimly lit room.

Destiny threw out her arms to catch her balance and waited for her eyes to adjust. When they did, she almost wished they hadn't.

In the corner of the room, next to a small bed, a young woman huddled on the floor, her features masked by the wild, unkempt mop of long blond hair covering her face.

One hand was bound to a bedpost by a long, thin strap, the other was clasped to her heart as she wept, her shoulders shaking with the silent sobs.

The air left Destiny's lungs in a rush, her stomach knotting. She had no need to see the young woman's face. She knew the eyes that would stare up at her would be a deep, dark brown, like fine, rich chocolate.

The nose would turn up and the lips would be pink, like little rosebuds. All set in the fine, porcelain frame of a heart-shaped face.

The face of her sister.

"Leah," she whispered, starting forward to comfort the young woman she had practically raised by herself.

Her progress was halted almost before it began, as if a transparent sheet of glass had been lowered between her and her sister.

"Leah!" she screamed, again and again as she beat her fists against the invisible barrier.

All to no avail. Her sister didn't hear.

"She inhabits the waking world as your own body does. Only your mind travels here, Desi."

"Daddy?" Destiny's voice broke as she uttered the name she hadn't used for so many years. She sank to the ground, her forehead against the barrier. "Why won't you help us?"

Wasn't it bad enough he'd left her to deal with everything on her own in the real world? Why wouldn't he help her now? She was so tired of fighting this battle all alone.

"I'm not strong enough to do this," she whispered. "I can't save her on my own."

"Destiny!" Her father's voice roared around her ears. *"Remember your mother's teachings and mind your words. Words have power. What comes out of your mouth can harm as well as help."*

Shaking, she rose to her knees, straining to search the darkness behind her for any clue as to the location of the voice. Was it only coincidence that she'd spoken those very words to Jesse tonight at dinner?

"Look to the vision, Daughter. A circle within a circle. Travel the line with the man who wears the mark. I can say no more."

She turned her head in time to see her sister's arm lower and her fingers open, freeing the object she'd clasped to her heart.

Their mother's necklace.

The necklace Destiny had so carefully wrapped up in a tissue after it had broken just days ago. The necklace she had carried in the bottom of her purse.

At the center of Leah's palm, light glinted off the shiny surface of the hematite stone bearing the odd marking of a striped snake with a line slashed through it.

The same symbol she'd seen earlier tonight in Jesse's tattoo.

There was no gathering of light to warn her this time, only the blinding bright radiance surrounding her as she felt her being, her essence, tossed through the time flow.

Destiny opened her eyes to a cold, inky darkness, at first unable to determine which world she inhabited. Her heart pounded and her breath came in short puffs of air as an overwhelming fear surrounded her, paralyzing her.

A fear for her sister.

A fear for herself.

Her arms and legs ached from being drawn into a tight, little ball, shivering. She wanted to search for some way to warm herself, but the thought of moving from that exact spot terrified her.

Anything could be out there in the night. Waiting.

As her eyes adjusted to the dark, she forced herself to sit up in bed and she recognized the room around her. Her covers lay on the floor, where she'd apparently kicked them as she'd dreamed. Cold air pumped out of a vent in the wall next to her and the huge T-shirt she wore provided no warmth at all.

T-shirt?

This must be the real world, but she certainly didn't remember having a shirt like this in her new things. She buried her nose in the fabric and the scent that lingered in the fibers of the soft cotton washed over her, bringing with it a promise of safety. There was only one place the shirt could have come from.

Jesse.

The realization brought with it an instant need for the man himself. A need so strong, it pushed her to crawl from the middle of the bed and place first one foot on the floor and then the other. One tentative step after another until she reached the door of the bedroom.

The security and safety Jesse represented outweighed the fear that threatened to consume her.

Out into the hallway she moved, stopping every few steps to listen for any noise, any clue that whatever it was that caused her terror might be lurking close by.

Nearing the stairs, she saw Jesse's door, open, just as he'd promised. He had, in fact, done everything he'd said he would, not just asking for her trust, but actually working to earn it, as if he really cared what she thought of him.

She realized with a start that he'd never even mentioned money, or how much all this was going to cost her. Instead he had, from the first moment they'd met, acted as if he was her personal protector.

That, of course, was ridiculous. His employer would, without a doubt, charge her a huge sum of money. But if they found Leah and brought her home safely, the cost was irrelevant.

Not that she could pay any amount right now. She'd spent every cent she had looking for her sister. Still, whatever the cost, it didn't matter. She'd gladly make payments on the debt for the rest of her life.

She'd reached his door, her feet drawing to a halt at the threshold. Indecision gnawed its way through her mind. She was torn between wanting to go to him and feeling that it was inappropriate for her cross the invisible line separating her from his bedroom.

The need to touch him, to lose herself in the sense of safety she felt in his presence, was strong, but once she crossed over into that room, she was admitting to herself that she needed him. Trusted him.

And that admission terrified her almost as much as the unknown fear hovering over her. It meant that she was once again opening herself up to the pain that would come if another person she cared for deserted her.

She waivered, not sure she was strong enough to go through that again, but not sure she was brave enough to go back to her own room, either.

A rustle of bedcovers was followed by his voice. "Des? Are you okay?"

He'd taken to calling her "Des," and somehow that small, almost intimate gesture touched her heart.

"Yes," she lied in a shaking voice, but then thought

better of it. "No." She wasn't okay. Not standing here in his doorway. Alone. Afraid.

"Come here."

She knew he was holding out his arms to her. Even though she couldn't quite make out his figure in the murky room, she knew it as surely as she knew she would go to him.

Heading in the direction of his voice, she reached his bed and found him standing there, his arms open, just as she'd known they would be.

He pulled her in, holding her close as he stroked her hair. "What's wrong?"

How was she supposed to tell him she was afraid of everything? Afraid of what was happening to her sister, afraid of that horrible Dermond Tyren coming after her again, afraid of dealing with all of it on her own. How could she tell him that right here with him was the only place she felt safe, but feeling that dependent on him frightened her as much as anything else. How stupid and pathetic would that make her sound?

Instead of answering, she shook her head, burrowing deeper into his embrace.

"I know you're worrying about tomorrow. Try not to. We're going to get your sister. I promise. Right now what you need is to get some rest." His words encouraged her to leave, but he made no move to loosen his hold.

And she didn't want him to.

Biting back her pride, she made her decision. "Please don't make me go away."

"I won't." He rubbed a hand up and down her back. "Strange house get to you?"

"Strange dreams is more like it. And your house is freezing." *Change the subject.* The last thing she wanted was to relive the horror of the nightmare she'd just had.

The dream was so different from her normal visions, even though her father's voice had been there. Perhaps it really had been no more than a nightmare.

And yet, it was so real. So vivid.

"You *are* chilled. Sorry. I didn't think to turn down the AC before I went to bed. I'm a hot guy, you know?"

Oh yeah, she knew. She also knew that if she could see him right now, he'd be wearing that lopsided grin. The one that made her want to rip off his clothes.

Not that he had all that many on right now anyway. Boxers, maybe? Certainly no shirt. And the legs touching hers were bare, too. Bare and strong and muscled and . . .

Think of something else!

"Why's it so dark in here?"

"Blackout curtains. I travel a lot and my schedule gets messed up sometimes. It's easier to get myself back in sync without daylight coming in."

For his work. He travels for his work. *Work like me.*

"Want me to go turn the temp up?"

"No." That would mean he'd walk away, leaving her here all alone.

"Then what *do* you want, Des?"

"Hold me." Just to be wrapped in his arms. Just to feel safe. Real or not." He pushed her toward the high bed. "Crawl in."

Sleep in his bed? With him? "I . . . I don't know."

"You want the cuddle thing. We'll stick to the

cuddle thing. But I'm not standing here all night. Now move it."

Another little nudge and she was climbing up, sitting, suddenly feeling the lines she'd worried about crossing were long passed.

He scooted in beside her, pulling her down next to him, snuggling her back into the curve of his body, his chin resting on the top of her head. "Don't worry. I'll be on my best behavior. Scout's honor. I'll keep my hands to myself." He chuckled as he tightened his hold on her. "Well, metaphorically speaking. Now, try to get some sleep."

She believed him. The problem was, at this point, with the warmth of his body surrounding her, she was much more concerned about being able to keep her hands to *her*self.

Chapter 15

⌒

$\mathcal{T}$he rattle of Jesse's cell phone dancing around the nightstand woke Destiny.

He was already climbing out of bed, grabbing for the unpleasant interruption to their sleep.

"Time to get up already?" She stretched and rolled into the warm indent he'd left behind.

"You can grab a few more z's. I'm going to hit the shower. I'll wake you when I finish."

She pulled his pillow close and breathed in his scent, her body missing his touch already. There was no way she'd be able to go back to sleep.

He'd been the perfect gentleman all night long, just as he'd said he would be. Not that he hadn't been interested in doing more—she knew that for a fact. She'd felt his *interest* pushing against her as he'd held her close.

Faint strains of music wafted through the closed door,

bringing a smile to her face. Who would have guessed he even liked the same old classic rock she liked?

Be sensible.

Neither his choice of music nor his behaving himself for one night meant anything. A real relationship was based on more than . . .

She slammed the door on that line of thinking. A real relationship? What kind of fool was she? Hadn't she already learned that fate didn't have that kind of fairy-tale life in mind for her?

She'd dated. She'd tried to find a serious relationship. It had never worked out. Men weren't that interested in a woman who had the responsibility of raising a teenager.

Well, not the men she'd met anyway. From what she could tell, most of them were only interested in having a fling, not in settling down in a real relationship. Though if she were perfectly honest, she'd have to admit she hadn't met any she'd trusted enough to even attempt the relationship thing.

If you kept the walls solid, if you didn't let anyone inside, they couldn't hurt you by leaving. And up to this point in her life, she'd never met the one she was willing to take a chance on.

That special one she waited to find. The man for whom she'd gladly dismantle those walls.

Her mother had always told the three of them that one day they would each find their true love. The missing match to their soul that would make them whole. And when they did, their own souls would recognize that love instantly and be willing to give up everything for them.

Though Destiny had ruthlessly worked to discount nearly every word that had come out of her mother's mouth as being nothing more than the ramblings of a drunk, deep down in her heart she knew better. Her mother had told them those same stories long before the disease had eaten away at her body, long before she began the heavy drinking to blanket her mind.

Like so many of the lessons Rainbow had taught her children, that little fairy tale of true love and finding one's Soulmate had worked its way into Destiny's psyche, burrowing its hooks in deep and taking permanent hold.

Apparently Rainbow's Soulmate had been a Faerie.

"Which just goes to show you," Destiny muttered to herself, sitting up. "Thanks a hell of a lot, Fate."

Though there may be Faeries in this world, there were no happy-ever-after fairy-tale endings.

So, again she asked herself, "What kind of fool am I?"

Here she had this gorgeous man who stirred emotions in her she didn't understand. Here he was, obviously interested in her, and she was busy worrying about what-if? Why couldn't she allow herself this one moment?

She climbed out of bed and nervously ran a hand through her hair as she tiptoed over and wrapped her fingers around the bathroom doorknob.

What if she walked in there and he rejected her?

What if she fell in love with him and he left her?

"No more what-ifs. For now I'm going with so what," she whispered defiantly for the benefit of any errant Fates who might be listening.

Taking a deep breath, she turned the knob and silently let herself into the steamy bathroom, shutting the door behind her.

If that hadn't been the hardest night of his life, it had to be damn near the top of the list. Lying in that bed all night long, holding that hot little bundle of curvy woman squeezed up against him.

And doing jack-shit nothing about it.

Jesse closed his eyes, lifting his face to the spray of water. He tried to lose himself in the music, wishing he'd turned the volume up full blast before he'd stepped into the shower.

But the hot little bundle was sleeping on the other side of the door. Sleeping with those perfectly shaped legs sprawled out on the bed. His bed. As if waiting for him to fit himself right into . . .

Biting back a growl of frustration, he grabbed the bar of soap and went to work on his chest and arms. He reached for the handheld showerhead to rinse off, stopping as he felt the mark on his arm tingle and the small hairs at the back of his neck rise in warning.

He spun in the glass stall, ready for anything, only to find Destiny standing outside the shower door.

She watched him, her eyes large and serious, but whether it was doubt or fear reflected there, he wasn't sure.

Adrenaline flooded his system at the thought of something threatening his home. Threatening her.

"What's wrong?"

He threw open the door as he spoke, and started to

step out, but she stopped him with a sad little smile and a shake of her head.

"Your question should be, What isn't wrong?"

She confused the hell out of him and he was getting ready to tell her so.

But she reached down and, grasping the ends of the big T-shirt he'd put her into last night, she lifted the whole thing up over her head. Over her head and floating away somewhere.

Not that he knew where or even cared. The instant she stood there, naked, every single square inch of her begging for his touch, all rational processes ceased to function properly. It was as if time slowed. His words, his thoughts, his ability to move tangled as the blood rushed away from his brain.

She placed one hand on the doorframe and stepped into the shower, gliding up against his soap-slicked body.

"Are you okay with this?" She waited, as if she expected him to send her away. The message in her eyes made sense now. It was fear, but not fear of anything outside their little glass cubicle.

What was left of his logical mind grasped at a last chance for reason, screaming for him to push her away and beat a hasty retreat, but his logical mind wasn't in charge anymore. Primitive Jesse had taken command. And the only message Primitive Jesse broadcast was, *Mine.*

One word, over and over. The refrain filled his mind as he embraced her, drowning out the rest of the world.

Mine, mine, mine.

She lifted her arms to his neck and he claimed her mouth as he'd wanted to all night, shifting as he did so, barely aware of the warm spray of water cascading over them.

When he slid his hands down her back, down under the firm round cheeks of her butt and lifted, she raised her legs, locking them around his waist.

One slick wiggle from her and any pretense of restraint was over.

"I want you." He hardly recognized the rasp of his own voice.

"I know. I want you, too." Her words escaped on a breath before she threaded her fingers in his hair, pulling his mouth back to hers.

All the scenarios he'd dreamed up since he'd first laid eyes on her. All the ways he'd imagined taking her. All the slow, methodical paths he'd considered for pleasuring her. All designed to drive her wild.

All gone.

He pressed her back up against the wet tile and drove into her, breaking the kiss as he did so. She felt so good around him—warm, tight, welcoming. He stilled, fighting for control, as she rolled her hips against him.

"Yes," she whispered. "Again."

Another roll, pulling him deeper, chipping away at what little *control* he had left.

"You got to slow down, babe, or this is going to be over before it starts."

"No slowing." She ran her tongue up the side of his neck, undulating against him once more. "If you can't hold out this time, we'll just have to do it again until you get it right."

She pulled his mouth back to hers and he slid out of her, driving back in again, and again, feeling the exquisite pressure build, urged on by Destiny's wild moans.

One last thrust and he felt his release coming, building, pulling from deep inside as all his muscles tensed.

Shit. What about protection?

Lifting her, he jerked out and pressed tightly against her as the now uncontrollable spasms hit.

Holy fucking shit. Pullout. He hadn't used pullout as a means of protection since high school. And even then he'd been smart enough to know it didn't work.

Her breathing was as ragged as his when she lowered her legs to the ground and trembled against him, her eyes closed.

"Sorry."

His apology sounded so lame-assed, he wasn't even sure why he'd bothered to utter the word.

She didn't respond, didn't even open her eyes. But she did rub her fingers back and forth on his chest. One little gesture of reassurance.

He was going to have to make this one up to her. Big-time.

She remained motionless as he ran the bar of soap over and around her beautiful breasts. One tiny gasp was the only indication that she noticed as he moved the soap lower, sliding it between her legs.

The gasp and her cheeks turning a dull red.

Amazing that two people could share a moment like they had and she'd still be embarrassed by this.

The water was starting to cool as he rinsed them both off.

She was silent as he lifted her to his arms and pushed out of the shower.

Across the floor and out the door, straight to his bed, where he lowered her to her back.

That got a response.

She struggled to sit up, but he held her down.

"We didn't even dry off! My hair's dripping. Your bed will be soaked."

He shrugged, grinning down at her. "And then we'll be dry."

Women. Like he gave a shit about the damned bed-covers.

He glanced at the drawer of the nightstand, remembering too late that he hadn't bothered to replenish the condoms after Lara had left. Since he'd pretty much sworn off women after her, he'd reasoned that he wouldn't have to buy more.

Yeah, right. That brilliant idea was working out real well.

How long ago had that been? Almost a year?

A lifetime ago.

No matter. There were other ways he could make it up to Destiny for his less-than-stellar shower performance.

He slid down her body, running his hands over the firm globes of her breasts before fastening them around her waist.

A small breathy moan was his reward.

He slid farther, off the side of the bed and onto his knees, pulling her along until her bottom was right at the edge. He lifted her legs, placing the backs of her knees onto his shoulders.

Her shoulders came up off the bed. "What are you—"

"Hush," he interrupted her, pushing her back down. "I'm just finishing what I started."

He kissed her stomach, enjoying the little moan as he ran his tongue into her belly button.

Her thigh muscles tensed when he ran his fingers over her mound, allowing his thumbs to glide lower, grazing over her outer lips.

When his thumb parted those lips and pushed inside, she bucked up off the bed.

Nothing got him all worked up quicker than a highly responsive woman.

An intended light kiss to the inside of one thigh suddenly became more intense as he fastened his lips tightly to the skin, sucking in.

Another reversion in his behavior to a decade past. He hadn't left a love bite on anyone since high school, but somehow the idea of possessively marking Destiny as his was too strong to resist. It was as if he needed to know she belonged to him.

No one would see it, but he'd know it was there. His mark. His territory.

Primitive Jesse had once again reared his head, the *Mine, mine, mine* chant stronger than ever, drowning out any attempt at reasonable thought.

What had she gotten herself into? It wasn't like she'd never had sex before.

But she'd never had it like this.

Not this focused on her needs, all-consuming, swallow-her-up-whole experience that tied her guts in knots and left her ears ringing.

She should be dying of embarrassment, legs splayed open for Jesse's inspection, but the sheer excitement, the mind-numbing pleasure of having his hands, his mouth hovering over her body was too intense for her to want to do anything to stop him.

His thumb plunging inside her almost toppled her over the edge, and when he withdrew it, massaging over the top of her clit, she wanted to scream, her whole body aching with need.

Large, warm hands slid back up her stomach and around, under her bottom, lifting her, and then . . .

Oh my God! Is that his tongue?

She couldn't think anymore, couldn't rationalize to think, as he fastened his mouth to her and wave after wave of tremors hit, her entire body convulsing with her orgasm.

The cool air washed over her as he lifted his head and she wanted to yell, whether for him to stop or go on she wasn't sure.

Finally she chose one.

"Enough." Had that breathless sound really come from her?

In reply, he laughed. Laughed! "Oh no. We haven't hit anywhere near 'enough' yet."

As if to prove his point, he delved a finger into her sheath, followed by a second, slowly pressing deeper, in and out until she found herself moving in unison to the rhythm he established. When he set his mouth to her, her body exploded into spasms again.

This time, when the tremors passed, she knew exactly what she wanted, lifting up, reaching for him to pull him to her.

"You," she said raggedly. "Inside me."

He stood, his erection proof he was more than ready to oblige. But rather than covering her with his body, as she'd expected, he pushed her legs farther apart and fastened his hand around her waist, pulling her toward him, entering her as he did.

Slowly, deeply, he pressed into her, holding her captive against him. Just as slowly, he pulled out, teasing her body with his nearness, waiting just long enough before reentering to make her squirm, trying to force him to move faster.

A deep, satisfied chuckle from above her and he began a second slow entry.

Accompanied by the ear-jangling ringing of the telephone.

"Fuck," he muttered as he moved away to grab the noisy instrument.

Destiny couldn't have said it better herself.

"What?" he all but yelled into the receiver, followed by a deep sigh. "Right. We'll be ready."

Then he was leaning over her, kissing her cheek. "Sorry, Des, I lost all track of time. Peter's on his way to take us to the airport. You hold that thought, okay? We'll have to finish this up later."

She nodded as he walked away to pull clothes from his dresser. But truly, at the moment, all she could think of was how much she hated that stupid Peter guy.

Chapter 16

⌒

As it turned out, she couldn't hate Peter for long. When he came to pick them up, he had brought her Dramamine for the flight. The nondrowsy kind, which earned him big marks in her book for thinking ahead.

Even better, he'd brought her a laptop. An extra he said he'd had at the office. Something to keep her occupied while they waited for their meeting with whoever held Leah.

They'd landed at the airport in Flagstaff a little while earlier and were just getting arranged in their rental car. Robert had folded himself into the back of the SUV, insisting Destiny take the front passenger seat. Jesse, on his cell phone, paced outside the vehicle.

She'd learned enough about him to recognize irritation when he displayed it, as he did now, snapping the phone shut and shoving it into his pocket.

Robert leaned forward as Jesse slammed his door shut. "Our boy genius has not been able to track the bastards, I take it?"

Jesse shook his head and tossed the papers he'd been carrying over to Destiny. "Not yet. Something about their having run it through too many levels of security. He swears he'll have it by the time we get to Sedona, though. Hang on to that map for me, will you, Des?"

The men were obviously in no mood to chat so they rode in silence, which was fine with Destiny.

Robert's presence prevented any discussion of what had happened between her and Jesse this morning, and maybe that was for the best. What was there to say anyway?

Destiny stared aimlessly out her window at the passing scenery, surprised when it occurred to her that dust spotted the glass, blurring her view just as in the vision she'd had. Ahead of them, she spotted the next bit she'd already "seen." Heavy timber poles like tree trunks holding aloft the weathered copper FLAGSTAFF sign.

"Keep an eye out, babe—our turnoff should be just ahead."

The feeling of déjà vu rolled over her as it always did in these moments. To think she'd lived with this sort of thing her whole life and yet could never bring herself to accept Faeries.

She'd spent her entire life with a closed mind. But all that was going to be different now. She'd already started down the path of change.

After her amazing morning, she couldn't decide if she should be ashamed of her brazen behavior or just plain proud of herself for having had the courage to do what she had wanted to do.

Whichever way she went with that, she had no doubt that what came next was where the difficulties would lie. Where did she and Jesse go from here?

She felt herself in completely foreign territory. She'd had a couple of relationships, but they hadn't amounted to anything serious. Totally her fault, she knew. She'd never allowed herself to trust a man before, to open up that protected, locked-away piece of her that you had to let someone into before you could build a real relationship.

But Jesse was so different. She trusted him. He'd been honest and open from the beginning, doing exactly what he said. Winning her over one kindness at time.

It was an entirely new feeling for her, this mix of trust and dependence. It was also scary as all get-out. With the exception of her family, she'd never allowed herself to *need* anyone.

With good reason. If those closest to her could abandon her without notice, what would keep an outsider from walking away?

It was her biggest fear. Abandonment. All those people she'd cared about had left her.

Not Jesse, she reassured herself. He wouldn't do that. He was different. She didn't know exactly what they had together, but she'd certainly felt something with him.

Working her way through the tangle of her thoughts and emotions, she found time passed quickly. They'd picked up speed after they switched roads, and within what seemed like a very short time they were less than a mile out of Sedona.

With five hours to spare.

The tinny music announcing Jesse had a phone call broke the silence and he flipped open the cell.

"Tell me you have what I want." He paused, obviously listening to the person on the other end of the line. "That's what I wanted to hear. Did you get reservations made? Good. Sending coordinates through to the GPS for both? You did good, Peter. Brews on me when I get back."

"Do we have them?" Robert spoke up for the first time since they'd left the airport.

"Sure as hell looks that way. We'll find out shortly."

Jesse slowed, staring at the little screen on his phone for a moment, looking up in time to take a hard turn on the first road they came to.

He grinned at her look of concern. "Sorry. Almost missed my turnoff."

"I thought we needed to go into Sedona to get to the Farmers' Market." She was certain of it, in fact. She'd checked the red circle on the map at least a dozen times.

"We're not headed to the market yet. And if all goes well, we won't have to go there."

"What do you mean? We have to meet those people at five thirty." Or she'd never see Leah again. Their message had been quite clear—this was her last chance.

"Maybe not." The grim smile on Jesse's face sent shivers down her spine. "Peter was able to track the email. We have a fix on their location."

He turned off onto a winding forested road, and from there to a tree-lined private drive.

"Overlook Creek Spa." Destiny read the sign out loud. "Is this where they're holding Leah?"

"No. This is where you're going to wait for us while we go get your sister."

"For a quiet lass she has quite the temper, does she no?" Robert asked the question without looking at him.

Which was probably a good thing, since Jesse could hear the laughter in his friend's voice, even over the blood pounding inside his head. He wasn't really in any mood to discuss Destiny or her bad attitude about being left behind.

And he certainly wasn't in any mood to put up with any of Robbie's shit right now.

"You just keep your eyes on that screen and let me know ahead of time before we get to the next turnoff."

He'd like to think that given more time, or at least a little privacy, he could have diffused her anger.

But with Robbie standing there listening to every word, he wasn't about to go into some long line about how he wanted her safely tucked away while he dealt with the Nuadians. Or about how having her around was too big a distraction for the work he needed to do. Or about how he wasn't sure how he'd deal with a direct threat to her.

Or about how he felt about her.

Instead he'd stuck to the standard line he'd give any client. Clients stayed in the background. Period.

She hadn't taken it well at all.

Didn't matter. If things went as he hoped, he and Robbie would survey the place where the Nuadians held the girl and be in and out long before the arranged meeting at the Farmers' Market.

And if that didn't work?

They'd go back, pick up Destiny, and make the appointment. A choice he really didn't want to resort to, because regardless of what Destiny might think, he knew in his gut that meeting would not result in her sister's release.

If anything, those bastards were aiming to grab Destiny.

These guys weren't your garden-variety kidnappers after money or publicity for a cause. They were maniacs, infected by an ancient evil, and neither Destiny nor her sister would be safe around them, not even in a public place like the Farmers' Market.

No, taking them down in their own backyard was his best option.

"We've a left coming up, but I dinna see anything resembling a road on this map." Head down, Robert scratched his chin as he clearly compared the GPS screen on Jesse's phone with the paper road map.

"What's that?" Ahead Jesse spotted a dirt track leading off the main road.

"Whatever it is, it's near the proper place, according to what Petey's sent over to us. I'd say we go for it."

Jesse slowed to pull off onto the rutted tracks, following them through the scrub trees and red rocks.

"Looks to me like they're getting ready to do some building here." Robert pointed to several wooden stakes positioned along both sides of the road, all with colored ribbons—blue, red, or yellow—whipping in the breeze.

Jesse agreed. Likely more of this pristine wilderness was being platted off for developing more expensive homes like the others they'd seen out this direction. The terrain grew rougher until at last they came to the end of the road. Nothing but trees, drop-offs, and desert.

"Let me see that GPS." It didn't make any sense. They should be almost there, according to the device.

"Well, damnation," Robert muttered. "Have a look at this, will you. We should have gone just a bit farther and we'd have found the road into that enclave." He pointed at the scattered mansions below.

Jesse propped his sunglasses on top of his head and studied the spot on the map Robert had indicated.

"Nope. Look at that. Gated community. We're not getting in there in daylight without raising a few eyebrows. I've got a better idea. Come on."

He climbed out of the SUV and walked to the edge of the cliff overlooking the houses below.

"I'm guessing it's that one. Right at the base of this cliff. I say we grab the binoculars and make ourselves comfortable right down there on that overhang."

"Wait." Robert grabbed his arm to stop him. "There's activity down there."

The big Scot squatted to his knee, closing one eye to focus in on the house below.

Jesse followed the direction of his friend's gaze.

Two identical black sedans sat in the driveway, the driver's door of one open. A moment later a big man emerged. Long blond hair, built like a football player.

"That's him." Jesse squatted to Robert's side. "Dermond Tyren, in the flesh."

"Then that one must be family." Robert pointed to another man emerging from the house. This one also had the long blond hair, but a slighter build.

"Who knows?" Jesse grinned at his friend, adrenaline rising as the excitement of imminent action kicked in. "Those Fae all look alike to me."

Robert snorted, not taking his eyes from the scene below. "You'd best no let the Prince hear you say that."

"You may have a point—"

Jesse stopped midsentence, the mindless banter completely forgotten as he watched Dermond open the back passenger door of the car as a woman stepped out of the house.

A tall redhead. The kind built to make men lose their minds.

Robert shook his head slowly. "I've always had a rule about avoiding redheads. But that one's a woman to make a man consider breaking the rules if ever I've seen one."

She did indeed look like she'd just stepped off the pages of a fashion magazine. And from the deferential nodding of the two Nuadians, Jesse was ready to bet the farm she was the one in charge of this mess.

Without looking back, she lifted her hand, reminding Jesse of a trail boss from one of those old Westerns he used to watch with his dad.

"Holy Mother," Robert murmured, drawing Jesse's attention away from the woman. "Likely that's our girl, is it no?"

"Very likely. Son of a bitch." Jesse bit off the words,

irritated they were this far away from the action below.

Two men had emerged from the house, half carrying a young blond woman between them, her wrists bound. She obviously struggled to break free of their hold, but to no avail.

They shoved her into the open car door, holding it respectfully for the elegant redhead to seat herself next to the girl before closing the door behind her.

Dermond slid into the driver's seat while the other two men got into the other car with the second Nuadian.

Both cars started up.

"Son of a bitch," Jesse said again, louder this time. "Let's roll. If we haul ass, we should be able to hit the highway at the same time they do. We are not losing these guys."

Robert was already on his feet, running back to their vehicle.

Once they were in the SUV, Jesse floored it, getting as much speed as the terrain and six cylinders would allow. If he lost Leah after getting so close, Destiny would be heartbroken.

When the SUV bounced over a rock, slamming them both sideways, Robert spoke up.

"You'd best slow it just a wee bit, my friend. A broken axle or worse will put us out of the chase entirely."

Robert should know. For a man who'd been born in the thirteenth century, he'd taken to machines like a kid to candy. He'd learned more about cars than anyone Jesse had ever met.

Jesse didn't bother to respond, but he did let up on the gas for the remainder of their drive back to the main road.

The asphalt was within fifty feet when they saw the two sedans pull out of the side road and onto the highway. One headed north, one headed south. With their dark windows, there was no way to tell which was which.

Jesse slammed on the brakes, waiting for the black car heading south to pass by.

Suddenly a rear window slid down and a long slim arm snaked out, something dangling from her fingers. As quickly as it happened, it was over, her arm retracted and the window gliding up.

"Did you see what she had? Did she drop it?"

"No, she dinna drop a thing," Robert responded thoughtfully. "Merely held whatever it was out the window."

It wasn't important anyway. What was important was that they'd spotted their man. Or in this case, their woman.

Turning south, Jesse followed.

"You will need to be brave."

Destiny jerked away from the strong arms that held her, staring up into Jesse's eyes. The words had come from his mouth, but the voice wasn't his.

"No," she groaned. "Not now."

Up to this point, she'd been having the most wonderful dream. Jesse had held her hand as they walked down a garden path, headed toward the most beautiful cottage she'd ever seen. When he'd lowered his lips to hers, enfolding her in his embrace, she'd melted into his delicious heat as if she belonged there. She'd been so happy, so sure this was a real, honest-to-goodness dream, not one of her visions.

But now?

Though the eyes holding her prisoner often seemed to shift from brown to green, the change they underwent now was drastic. As she watched, the corners tilted up and the green darkened, morphing into deep pools of emerald.

"This is but the destination your heart desires, my child. You must be brave, you must trust to have any hope of reaching it."

It was her father's face she stared into now, her father who spoke to her.

"I don't understand. What am I supposed to do?"

Even as she tightened her hold on his arm, he turned to smoke and she was alone. Alone, surrounded by the dark, clammy mist she recognized as the Time Flow of the All-Conscious.

"What if she doesn't come?"

Destiny froze, her heart pounding in her chest. She knew that voice. It was the Nuadian, Tyren. Though she couldn't see him, his words seemed to echo off the walls around her.

She resisted the urge to fold into herself, to try to hide in the dark mist, forcing herself to take one step forward. And then one more.

"If she doesn't come?" a woman's voice repeated, low and melodious. "Then we'll leave as we planned. It will be her loss. Hers and her sister's."

"You must go with them if Leah's to have any hope. Only in that way will you find her." Her father's voice again, feathering against her ear as if it were the mist itself.

"But Jesse's gone to where they're holding her. He and Robert . . ."

"No!"

The mist buffeted her face like tiny stinging needles and she closed her eyes against the onslaught. When she opened her eyes, she stood in a ghostly marketplace, tables filled with a variety of semitransparent vegetables.

"Be strong, Desi. Trust in yourself. You alone must go to this place in order to find the way. A circle within a circle. Travel the line with the man who wears the mark. You must follow the narrow path to reach your destination."

His words echoed in her ears as a blinding flash of light burst up around her, engulfing her, squeezing the breath from her lungs as it seemed to pierce her body.

Destiny's eyes flew open and she gasped for air, her head cradled in the crook of her arm, propped on the table next to her open laptop. Her neck hurt and her stomach felt weak with fear and confusion as her father's words throbbed in her mind. Go with them, go alone—what could the contradictory statements really mean?

She rubbed her hands over her face. How long had she slept?

The bright blue 4:58 showing on the bedside clock across the room did nothing to settle her stomach.

A glance to the lower right-hand corner of the computer screen confirmed that the clock wasn't wrong.

She stood and walked to the door leading into the suite she shared with Jesse and Robert. An empty silence greeted her. Though time was running out, they weren't back yet, and a quick glance at the telephone's dark message light showed there had been no calls for her.

"Where are they?" she groaned, running a hand through her hair.

If they didn't return soon, what should she do? Jesse had told her to stay put inside this room when he'd left.

"Aren't you going to call in the police?" she'd asked as he'd prepared to leave her here to go find the men, the Faeries, who held her sister.

But no. Jesse explained that these Fae had the ability to control the minds of Mortals. Something he'd called a *compulsion*. He didn't want to take a chance on the bad guys being tipped off by anyone on the police force who might be under their control.

So he and Robert had gone off like rogue cowboys, on their own, to rescue Leah, promising to call the minute they had Leah safely in their custody.

Obviously they hadn't been successful or she would have heard.

Again she glanced at the phone. There'd been no call.

Her stomach knotted with worry, both for Leah and for Jesse. The old familiar panic began to build, its tiny icy fingers tightening around her throat as she returned to her bedroom.

What if the whole origin of the email thing had been a ruse, leading Jesse and Robert off on a wild-goose chase? She had absolutely no idea how far away they could have gone following those coordinates Peter had sent. What if the bad guys had managed to look like they were somewhere else entirely?

What if Jesse wasn't coming back? Was that what her father's words in the vision had meant when he'd told her she'd have to do this alone?

She couldn't think about it anymore. Just like always, she was driving herself crazy with what-if, opening the door and inviting the panic in to control her.

Fighting the approaching terror, she paced the length of the room. What was the smart thing to do?

Call Jesse. Of course. He'd left his number for her on that little sheet of paper. She'd picked it up while they were arguing about her staying here and she'd . . . what? What had she done with it?

Not on the table, not on the bed.

Destiny checked the bathroom counter before racing into the main communal area of their suite. A quick glance around showed no papers anywhere.

She hurried back into her bedroom and spotted her new purse on the floor by the bed. Dumping it out revealed the only things in her little pink bag were her driver's license, two tissues, and a little roll of Dramamine.

The sheet of scratch paper was nowhere to be found, and another glance at the clock warned her she was running out of time.

Panic bubbled up from her stomach and into her chest, tightening around her lungs like a too-small corset. She couldn't go alone to meet her sister's kidnappers. She wasn't brave enough for that. Besides, hadn't the words in her vision said she was supposed to "go with them"?

She had to stay calm. Had to think clearly.

What mattered now was, if they hadn't already located Leah, someone still needed to be at the Farmers' Market in . . .

Another look at the clock.

Only thirty minutes until she was supposed to be at the most important appointment of her life. If Jesse wasn't coming back, that left only one alternative. Her vision had told her she must be strong enough to do this.

She picked up the telephone and punched the speed dial.

"Front desk, this is Cindy. How may I assist you?" The cheery feminine voice did nothing to alleviate Destiny's dark mood.

"This is suite two-oh-two. Can you tell me how long it would take to get a taxi out here and then get into town?"

Just to be on the safe side. If Jesse and Robert didn't show up in the next few minutes, she'd need to be prepared, and the best way to do that was to check out all her options.

"A taxi?" the young woman parroted. "We have a courtesy car that can take you into town."

Perfect! "Who do I need to talk with to arrange that?"

"I'd be happy to handle that for you. When will you be wanting to go?"

Another glance at the clock. She couldn't afford to wait any longer. She was out of time.

"Now, please."

"Umm . . ." The voice on the other end of the line suddenly didn't sound so cheery. "Normally we request that our guests give us advance notice so we can have a driver available. I'm not sure we have anyone here right now. Hold, please."

"I don't have time to . . ." But it was too late. The canned music playing in her ear told her holding was exactly what she was going to do.

After what seemed like an hour, though the blue numbers assured her it was less than two minutes, the music stopped.

"Miss? I'm really sorry, but the driver and the car are already out with another guest."

"Look. Cindy. It's extremely important that I get into town right away. I have an appointment that I just can't miss. Can we call a taxi?"

"Well . . ."

The girl's habit of dragging out her words was starting to seriously irritate Destiny.

"I suppose we could. Oh! Wait a second. Hold, please."

The music was back before Destiny could protest. Someone really should have a chat with this Cindy about the etiquette of putting someone on hold.

"Sorry to keep you holding. We don't normally do this, but the lady who runs our gift shop is closing up early today and getting ready to head into town. She says she'd be more than happy to drop you wherever you need to go, if you're ready now."

No time to dash off a note telling Jesse and Robert where she'd gone. They should know anyway. No time to debate how stupid it might be for her to go to this appointment by herself. It didn't matter. The email had said it was her sister's last chance and her vision had shown her she must be there. No matter how frightened she might feel, she wasn't willing to risk Leah's life to protect herself.

"I'll be right down."

Destiny hung up the phone and grabbed her purse, heading out the door.

She'd have to remember to tell Jesse to leave this Cindy a great tip.

Glancing at the elevator, she immediately rejected the idea, remembering how slow it had been on her way up to the room. Instead she hit the stairs, arriving in the lobby out of breath but in record time.

The perky young blonde at the front desk, apparently Cindy, looked up and smiled as she approached. "You must be the lady headed into town. Miriam has gone to get her car. She's parked out in the employee lot, so it'll be just a minute or two."

"Thanks. I really do appreciate your coming up with a way to help me out so quickly." Even if it hadn't felt quick at the time.

The girl grinned again. "Not a problem. I'm just so sorry Mr. Coryell didn't tell us you'd be needing the car when he and the other gentleman left. We could have had it all set up."

What had she called Jesse?

"I think you might be mistaken. The company that reserved the suite for us is Coryell Enterprises, not Jesse. He probably used a company card to sign in."

The girl looked confused for a moment before shaking her head. "No . . . I checked him in myself. I'm always so good at names." She turned to open a small card file, thumbing through recipe-sized sheets of paper. "Yes. Here it is. See?" She handed the card to Destiny. "He signed it himself."

As if she moved in slow motion, Destiny took the card, scanning the lines of information.

Jesse J. Coryell, home address on Adams Street in Denver, Colorado. And there at the bottom, his signature.

Shocked, she handed the card back.

Why hadn't he told her?

"There's Miriam now, in the green car out front. Is there anything else I can do for you?"

Destiny shook her head and made her way out to the waiting car, sliding into the front seat with a mumbled "Thank you" to the driver, a cheerful lady who looked to be at least eighty-five if she were a day.

"Where shall I drop you, dear?" The woman smiled and waited expectantly as Destiny struggled to gather her thoughts.

"The Farmers' Market off Eighty-nine-A. Do you know where that is?"

"I sure do. I go there every Saturday morning with my granddaughters. The oldest one—her name is Celia—she loves to . . ."

Destiny lost track of the conversation as they drove. Fortunately Miriam proved to be one of those happy talkers who didn't need any response to keep them going, carrying on about all her grandchildren and what their favorite activities were.

Destiny had never even thought to ask Jesse's last name. How could she have been so stupid? So careless? She'd slept with the man, for God's sake. Without even knowing who he was. Without even knowing his last name.

Jesse Coryell. *The man* is *Coryell Enterprises*. No

wonder he hadn't said anything about what the company would charge her. Maybe he'd just assumed she'd be working off her bill in his bed.

Her face heated at the idea.

Miriam interrupted her own story to chuckle. "We're almost to the market, dear. If you're getting too warm, feel free to roll down the window. I save the air conditioner for the really hot days."

"I'm fine, thank you."

She was hardly fine. She felt as if her whole world had been shaken like a snow globe and tossed to the ground to shatter.

Damn. All the winks, all the grins, all the reassuring touches. She'd been completely taken in by them. Jesse wasn't just good-looking. He was good-looking and rich. The worst possible combination in the world.

Good-looking, rich, and gone.

And she hadn't been any better at resisting that tantalizing combination than her mother had been at resisting her father.

Karma. It had to be karma biting her in the butt for all the awful things she'd ever thought or said about her mother's stupid choices in men.

What if he hadn't called or shown up in time for this meeting on purpose? He had what he wanted. She'd seen to that this morning, throwing herself at him like some cheap streetwalker.

Her vision had warned that she'd have to face this alone.

Her heart raced, her head pounded, and she found herself struggling to catch her next breath, fighting an impending full-fledged panic attack.

Reason tried to rear its head and she scrambled to hang on to it. A man like Jesse would hardly spend all that time and money to fly her across the country just to sleep with her. *Her*, for crying out loud. There was probably a very good reason he hadn't come back or called the room.

But what was it? If he hadn't willingly deserted her, had something happened to him? It wouldn't be the first time someone had left her through no fault of their own.

She felt too weak to fight off the what-ifs this time. Too numb. Neither reason nor logic controlled her emotions at the moment. Too much of her past had returned to haunt her in the last couple of days. Too many issues she'd refused to deal with her whole adult life had stepped out front and center, demanding her attention. Her emotions were too raw for her to rationalize her way out of this emotional pit.

Her battle was lost to the black despair.

Either he was dead or he'd dumped her at that stupid resort. The facts were he hadn't called and he hadn't come back. And worst of all, he hadn't been honest with her.

Regardless of the reason, once again she was on her own. Alone.

"Here we are, dear. Are you sure you're all right?"

Destiny nodded and forced a smile for Miriam's benefit. "Yes, thank you. Just a little headache. Do you happen to know what time it is?"

The woman lifted the watch she wore pinned to her blouse. "Five twenty-five. I hope I got you here in time."

"You did. Thank you so much."

Destiny hopped out of the car and threaded her way through the people on the sidewalk. She'd made it, with five minutes to spare.

Her emotions in turmoil, she entered the Farmers' Market and hurried past the fresh vegetables and fruits on display, scanning the faces around her. There was no one there who looked even remotely like the Nuadian she expected.

Her steps slowed to a halt as she realized she had no idea what came next. The vision hadn't shown her what to do, only that she had to be here.

Panic slammed her full force, bringing with it the threat of tears.

Be strong, strong, strong. Her father's caution rang in the back of her mind, beating in time to the throbbing in her temples.

Okay, so she was here alone and she didn't have a clue what she needed to do next to save her sister.

It didn't matter. She was supposed to be here. She could do this. She didn't need Jesse. She didn't. It wasn't like she'd really cared about him or anything. Not like she'd actually let herself fall in love with him. Not someone she hardly knew. Not any man. Not ever.

She wasn't that stupid. Was she?

Who was she kidding? She'd been beyond stupid. She'd been gullible. And now she was in a situation way over her head.

The threat of tears turned to reality and she dug in her pockets, hunting a tissue. Instead she found the missing paper with Jesse's number scribbled on it.

The little scrap of paper felt like a lifeboat to reality.

He wouldn't have given this to her if he'd intended to abandon her. So where was he?

Only one way to find out.

Praying no one would notice the crazy lady crying in public, she headed to the far end of the market area searching for a public telephone. If she kept her head down and didn't make eye contact with anyone, chances were no one would notice her.

"Ms. Noble?"

Destiny looked up with a start as a hand lightly brushed her shoulder. "Yes?"

She didn't recognize the man who spoke, or the one who accompanied him, but thankfully, neither of them looked at all like the Fae she had seen so far.

"You'll need to come with us."

"Are you the police?" Both men wore nondescript black suits and dark sunglasses, hiding whatever their eyes might tell her. Had Jesse changed his mind and confided in the local authorities after all?

"It's not safe to speak here."

The second man moved closer, one of his hands now on her lower back, urging her forward, through the throng of shoppers rushing to make their choices as the market prepared to close.

"Where are we going?"

"We're taking you to your sister." The two men crowded closer, pushing her toward the street.

They must be the police, though something didn't feel right about them. She just couldn't quite put her finger on what it was that bothered her.

On the sidewalk, they directed her toward a large

black sedan parked at curbside that looked more like a limo than a police car.

Slowing her steps, she looked from one to the other of the men flanking her. "Wait a minute. I want to see your badges before we go any farther."

Rather than answer, the two men closed in, boxing her in between them. Ahead, the driver's door of the car opened and a man stepped out. A tall man with long blond hair.

Now that she knew what to look for, she had no doubt this man was Fae.

A shot of fear surged through her and she attempted to run, but the men on either side of her grabbed her arms, shoving her forward as one clamped a hand over her mouth. She pulled against their hold, to no avail. Neither man loosened his grip.

She twisted against one of the men and the top of her head dislodged his sunglasses. They hit the pavement and crunched under his feet without his seeming to notice. When she looked into his eyes, it was as if he had no expression there at all. Completely blank.

No Jesse to save her this time, but there were plenty of other people everywhere, although no one had yet seemed to notice her dilemma. All she needed to do was create a scene. Surely someone would come to her aid.

Before she could act, the Fae waiting beside the car spoke up, his words quiet, clearly just for her benefit. Though his eyes were hidden behind dark glasses that matched those of the other men, the sickly sweet tone he used sent shivers down her spine.

"Ah, Ms. Noble, at last. I'd caution against any resistance, my dear. If you have any intention of seeing your sister alive, you'll allow these gentlemen to assist you into the backseat. Quietly."

He stepped to the back of the car and opened the passenger door, sweeping an arm out in invitation.

With a shock, she heard her father's words from the vision ringing in her mind.

"You must go with them if Leah's to have any hope. Only in that way will you find her."

The first of her two captors slid into the backseat and Destiny followed without word.

She had no choice.

It was what she was supposed to do. What her father had told her to do in her vision. For Leah.

Chapter 17

—

"What the hell are you doing over there?"

Jesse had watched for the last five minutes as Robbie sat propped against the large red boulders, the fingers of one hand moving rapidly in the air while he pumped his elbow up and down.

"I'm playing the pipes in my imagination. Taking myself to another place while we wait out the boredom here. I'm more of an action man, you ken? I've never learned to like the sit-and-wait part of this job."

Jesse shook his head and snuck another look around the rock they hid behind.

In the drop-off below them sat the black sedan they'd followed, obviously waiting for something.

Or someone?

It was whatever they waited for that interested Jesse.

What the hell could they possibly be planning out here in the freaking-hot middle of nowhere?

He and Robert had hiked in to this location, leaving their vehicle hidden about half a mile away. Sound traveled out here and bringing the SUV any closer could have given their location away. Stealth and surprise were about all they had on their side at the moment.

Through his field glasses, he could clearly see Dermond Tyren in the driver's spot, his seat pushed back. Less clearly, he could just make out two figures in the backseat.

Leah and the redhead.

They'd determined right away that there was too much open ground around the car for them to hope for any kind of a successful surprise attack. A frontal assault on the auto would either result in harm to the girl or, more likely, Dermond burning rubber and leaving them in his dust.

So they waited. Waited to see what the people holding Leah had planned next.

"I suppose I may have mentioned once or twice before I'm no much a man for the desert heat." Robbie wiped sweat from his forehead without opening his eyes.

"Once or twice." Jesse couldn't say he was all that fond of it, either. He'd much rather be on that sweet little spread he'd bought for himself in the highlands of Scotland. "You'll have to remember your discomfort when we finally get to chat with our friends down there."

"Oh, I'm no likely to forget it. I think of it each time I take a peek at that bastard with my fine friend here." He patted the rifle with scope lying across his legs.

"And then I think on the poor wee lassie they're holding in that auto with them. Oh, I'll have plenty on my mind when we finally get to chat with the lot of them."

They both would. This wasn't the sort of experience even the most mature sixteen-year-old would get over easily. The Nuadians holding Leah needed to pay for what they'd done.

Too bad Dermond hadn't gotten out of the car to give Robert and his "friend" a clear shot. They couldn't risk the chance of bulletproof glass. That would only warn the Fae they were here.

"Though sitting down there in that car with the air conditioning on is certainly a much better way to spend a day in this heat, beautiful though this place may be."

Jesse agreed. Maybe they'd get lucky and the cocky Nuadian would run out of gas.

"Or back in that fancy hotel Peter arranged for us. Destiny, at least, is nicely cooled while she waits."

Goddammit! Destiny.

Jesse grabbed Robbie's arm, scowling at the man's watch.

"Fuck!" Five minutes to six. Staking out the sedan below, he'd totally forgotten about calling Destiny.

He grabbed for his phone as Robbie looked at the watch and chuckled.

"Uh-oh. Yer arse end up now, are you no? You forgot to check in. The lass is no going to be so happy with you, my friend."

Not happy? She was going to be royally pissed.

"Thanks for helping me remember." Jesse injected as much sarcasm as possible into the remark as he listened to the first ring.

"It's no my fault. I was having such a lovely time sweating like a pig, I couldna be expected to be thinking of yer woman."

"She's not my . . ." Jesse stopped as the hotel switchboard answered.

"Put me through to Suite two-oh-two." He hoped she wouldn't hang up the second she heard his voice.

"Are you trying to reach the lady there? This is Cindy. At the front desk. Is this Mr. Coryell?"

"Yes. Could you please put me through to the suite?"

"I knew I was right about your name." The girl laughed. "I told your lady friend I was sure I was when she was waiting for the car. I'm always good with names."

Waiting for the car? Jesse felt a surge of something very like fear.

"Where's Destiny now?"

"She said she had an appointment in town. Miriam—the lady who runs our gift shop? She agreed to drop your friend off on her way home. We don't normally do that sort of thing, you know? But the poor thing seemed so anxious and our regular driver was already out with other guests."

Jesse's first instinct was to yell at the girl to shut up her rambling, but that wouldn't get him the information he needed. Instead he made a conscious effort to calm himself.

"What time did she leave the hotel?"

Not before five thirty. Please not before five thirty.

"It was about an hour ago, I think. Right about five o'clock."

"Fuck!" he spat, snapping the cell shut and shoving it into his pocket.

Why the hell hadn't she called him before she'd taken off on her own? He'd written his cell number down and handed her the piece of paper himself.

"Problems?" Robbie was watching the sedan through the scope on his rifle.

"Even my problems have problems. Looks like Destiny went to the Farmers' Market to make that meeting. By herself. I can't believe she'd do something so stupid. Thank God the people who were supposed to meet her are down there where we can keep an eye on them."

Robbie turned back to look at him, one eyebrow raised. "No all of them, Jess. Yer no thinking clearly. We've no idea where the other auto went when we followed this one."

Jesse felt like he'd taken a fist to the gut. His friend was absolutely right; he wasn't thinking clearly. He hadn't been able to concentrate on business since the moment he'd met Destiny Noble.

He rose to his feet, crouching so he wouldn't be seen by the people in the sedan.

"I've got to go find her. You stay here and keep an eye on them. I'll be back for you as soon as . . ."

"Hold on." Robbie, eye fastened to the scope, held up a hand. "Perhaps our wait is at an end. I believe yer missing car has arrived. Might no be the best time for you to leave."

Jesse fell to his knees, grabbing up his field glasses in the process.

Sure enough, it looked like the party was about to begin.

The leggy redhead had emerged from the sedan, followed by Tyren leaning in and dragging Leah out. He held the girl around the waist, her back pinned up against his body like a human shield.

"No a clear shot yet. No with the other car coming to a stop," Robbie murmured, as if he read Jesse's thoughts.

Three doors on the newly arrived sedan opened simultaneously and the three men they'd seen at the mansion earlier today all climbed out.

Followed by a fourth person.

"Aw, shit."

Jesse's fingers tightened around his field glasses as he watched Destiny jerk her arm from her captor's hand and race toward her sister.

The windows of the sedan were so dark, Destiny could barely discern the passing scenery. By shifting her weight against the man on her left, she could catch glimpses out the front of the car, and she didn't like what she was seeing one little bit.

It appeared they were headed into the desert.

Great. No one to help her out there.

The men who sandwiched her in between them were more like robots than people. No Sunglasses was a completely blank slate, emotionless, like some kind of doll, and she suspected that under those dark shades the other guy wore a matching nonexpression. No wonder she'd thought there was something odd about the two of them. Neither spoke again or responded to anything but instructions from the big blond guy driving the car.

Driving them out into the middle of nowhere.

Though logic told her there was nothing she could do now but wait until they reached their destination, she was hanging on to logic by her fingernails. Her trepidation built, swirling and writhing around in her gut, until she thought she'd scream.

And then the car stopped.

Destiny's stomach lurched. A moment earlier she couldn't wait for them to arrive. Now that they were here—wherever here was—she realized she was much more afraid of the destination than the journey.

The men opened their doors and exited, With Sunglasses reaching back in to grasp her arm and drag her from her seat.

Once on her feet, it took only an instant for her to assess her situation.

Yep, just what she'd feared. Smack in the middle of nowhere.

Another black sedan was parked nearby. Destiny's gaze was immediately drawn to the man standing by the car. Psycho Blondie, Dermond Tyren, in all his arrogant glory, his arm wrapped around . . .

"Leah!" She jerked her forearm from the zombie's light grip and ran across the open space.

Dermond released his hold on Leah and the girl raced toward her, meeting her halfway between the cars. Destiny grabbed her sister, hugging the girl to her, both of them dissolving in tears, sinking to their knees on the rocky ground.

"I didn't think I'd ever see you again," Leah sobbed. "They showed me your necklace. Mama's necklace. They told me they'd found you. Captured you."

Nothing to be gained in pointing out to her sister they'd done exactly that. Leah was upset enough already.

"I know. It's okay, baby. I'm here now. You're okay." Destiny found herself murmuring the same reassurances that had made her feel so much better when they'd come from Jesse. Found herself wishing he were here with her. Found herself feeling almost as if he were.

Damn him.

She fought to gather her emotions and shove them away. She had to be strong now. For Leah. She had to be clearheaded if she was going to get them out of this mess.

"Ah, my pet." A tall, elegant redhead stepped forward, running her hand over Leah's hair as if she stroked a favorite dog. "But don't you see? We did find your sister. We did capture her. Just as I said we would. And all for you."

"Get your hands off her," Destiny snapped, shoving her sister to her side, away from the redhead's touch. She might not know the woman, but she recognized her voice from the vision she'd had.

The woman smiled, an eerie, frightening expression that never reached her cold, hard eyes, and Leah began to shake as Destiny embraced her sister again.

Destiny glared up at the woman, tightening her hold on Leah. "Tell me what you want from us so we can get it over with and then let us go."

"Let you go?" The redhead laughed, a sharp trilling sound as she brushed a finger over Leah's head. "Don't be ridiculous. I'll never let this one go. She's mine. As for you? We'll have to see how valuable you really are,

Ms. Noble. I certainly hope you prove worthy of all the trouble you've caused me."

"You leave her alone!" Leah shouted up at the woman.

Dermond came to stand over them and Leah shrank back against Destiny, her eyes large and frightened.

Destiny pulled Leah back to her, turning to place herself between Dermond and her sister as she kept an eye on their captors.

She needed to be alert, ready for anything that might give them an advantage. Unfortunately her vision had shown her nothing of this.

"Where to now, Adira?" Dermond was intimidating in his closeness, but he seemed to completely ignore them, his attention fixed on the redhead. "Home?"

"No, my darling. I'm afraid that, thanks to the traitor, Ramos, Switzerland is no longer safe for us. We'll have to choose one of the other properties. No matter. Reynard loved to buy land so we've many alternatives his son never knew about."

Dermond sighed. "As you say, my queen. I hope it's far away from these barren red rocks. I detest this place."

"I know, my darling. How about someplace green? Equally as barren, perhaps." Adira looked around with distaste and shrugged. "But that suits our needs for now. I was thinking of the castle near Fleenasmore. We haven't been there in ages. Would you like that?"

"Yes, my queen." Dermond inclined his head in a respectful bow. "Thank you. I'll be happy to see the last of this country."

"I know." Adira briefly caressed his cheek before

turning away, walking off toward the rocky incline behind them. "Bring the girl. Flynn! Bring the new acqui-
sition. And make sure your Mortals cover our tracks."

"Yes, mistress." Flynn, the Fae who had driven
Destiny out to this place, grasped her arm, wrenching
it up behind her as he forced her to her feet. "Follow
along nicely now. I've no wish to harm you."

Dermond lifted Leah from the ground with an arm
around her waist. "You heard Adira. It's time to go,
pet."

Destiny's mind raced as she followed the others up
the rocky incline. This Flynn didn't seem to have his
heart fully in the job; his hold on her upper arm wasn't
really very tight now that they were climbing. She
might be able to break free.

But where would she go? Back to one of the cars?

And what of Leah? Her sister was her whole reason for being here. She couldn't very well try an escape without Leah. Psycho Blondie was living up to her
nickname for him, giving her sister no room at all.

Still, whatever that woman, that Adira, had in mind,
it couldn't be good. Had Dermond only meant this
particular place when he'd spoken of leaving this country? Or did they actually mean to take them out of the
United States? That wasn't possible. Neither one of
them had passports. And surely this Adira realized that
both women would give her away at the first sign of any
authorities. That should complicate her plans.

Destiny's foot slipped on loose gravel and she nearly
lost her balance as another thought struck. Adira hadn't
said anything about taking Leah and Destiny to that
castle in Fleena-wherever. Did she plan to murder them

out here in the desert and hide their bodies before leaving the country? What possible reason could she have for wanting them dead?

What exactly had that horrible woman said? Destiny had been so concerned with Leah's shredded emotions, she hadn't paid close enough attention.

Think! She had to be logical and reason out a plan.

If she believed what Pol had told her and Jesse, these people were blood-drinking, vampire wannabes.

That was it, then. That had to be her answer. They planned to murder her and her sister, drain their bodies of blood, and leave their carcasses out here in the desert rocks to rot.

A shudder raced through her body at the realization.

That might be their plan, but Destiny wasn't willing to let that happen. If only she could get free, disable this Flynn guy somehow, then she could go after Leah. Maybe, if they were lucky, they could get back to one of the cars and get away.

It was better than following these crazies farther into the desert to be murdered.

They were nearing the summit of the mount. She'd lost sight of the redhead already. Dermond and her sister were at the crest, starting down the other side.

Whatever she planned to do, she'd have to do it now.

Planting her feet in the center of the trail, it was easy enough to pull her arm from Flynn's light grasp. Disbelief was evident in his expression as his hand shot out to reclaim her wrist.

She hadn't counted on his being so quick. Or so strong.

Faster than she could think, he had her pinned, her arm bent behind her back, her chest slammed up against the rock face.

"I thought I warned you to behave yourself," he grunted. "And here I was trying to be nice to you."

What had Jesse told her? Something about how she should have fought Psycho Blondie. Some nerve thing on his shin.

She visualized her moves exactly and sprang into action. She'd seen this sort of thing on television a hundred times. She could do it.

Using her free arm, she shoved off from the rock as hard as she could, backward against Flynn. She reared her head back into his face, hoping to break his nose, while at the same time she stomped against his leg with her foot.

The techniques, so effective in her imagination, didn't work at all as she'd planned.

The top of her head barely grazed his chin, the back of her head smashing against his breastbone. Though he was cursing a blue streak, she didn't think her running shoes had delivered the necessary punishment to his leg, either.

Wherever in his shin that incapacitating nerve bundle was, she obviously hadn't managed to find it.

If anything, she'd only managed to anger the Fae.

No matter. She was committed now.

Again, she slammed her head backward. Feeling the impact down her spine as her skull whacked against Flynn's chest once more, she fully expected a headache that would last a week from this little episode.

Assuming she lived a week.

"Stop it!" he ordered, pulling her arm painfully up behind her. "I'll break it if I have to."

He shifted his hold, turning her around to face him in order to gain better control of her, but she was having none of it. She'd started this and she planned to finish it.

He was too tall for her to reach his face with a head butt, but she reared back her head all the same to slam it against his chest yet again.

Just before she made contact, a crack echoed through the canyon and Flynn's body twisted. Screaming, he fell to one knee, dropping his hold on her to grab his other arm.

The momentum of her would-be head butt carried her forward, her legs tangling as she stumbled over the crouching Flynn and down, over the edge of the trail they'd just wound their way up.

"What the hell happened?" Jesse yelled, already running down the slope and across the open ground. Surely Robbie hadn't hit Destiny with that shot. His friend never missed.

But no, he'd seen the Fae fall as the bullet struck his arm.

He'd also seen Destiny pitch over the side of the hill, tumbling down the steep, rocky face.

If anything had happened to her, he'd kill them all with his bare hands.

The two men who'd climbed out of the car with Destiny were only yards away now, moving in his direction as he raced toward the spot where she'd landed. He didn't have the time to mess with them.

He had to get to Destiny.

"Go on. I've got 'em," Robbie roared from behind him.

She had fallen about halfway down the slope. Her body lay lodged against the tall brush on the rocky outcropping, ominously still.

Jesse sprinted up the hill, squatting down as he reached her side. He placed two fingers against her throat while he fought to control the shaking of his hands.

Strong pulse. Good sign.

Breathing normal. Good sign.

His mind slipped into automatic, all his emergency field training kicking in as he ran his hands down her body, checking for any obvious fractures. Her arms were scraped and bloody, but nothing felt broken, though she had a bump forming on the back of her head that concerned him.

"Is she . . . ?" Robert left the obvious question hanging as he drew near.

"So far, so good. Go!" Jesse shouted, urging his partner to follow after the others.

A low breathy moan escaped Destiny's lips seconds after Robert passed by, and her eyes fluttered open.

"Jesse?"

Her unfocused look of confusion worried him. Head trauma? But the confusion cleared immediately as reality crashed back into place for her.

"Oh God. Leah. They have Leah." She struggled to get to her feet as he held her down.

"Give yourself a minute, babe. That was quite a tumble you took."

"No!" She slapped at his hands, still trying to get her legs under her. "I have to go. They're going to kill her. They're going to drain all her blood!"

She teetered on the edge of hysteria, her eyes brimming with unshed tears.

Taking her face in both his hands, he kept his voice modulated as he calmly spoke directly to her, making sure their eyes connected.

"Robert's up there. He won't let that happen. You promise me you'll sit here on your butt without moving, and I'll go get Leah. Can you do that?"

Her breathing continued in erratic puffs and big tears rolled down her cheeks, but she nodded her head in agreement.

Staring into her eyes, his feelings for her hit him hard. She wasn't just another client, no matter what he might try to tell himself. When he thought something had happened to her, he'd all but lost his ability to think rationally. Now, seeing her hurt, he hurt. At this moment, he wanted nothing more than to hold her until her pain was gone. But pretty words and strong arms weren't going to solve Destiny's problems.

Only rescuing her sister would do that.

Gently he brushed a thumb across her cheek and jumped to his feet, heading up the trail to follow Robbie.

As he neared the summit, he saw Robbie with his rifle to his shoulder, scope to his eye. The man's back tensed and he lowered his gun.

"Holy Mother," he said, obviously aware of Jesse's approach. "I dinna believe what I've just seen with my own two eyes."

At Robert's side, Jesse looked down into the canyon below.

The *empty* canyon.

"Where the hell are they?"

As Destiny got to her feet, the dull thud in the back of her skull turned into a major pounding. Her head hurt so bad, she could feel her pulse beating behind her eyes. She doubted there'd be enough ibuprofen in the entire state to dent this headache.

The cuts and scrapes on her arms stung and she felt like she'd been whacked in the shoulder with a baseball bat, but she started up the hill nevertheless.

Leah was up there somewhere and needed her.

"Hey!" Jesse came running toward her, grabbing her shoulders, forcing her back down to a sit. "What do you think you're doing? You promised to stay right here, on your ass, where I left you." His face was all pink, like he'd been out in the sun too long.

"I never said I promised. Where's Leah?"

"Gone."

Jesse glared up at the approaching Scot who'd answered her question.

Gone? They'd been too slow? The terrors she'd felt before were nothing compared to this. Not when she'd been so close to saving her. It couldn't happen like this. She couldn't bear losing her sister.

An all-consuming pain squeezed in on her heart as she visualized Leah's limp body lying at the bottom of the canyon.

"Dead?" she squeaked, fighting to catch her breath.

"You let them kill my sister?" Once again she tried to get to her feet, but Jesse held her firmly down.

"No," he and Robbie answered in unison.

"Not dead. Nobody said anything about dead. He said *gone*," Jesse finished alone.

"What do you mean gone? They went right over that ridge. I saw them. They have to be there. They must be hiding." And if she had to go find them herself, that's exactly what she'd do.

This time when she surged up, she broke his hold, making it all the way to her feet before he reclaimed her shoulders.

"No, lass." Robert's quiet voice stilled her movements. "One second they were there, and then they were gone. Vanished into thin air. I saw it happen with my own eyes."

"Vanished into . . ." she echoed, her voice loud in her ears.

Blood rushed to her head and her leg muscles seemed to give up any pretense of ability to hold her upright. She would have fallen but Jesse swooped her up into his arms, one arm under her knees, the other around her back.

What the hell had those monsters done with her sister?

Chapter 18

~~~

Destiny pushed away the food Jesse tried to hand her. "I said, I don't *want* anything to eat."

She knew her voice sounded whiny. She didn't really care. She was empty but for the black horror that filled every corner of her heart.

They should be out there scouring the floor of that desert canyon right now. Again. Not sitting here in this stupid hotel suite ordering room service.

"Fine. Suit yourself." He slammed the plate onto the table in front of her, sending raw carrot slices skittering off her plate and across the polished wood. "But you'd be better off with food in your stomach, because we're keeping at this all night until you remember every word you overheard that might give us a clue about where they were going next." Jesse towered over her, his hands on his hips, a dark scowl on his face.

"I already told you. What they said about some castle made no sense."

No more sense than Pol had made when Jesse had called him, carrying on about the Exiled Ones having used some kind of mysterious energy to travel from place to place. "There'd be no way they could get Leah out of the country. She didn't . . . doesn't even have a passport, for God's sake. Neither one of us ever did."

She couldn't think reasonably. The thoughts hurt too badly and she didn't have the strength to fight the black horror anymore. Nothing mattered. Somehow Jesse and Robert had allowed those bloodsuckers to slip away with Leah and now it was too late.

Her vision had been wrong. Her father had said that her going with those men was the only way she'd find Leah. She'd gone and . . . she'd failed.

They'd slice her sister open, drain every drop of her blood, and then leave her body out there in that canyon somewhere for wild animals to gnaw on until no one would ever recognize . . .

Hot tears tracked down her cheeks again as she pictured all the horrible possibilities.

"Aw, Des. Come on, don't cry anymore."

Jesse's stern expression crumpled. He wrapped his arms around her, lifting her to her feet, murmuring how it would all be okay as he held her close.

She allowed him to hold her. It felt wonderful to have someone share this burden. To have someone care about her feelings. Even if he didn't really mean a word of what he said.

Granted, he hadn't technically deserted her as she'd feared. He'd been tracking Leah. But it was only a matter of time. He'd hidden from her the truth of who he was, and that told her as much as she needed to know.

"It'll be okay, Des. We'll find her. But we need your help to do that."

Yes, they did. And what was she doing? She was being a total wussy-girl. The kind of female she always made fun of at the movies.

That was absolutely *not* who she was. Time to stop wallowing and get her act together. It might be too late to save Leah, but if it was, she wanted to catch the people responsible for her sister's death and make them suffer horribly.

She couldn't do that from her suffocating, self-imposed cave of black terror and pity. Really, what did she have to fear anymore? What was the worst thing in the world that could possibly happen to her? She could lose everyone.

Already happened. That meant there was nothing else they could do to her. She had nothing left to lose and everything to gain.

Leaning back from Jesse's embrace, she placed the heels of her hands over her eyes and rubbed, smearing them down over her face to wipe away the wet streaks.

"Okay," she said, as much for her own benefit as for that of the men in the room. "Okay. Everything I can remember. Let's go through it again. Every single thing I can remember. The redhead's name is Adira. She was totally in charge. Psycho Blondie called her his queen."

"Good. We have that." Jesse scanned the notes he'd taken earlier as she spoke.

"He wanted to go home but Adira said they couldn't because some traitor—Ramos, I think she called him—

messed up Switzerland. And somebody's son didn't know about a lot of places, including this castle in Fleenas-something. Fleenasmore."

Jesse's head snapped up. "A traitor named Ramos? Are you sure that was the name?" Jesse scribbled furiously on the notepad. "I can't believe we could get that lucky." A nod toward his friend and Robbie flipped open his cell phone, moving into one of the bedrooms as he punched buttons.

"You know who this Ramos guy is?"

Jesse smiled grimly as he pulled out his own phone. "If it's the same one, and I'm betting it is, he's family. Anything else you can remember? Anything at all?"

She shook her head. That was all she could think of, and she'd scoured her memory for that much.

"Okay. We'll go with that for now. If you think of anything else, you let me know."

Before he lost himself in his next phone call, he kissed the top of her head and smiled at her in a way that would have melted her heart if she'd allowed it to. But he wasn't getting to her again. Now that she knew who he was, she understood the ground rules.

This was supposed to be a purely business relationship and she was keeping it that way. No matter how hard it might be. And that nagging little emotion eating away at her insides promised that it was going to be awfully hard.

She picked up a piece of broccoli from the plate in front of her and popped it in her mouth, surprised to find it was still warm.

"That's it, then." Jesse put away his phone and seated himself at the table, pulling his plate closer. "Did you get him?" he asked, as Robbie came back into the room.

"Aye." The Scot winked as he joined them at the table. "And the pieces all fit. That Adira woman was his father's wh- . . . um . . ." Robbie stuttered to a stop, his face turning a dull red as he glanced over at Destiny. "Live-in lady friend, we'll call her. She sounds to be a vile one."

"She is." Destiny had no doubt about it. "She said she'd never let my sister go."

The words were barely out of her mouth before their import hit home. That awful, hateful woman needed Leah for some reason. Needed her badly.

And that meant there was no way Adira was going to allow anything to happen to Leah.

Destiny's breath caught in a hitch as the realization settled on her. Her sister was alive. This was still a rescue operation.

She tuned back in to the conversation between Jesse and Robbie just in time to catch a phrase she didn't particularly like.

"What do you mean you'll stash me in Denver before you go? Go where?" Stash her? That made her sound like she was hot property from some bank heist.

Jesse was wearing that imperious "I'm in charge" look of his again. "I mean exactly what I said. We'll fly out of Sedona tomorrow around two o'clock, and when we get to Denver we'll drop you in a safe location while Robbie and I head to Scotland."

"Scotland?" Destiny sat back in her chair. Jesse actually believed those maniacs had been serious about leaving the country?

"Peter's located at Fleensamore. It's a village in the north of Scotland. It's the best lead we have."

"Why are we leaving so late?" Robbie interrupted around a bite of his steak.

"Mechanical problems. They're waiting on a part to repair one of the hatches." He rubbed the heel of his hand over one side of his forehead as if he could physically clear his mind. "I think I'll have Peter run Destiny up to Cate's when we get in."

That's what he was thinking? Well, he could just think again. "Peter isn't running me anywhere. It's my sister we're after. I'm going with you."

Jesse arched an eyebrow arrogantly. "Oh, I don't think so. Try some logic, babe. You said yourself you didn't have a passport. And we sure as hell don't have six weeks to wait for you to get one, now do we?"

Of course the answer was no, but she wasn't going to give him the satisfaction of acknowledging he and his stupid logic were right. Instead she snatched a roll off her plate and stormed away from the table, leaving the two of them to their plans.

Plans that didn't include her.

Or so they thought.

Her head was clear now. In facing the possibility of her sister's death, she'd fought her way through the black morass of her fear and she didn't intend to ever let it control her again.

She was in charge, at least of herself if not the situation.

Picking up her borrowed laptop, she switched it on and made herself comfortable on the bed.

In spite of Jesse's logic, there were still things that just didn't add up for her.

Like . . . if she couldn't get to Scotland because she didn't have a passport, how the heck were the bad guys planning to get Leah there?

And what had Pol meant about the Exiled Ones, the original vampire Fae, using some kind of energy to travel? Everything the man had told them so far had been fact. Weird fact, but fact, so she couldn't discount this part, either.

She leaned her head back against the wall, wincing at the pressure on the lump she had there.

Answers were what she needed, but questions were all she had.

The computer in her lap beeped helpfully to let her know it was all ready to work.

Somebody, somewhere in the world must have touched on at least one of the things she needed answers for, and here she sat with the world's best answer machine right in her lap.

Signing on to the internet took only a moment. When the search box came up, she typed in

`Energy sources, Sedona, AZ`

She'd barely made her way through the first page of responses when a knock sounded at her door.

"You okay, Des?"

Her stomach knotted as she pictured him standing there on the other side of the door. He'd be wearing that concerned expression, the one that could melt into his breath-stealing grin in the space of a heartbeat.

"I'm fine."

"You need anything?"

"No." She didn't. Not a thing. Especially not him, no matter what her traitorous heart might be screaming. "Just sleep. And privacy."

"Okay, then." He paused, and for an instant she wondered if he'd left. "You know where my room is if you need me. I'll leave the door open."

Yeah. She just bet he would. But he was going to be in for a big surprise if he expected her to come crawling to him tonight. No way. He needed to learn that simply because he was rich, it didn't mean he could just wiggle his finger and she'd come running. No matter how attractive the man that finger was attached to. No matter what she might feel every time he looked at her. No matter how much she might want . . .

She forced herself to focus her attention back on the little screen in her lap as she heard his steps fading away on the carpet.

By the time she looked up again, her back had cramped and her head was splitting. The little scrapes and cuts along her arms, which Jesse had so carefully cleaned and bandaged earlier this evening, were all stinging like crazy.

It was very late and she needed to be sharp tomorrow for whatever happened. She climbed out of bed and headed for the bathroom.

As she slipped into the T-shirt she'd brought along to sleep in, she tried to ignore the scent of aftershave that clung to the fibers of the soft cotton. For a moment she considered taking it off, but that would be too much like giving in.

Destiny Noble wouldn't give in. Not anymore.

She wouldn't think about the last time she'd worn

this thing. Last night when she'd gone to Jesse's bed . . .

No. That was all in the past. Never happened. Certainly wouldn't happen again. She'd make sure of that. She'd resisted him earlier tonight when he'd come knocking on her door, hadn't she? Damn straight she had.

Jesse Coryell was too dangerous. It would be too easy to wake up and find herself in love with a man like that. Too easy to let herself believe he might be the one. And then where would she be?

She didn't plan to turn into Rainbow. Ending up alone and miserable was not the way she wanted her life to go. No sir. Not her. She might be alone, but at least she wouldn't have to live with the thought of having been deserted by the love of her life, her Soulmate.

She stretched her back and reached for the ibuprofen bottle. Two should knock the edge off the pain enough to allow her to get some sleep.

How long had she sat there anyway, hunched over the computer, hunting through page after page of information? Long enough to have bumped into every wacko in the world, it felt like. Energy vortices, spirals, magnetic grids—she'd found them all. Each one more wacked than the one before.

When she finished brushing her teeth, she padded back to her bed, and turned off all the lights in the room save for the small one on her nightstand. She had started to close down the computer when another idea floated into her mind.

Of course, it was ridiculous, but who was she to discount ridiculous? Come to think of it, she hardly had any room to be proclaiming people wacko because of their beliefs. Especially considering all she'd learned to be fact in the last two days.

Especially considering she was supposedly the daughter of a Faerie.

Again she fingered the keys on the laptop before typing once more into the search box:

```
Energy vortex, Faeries
```

An hour and a half later she closed the screen on the laptop, gently setting the little black machine on the floor beside her bed.

Switching off the light, she snuggled into her pillows, pulling the covers up around her chin, seriously doubting she'd get any sleep at all.

She'd be too busy trying to figure out how all the things she'd discovered could possibly fit together. What it all meant.

Especially the bit about something called ley lines. She might have dismissed the lines themselves and those sites that mentioned them as nothing more than the standard made-up fantasy stories she'd run into if not for one small commentary she'd found.

It was on the one site that appeared to be more of a personal diary than anything else. It certainly hadn't had the professional, polished look of the sites out there aimed at selling something or even entertaining.

The writer had journaled about the experiences he'd had with encountering those ley lines and the supposed energies surrounding them. But that wasn't what caught her eye. It was the other name he used for the lines.

Faerie Paths.

Chapter 19

*I*t was official.

Not only did Jesse not understand women in general, he most definitely did not understand this one in particular.

He watched Destiny marching across the parking lot ahead of him, her back rigid with irritation.

After learning the clerk at the hotel had told Destiny his last name, he was ready to bet the farm that her whole attitude would change.

Especially in light of what had happened between them only a day earlier.

It had changed, all right. But in a totally opposite direction from what he'd expected. Instead of clingy, needy, ready to move into his house and take over his life, she'd gone into full off mode: stand off, put off, and pissed off.

Obviously she was upset about her sister. He'd tried to talk to her last night, but she was having none of it. None of him. She wouldn't even open her door for him.

And today?

Today she wouldn't shut up about going back out to that canyon to find some freakin' ley line energy vortex thing she'd read about on the internet. He understood better than most how many truth-is-stranger-than-fiction things actually inhabited the world, but he also recognized the abundance of New Age wackos in fantasyland writing blogs on the internet. He couldn't spend valuable time chasing down worthless leads. As it was, they'd be arriving in Denver with no time to spare to make their connecting flight to New York for the hop over to Scotland.

"I'm supposed to find her there," she'd argued.

"Did you have a vision that told you that? Specifically? That we're supposed to search the desert with a fine-tooth comb to locate some doorway?"

"Not exactly," she'd admitted.

"Look, Des, your sister's not out there," he'd tried to reason.

"I know that." She actually clicked her tongue at him. "That's why I want to go back. To follow her. And you're supposed to go with me."

She'd exhausted his patience as he tried to push her toward their SUV. "Following her is exactly what Robbie and I are going to do, babe, if you'll just stop making life difficult and get your stubborn little butt in the car."

She hadn't taken the whole thing very well, as evidenced by the fact that even now that they'd arrived at the airport, she was still angry.

It wasn't bad enough the problem with the part for the hatch had cost them half a day; now, thanks to Destiny's stalling, they were running late to meet the plane.

Jesse hated being late anywhere, but he hated it especially much when it could cost him his connecting flight.

Still, he couldn't say he minded watching her stalk off ahead of them, her back stiff, that perfectly rounded little ass swaying as she made every attempt to ignore him as if he didn't exist.

Destiny wasn't like the other women he'd known. There was something special about her. Something that made him want to try harder, to do more. Something that made him want to see her smile, to feel her touch. To simply enjoy watching her walk ahead of him.

Robert ruined the moment, shoving an elbow into his ribs. "If I dinna ken the truth of it, I'd swear you'd been at that bottle of Nectar again, my friend. Yer wearing that same goofy grin."

Jesse chose not to dignify Robbie's teasing with any response. He knew from experience it would only encourage the big Scot.

They'd reached the end of the terminal, nearing the gate for their boarding, when Jesse remembered the keys to the rental car.

"Dammit. I forgot to drop off the friggin' keys."

Robert shrugged. "We're already past time for being on board. You've no much of a choice. Leave them with the lass at the gate. She can drop them in the box for you."

True. And if they didn't want the responsibility, he'd simply have Peter overnight the keys to the rental company once they got home.

Ahead of them, Destiny suddenly stopped and turned back to where the two of them followed. As she approached, her face was an unreadable mask.

She sidled very close to him, her body almost touching his, before she lifted her gaze to meet his.

"This is your last chance. Won't you please reconsider and come with me out to that canyon?"

Her eyes glittered suspiciously. More tears coming? Or an all-out tantrum?

He had to be firm. "No, Des. That's not happening. We've been all through it. We're doing this my way."

She was so near the fruity scent of the shampoo she'd used this morning wafted into his nostrils. So near he'd only need to lean down a few inches to capture those pouty lips.

As if he couldn't stop himself, he placed his hand on the back of her neck, edging her ever so much closer.

Close enough he could feel the tremble in her body.

"Are we clear on that now?"

"Crystal clear," she whispered.

She smiled then, placing her palms on his chest and sliding them down and to his sides, causing his muscles to jump in response to her touch. Farther down she trailed her fingers, slipping into his pockets, the heat from her hands burning through the fabric as she eliminated all space between them.

"I'm sorry, Jess," she whispered, rising up on her tiptoes and luring him in for the kiss he'd only briefly considered before.

Another radiant smile and she backed away, giving them both space to breath.

"I have to run to the ladies' room before we hit the plane, okay? I'll only be a little bit." She traced her fingers down his cheek before turning her back and heading up the terminal toward the restrooms.

"Shit," he muttered under his breath, trailing behind Robert to the nearest bench, where they waited.

The physical attraction between him and Destiny was undeniable, and after what they'd shared before leaving Denver, he'd allowed himself to think she might be feeling something more for him. But she was so goddamned hot and cold. A Fury one minute, a sex kitten the next. Was any of it real or was it all a well-calculated act because of who he was?

He was, after all, a Coryell. If she were like all the others, no matter how she really felt, she wouldn't want to piss him off for too long and ruin her shot at having her own walking, talking private bank account.

And he was beginning to realize that when it came to Destiny, he just might be fool enough to let her get away with whatever she did. Just to keep her close.

"Shit," he muttered again, disappointment clouding his thoughts, though whether it was disappointment with what she might be doing or with himself, he'd be hard-pressed to say right now.

Robbie was back on his feet within minutes, pacing as he alternated glaring first at his watch and then down the hallway where Destiny had gone.

"How long can the woman possibly take?" he growled. "At this rate, we'll miss our connection in Denver."

Jesse was beginning to feel concern himself. She had

been gone for an excessively long time. What if all the Nuadians hadn't left after all? What if they'd been followed to the airport? He'd gotten sloppy thinking they were out of danger.

"I shouldn't have let her out of my sight." He rose to his feet to follow, but Robbie stopped him with a hand to his shoulder.

"Give me the auto keys. I'll explain to the gate attendant about getting them to the rental agency. With that out of the way, we'll no have that to slow us down when the two of you get back."

"Good idea."

Jesse reached in his pocket to find it empty.

"Son of a bitch," he bit out, turning to stare down the hallway. "She took my keys."

A small thrill of excitement threaded in around what should have been anger. She'd tricked him, all right, but not because she was trying to stay on his good side because of who he was. Her little act had nothing to do with how she felt about him at all. She'd only been after his keys because she was so determined she was right. There was hope for her after all.

At the moment, though, it was hard to feel relief that she honestly wasn't like all the other women he'd known, when all he could think of was what kind of danger she was facing.

"What now?" Robbie shook his head in irritation.

They really only had one choice.

"You go deal with the pilot. I'll have her back as soon as I can. Get hold of Peter. Have him reschedule our flight to Scotland."

"How in the world do you think to find her?"

Jesse didn't bother to answer as he jogged away, his stomach tightening with fear as his mind rapidly flipped through a variety of scenarios, all of which ended badly for Destiny. He had to get to her and fast.

Tracking her wouldn't be difficult because he knew exactly where she'd be headed.

He had only to make his way out to that canyon in the desert before she could do something really stupid.

Like get herself caught again.

Destiny glanced down at the speedometer and eased her foot off the accelerator. At this rate she'd find herself on the side of the road getting a ticket from one of Arizona's finest long before she reached the canyon.

Besides, she couldn't go fast enough to escape her own guilt demons so she might as well slow down.

Guilt for having tricked Jesse. Guilt for stealing his car.

"So I misled him a little bit," she reasoned out loud. Being that close to him, forcing herself to concentrate on snagging his keys while she was kissing him, surely that had been harder on her than on him. It wasn't totally dishonest. She'd really meant it when she'd told him she was sorry.

And it wasn't really like she'd stolen anything. Jesse would come after her and get his car back.

Or she hoped he would. He was supposed to be there with her. She might not have seen that specifically in her vision, but that had to be what her father's words had meant.

"A circle within a circle. Travel the line with the man who wears the mark."

The words had come to her again last night as she'd slept, along with a confusing jumble of desert and woodland scenery, as if she'd sat through someone's home made vacation videos.

It was only later this morning as she'd scoured the internet looking for more clues that the words had finally clicked for her.

The Faerie Paths, the ley lines, must be the energy source the Nuadians had used to escape. They were also her route to follow after Leah. They had to be. And Jesse Coryell was the man who wore the mark. His tattoo being a match to the carving on her mother's stone necklace was too much of a coincidence not to be another piece of the puzzle.

She'd tried to convince Jesse they needed to pursue these Faerie Paths in the desert, but her visions being so nonspecific only supported his case. He'd made up his hard head that they were doing things his way.

His way meant leaving her behind to sit and chew her fingernails while he chased off all over the world hoping to end up in the right place. In spite of what he thought, she knew that her way was better.

So at the airport, when she'd overheard his comments about still having the keys in his pocket, she'd known what she had to do.

Leaving the paved highway, she bounced along the rough excuse for a trail until she came to the end.

Climbing out of the vehicle, she considered taking the keys with her, ensuring Jesse would have to follow.

But this was too important.

Instead she left them easily visible in the seat. If he was only after the car, he could take it and go.

But if he was there for more than just the SUV, if he came for her, because he was supposed to be there with her, because he *wanted* to be with her, he'd follow her up the side of that rocky outcrop and down into the canyon beyond no matter what.

With that decision made, she began the steep ascent.

She'd barely reached the summit when she heard the noise below.

Dust billowed around the quickly approaching car and hung in the air as he pulled to a stop.

Jesse jumped from the driver's seat, making a beeline to the parked SUV.

She knew he'd found the keys when he opened the door.

She knew he'd made his choice when he slammed it just as quickly, hard enough for the sound to echo off the rocks around them. He started up the incline after her.

Damn, he moved fast!

Gravel skidded under her feet as she scrambled to make her way down into the canyon before he could catch up to her.

"Stop right there," he yelled from somewhere behind her.

No way. Not now. She was too close.

"Destiny! I'm warning you!"

His voice sounded nearer, so she picked up her speed, almost running.

Halfway down to the canyon floor, he reached her, his fingers closing around her forearm like a band of steel.

"What the hell do you think you're doing?" he demanded. Unlike her, he didn't seem the least bit winded. "Don't you realize this little stunt of yours has only delayed our getting to your sister?"

"I knew you'd come." Well, she'd hoped he would anyway.

"Damn straight. You saw to that by running off with my keys. Not to mention the rental car I'm responsible for."

"Well, you're here now." She pulled against his hold without any results. "We've got to go down there and at least try. I told you about the ley lines, the Faerie Paths."

"Yeah, wacko New Age bullshit you found on the internet," he grumbled, not releasing her. But not dragging her back up the mountain, either. "I asked you before if you'd had a vision about this. About coming out here in the middle of nowhere and finding some mysterious energy pathway?"

"And I told you, not exactly," she admitted. But her visions had told her to travel the line with the man who wore the mark, and though she had no proof to convince him, she felt sure she was right on this. This was where she'd find the way to rescue her sister. "Give me half an hour to look around. We're already late. What harm is half an hour going to do? Besides, I feel certain that if Scotland is where they've taken Leah, we'll find a way to get to Scotland from right out there."

The internal debate was evident on his face, his jaw muscle working, tightening and releasing, as he obviously considered her request in spite of his irritation.

"Fifteen minutes, then. What about just fifteen minutes?" she bargained.

"It's a big canyon floor, Des. Where would you even begin?"

He hadn't agreed to her request, but he did release his hold on her arm.

She scanned the terrain below them. Something shiny caught her eye, as if the sun glinted off a piece of metal. Searching for the source of the twinkle, she noticed something even more interesting.

"Over there." She pointed to her right. "See that outline? That's not a natural feature. Someone has gone to the trouble of lining those stones up in a circle. That's where we start."

"Fifteen minutes. But that's it. And you promise never to pull this kind of crap again."

"Deal." She'd agree to whatever compromise she could get out of him as long as it got her what she wanted right now.

He didn't look happy, mumbling something about taking chances on getting caught as he followed along until they reached the level ground of the canyon floor. Once there, he moved in front of her, leading the way to the circle of stones.

There were maybe twenty-five of them, none any larger than a loaf of bread, all laid out in a perfect circle.

"A circle within a circle." She whispered the words from her vision, trying to figure out what they could mean as she followed the outside perimeter of the stones, waiting for something to happen.

Nothing did.

Slowly, hesitantly, she stepped inside the circle, murmuring the words to herself again. "A circle within a circle."

This time she walked the perimeter inside the circle and waited after one full circuit.

Nothing.

"A circle within a circle," she said aloud, looking straight at Jesse. "What do you think it means?"

"I don't know." He shrugged. "But you have about five minutes left to figure it out and then we're out of here."

"Thanks so much for the news flash, but pressure's not exactly my friend right now," she muttered, not really expecting him to hear.

If walking the perimeter hadn't worked, maybe she needed to cut through it. Nearing the center, she felt something. A pull or a pressure, she couldn't be sure which. She crossed over again, this time searching the surrounding cliffs for anything that might give her a clue.

Once again, near the center, she felt something, though she'd be hard-pressed to describe what it was.

Did she need to concentrate on where she wanted to go? Say some magic words? What was she missing?

She remembered the sun glinting off something, which had originally caught her eye, and made her next crossing more slowly, directly through the center of the circle, searching the ground at her feet.

Barely halfway across, she spotted the source of the reflection, lying near the exact center of the circle.

The large, shiny hematite stone from her mother's necklace. The one with the symbol carved into it.

Leah must have left it behind, like Hansel and Gretel dropping their bread crumbs.

"Look at this! I knew it. We're on the right track." She held up the stone as Jesse approached.

When he reached her, he fastened onto her arm, spinning her around to face him. His expression surprised her as much as his words.

"Didn't you even stop to consider what I'd think when you were gone? Didn't it ever occur to you I'd worry?"

She'd just made this wonderful discovery and all he could think about was what happened at the airport? She was about to tell him how petty he was being when he spoke again.

"I thought at first they had you. And then, all the way out here, all I could think of was Dermond or that other damned Fae waiting out here for you, dragging you away, just like yesterday. I didn't like the way it made me feel, Destiny. I don't ever want to feel that way again."

"Oh!" She blinked against the stupid emotional tears she felt forming at his little speech. He'd been frightened. For her. He really did care for her. "That's the sweetest . . ." She lifted her hand to his arm, caressing the hard muscle, running her fingers up and under the sleeve of his black T-shirt, right onto the tattoo that tingled under her fingers.

Tingled and pulsed. Or was it the air around them pulsing?

She looked down at his hand on her arm, her hand on his. They'd completed another circle.

"That's it! A circle within a circle. *We're* the circle within a circle."

The hair on her arms stood on end as some sort of

energy engulfed them, surrounding them in a shimmer of colors, like vibrating curtains of liquid rainbow. A wind that hadn't been there moments before swirled violently around them, whipping the ends of her hair against her face in tiny stinging lashes.

"Hold on!" Jesse ordered, crushing her to him just as the ground beneath their feet disappeared and the world around them exploded in a shower of multicolored sparkles.

Chapter 20

When the last sparkle faded, the wind died as abruptly as it had begun, and Destiny found herself lying on the ground on top of Jesse, struggling to catch her breath.

"What the hell?" Jesse's outburst shattered the dark silence around them. He rolled them over, putting his body over hers as if to shield her and dropping his head to the crook of her neck, breathing hard.

The smell of moist earth, the feel of wet grass against her exposed skin surprised her.

"Where are we? Why's it so dark?" Afternoon in the Arizona desert was not like this. She peered straight up over Jesse's shoulder at . . . the moon?

"I'm not sure," he answered, his words muffled against her neck, his breath hot and moist against her skin. "You okay?"

His question caught at her heart and she wrestled with her emotions, not sure if she was going laugh or cry. Somehow they'd lost hours, a whole afternoon and evening, and all he could ask was whether she was okay.

"Uh-huh," she murmured into his ear, and tightened her arms around his neck. She wanted to hold him close, to memorize the feel of his body next to hers, knowing any second now he would break the embrace and be on his feet.

Why had she thought this was bad? Why had she ignored him and sent him away from her bedroom door last night?

Oh yeah. She was angry with him for deserting her.

Only he hadn't. And then she'd been too frightened by that to let go of her anger, as if it were the last of her emotional barriers. Her last line of defense against laying herself open to whatever might happen between them. Her last chance to protect her heart. Her last chance not to end up like her mother, broken and alone. She'd lost everyone who was ever important to her. The thought of finding, and then losing, the most important one of all terrified her.

He nuzzled his head against her in what felt suspiciously like a kiss to the area just under her ear before pulling away and rising to his knees.

"Come on. Let's figure out what you did."

"Me?" she squeaked, allowing him to pull her up. "I didn't . . . oh! Look out!"

A huge figure loomed behind Jesse. Without taking time to think, she threw her weight against him, knocking him onto his back, throwing herself over the top of him.

In less than a heartbeat, he'd flipped them, once again covering her body with his own. "What?"

From this position, she could clearly see the "figure" looming behind him was an enormous rock.

Well, damn. This was the second time she'd mistaken something purely harmless as a danger to him and made a fool of herself. Third time if she counted the dream in the car. She totally sucked at this chasing-the-bad-guy stuff.

"Sorry. I thought it was a person." She pointed at the enormous stone.

"Lucky for me it's not." He rose to his feet, pulling her up once again, keeping hold of her hand even after she stood. "I think a guy this size might be a little much. Even for me."

There wasn't just one stone, she realized as she looked around. They were surrounded by them. Moonlight reflected off their light surfaces. Each one standing up on end, tall and straight, as if they'd been placed there in some sort of a pattern. Though they all varied in size, the ones she could see clearly were considerably taller than Jesse, and that was saying something.

"So, you have any idea where we are?" she asked, not really expecting an answer.

"As a matter of fact, I do have an idea," he answered, dropping his hold on her hand to reach into his pocket. "But it's crazy. You stay right there. Don't move. I want to check something." From his pocket he pulled a tiny, flat key chain flashlight and switched it on.

He strode away, quickly blending with the darkness. He disappeared among the stones, a tiny bobbing light the only telltale sign of his presence, like one lone firefly in the distance.

Destiny placed a hand against the nearest stone, realizing the moisture she'd felt initially hadn't been her imagination. The face of the stone was damp. So was the back of her shirt. And her butt. And the back of her hair.

"Great," she muttered, wiping her hand on her jeans. Lost in a strange, dark, wet place. Could their problems get any worse?

A full moon certainly would have been welcome, but the one shining down on them, when it wasn't hiding behind what appeared to be clouds, was no larger than the one she'd seen last night. The light it cast gave her maybe three or four feet in any direction to actually discern anything more than vague shapes.

One of those shapes, at the boundary of what she could see, was another stone. Roughly as tall as the others, but wider. She made her way to it, taking small steps to avoid slipping in the wet ankle-high grass and mud.

There was something different about this stone. As she got closer, she could make out a carving on the face of it. A slanted bar, a snake curled around it . . .

"Look at this," she called, hoping Jesse was still within hearing distance.

"Keep your voice down," came his response from somewhere out in the dark. "And stay still like I told you."

"Whatever," she muttered, tracing her fingers over

the familiar markings before she began backing away. "You're not going to believe what I . . ."

As she spoke, her foot sank into a puddle of water and she jumped when she felt mud ooze over the side of her shoe. Her other toe caught on one of the wet clumps of grass and mud, pitching her forward into the big carved stone.

Into and through it, as if a door had opened.

Destiny landed on her stomach, her arms thrown out in front of her to protect her face. The wind was knocked from her lungs with the force of her body hitting the ground.

She lay still for a moment, catching her breath.

In that moment, she realized the problems she hadn't thought could get any worse just had.

It wasn't dark anymore, though it wasn't exactly daylight, either. More of a twilight glow all over.

The ground wasn't wet. Or even damp.

And instead of stones she was surrounded by hills and forest.

"Not good. I am so not liking this. Not at all." She spoke aloud to keep her courage up.

"Jesse?" she called quietly, straining to hear any response as she lifted herself to a sitting position.

When he'd told her to be quiet just minutes ago, his voice hadn't sounded very far away.

At least, not very far from where she had been.

"Jesse!" she yelled, knowing even as she did so he wouldn't answer, because he wasn't here.

Here, wherever *here* was, wasn't where she'd been a moment before. Where Jesse still was.

"Well, what have we here? A lost damsel?"

Her head snapped around at the sound of a man's voice to see a horse and rider picking their way through the trees toward her.

Too frightened to stand and run, she scrambled backward through the grass like a desperate crab on the shoreline, staring up into a face she knew all too well. The face of Dermond Tyren.

"Destiny?"

He had left her in this exact spot. He was positive of it. In the glow of the small flashlight, he could see her footprints marking the soft mud all around him.

Goddammit! He'd told her to stay right here. Where had she gotten herself off to this time?

When the lights had surrounded them in the desert, he'd known they must have stumbled into the vortex Destiny sought. What they'd experienced was too much like what he'd seen years ago when his sister Cate had swept him through time with her to rescue her husband.

All he could think of when the lights stopped and the winds calmed was that wherever he was, whenever he was, he had Destiny safely at his side. His ego hadn't allowed him to consider any possibility other than his own ability to protect her from whatever they might encounter.

His feelings for her had clouded his judgment.

Once he saw the stones, he'd had a suspicion of where they had landed. He'd been here before, though not in the dark. Making his way to the outer perimeter of the big stone circle and around to the signposts confirmed his suspicion.

They were at Callanish, on the Isle of Lewis. Scotland.

They had ended up in Scotland, just as Destiny had predicted they would.

Once again, Pol had known what he was talking about with his legends of the old Fae traveling long distances using energy lines. One day of researching the internet, of all places, and Destiny had more or less figured out the mechanics of the process.

So, too, it would appear, had the Nuadians. It certainly explained what had happened to Leah and her kidnappers. They'd come through here yesterday.

He could only hope none of them had remained behind as sentry.

"Des!" He fought to control his voice as the panic started to swell. "Answer me!"

This was the same way he'd felt at the airport earlier today. Frightened, helpless. To experience these emotions on a personal level was foreign to him.

Not that he hadn't tasted fear in the past. He had. He'd experienced more than his share of danger in his line of work, but always he had felt in control. What he'd known before had been an entirely different flavor of fear. One that motivated and empowered him to change his circumstances. Not like this.

This new fear stripped him bare and dug into his gut, burrowing around like some animal.

If anything happened to her . . .

He'd tried to tell her that back in the desert. Tried to explain how he felt about her. Though explaining his feelings to her was damn near impossible when he didn't completely understand them himself.

What he did know was that he cared about her more than he had any woman in his past. He also knew that in spite of his feelings for Destiny, he had to stay calm so he could think clearly. He'd been in much worse situations than this before.

But he wasn't the one in trouble this time. Destiny was in trouble. She was the one who was missing. His stomach knotted even as the thought formed.

One minute she'd been here, calling out to him to come look at something she'd discovered. Then her words had cut off with a little squeal and he'd come running, not sure what he'd find.

Her disappearing completely was not on the list of things he might have expected.

Dammit! If she'd just done as she was told, neither of them would be going through this now. He should have kept her with him. At the time, though, he'd wanted to check for tracks, to make sure no one else was around. No one who might want to harm her.

Squatting down, he studied the ground around him, tracing her footprints. She'd moved from their original spot, in spite of his orders. That didn't really surprise him. Her staying still and quiet as he'd asked—now that would have been a shock.

The fact that there were no other prints, only hers, was a small relief.

He followed her tracks over to a large stone, wider than the others nearby. From the slide of her shoe print, it looked as though she might have slipped in a mud puddle, but there the prints ended. Right at the stone.

Turning his light on the face of the large obelisk, he

saw nothing. Not even rubbing his hand over the surface showed any difference between this stone and any of the others.

Not that he actually expected to see anything.

He'd learned many things during the time he'd trained as a Guardian in the Realm of Faerie. One of these things he'd learned had to do with stone circles such as this one.

Long ago, the ancient stones had been gathering centers for the Fae, places where the entrances to their world, Wyddecol, as Pol had called it, were located. For the most part, these entrances had been permanently sealed.

For the most part.

Some entrances remained, though they were usually under the care of a Guardian. And, of course, they couldn't be seen by anyone who hadn't passed through the doorway.

Anyone except a female descendant of the Fae, that is. The women, Faerie women, could always find the entrances. That was why the Nuadians had searched for female descendants for centuries. To make their way back into their home world.

This circle, these ancient stones, resonated with the power of the Fae. When he concentrated, Jesse could smell them. He could feel the essence of their having been here in the very air he breathed.

But he couldn't feel Destiny any longer. Wherever she was, it wasn't here.

To make matters worse, he had a horrible suspicion that he knew where she'd gone.

Wyddecol.

"Don't you come any closer to me, Tyren!"

Destiny continued her backward crabcrawl until she bumped up against a massive tree trunk. She didn't dare take her eyes off the approaching Faerie.

"Tyren? Do I know you?" His blond hair, longer than she remembered and worn in a low ponytail, swept over his shoulder as he dismounted. In his hands he held a wickedly lethal-looking sword.

It was hard to take the high ground when she sat on her butt looking up at the huge man, but it wasn't like she had much choice.

"You stop right there!" She pressed her back into the rough bark of the tree. There was nowhere to run. "I mean it. Jesse's here . . . somewhere. And if you even think of touching me, he'll kick your ass again."

There. That should slow him down for about a second and a half.

"Jesse?" In spite of her warning, he closed in, his head tilted to one side. "I fear I am at a disadvantage, my lady. I have no idea who either you or this Jesse you speak of may be. And I certainly have no intent to . . ."— he paused, his eyes tracking her from head to toe and back again before his lips curled in a knowing smile— "to harm you."

He sheathed his sword and leaned over, reaching out a hand as if to help her to her feet.

In response she slapped his hand away and he laughed.

The nerve of the guy! Acting so innocent, giving her an obvious once-over and that flirty grin. Who did he think he was? It set her blood boiling.

"Oh, and I suppose you don't intend to harm my sister, either, huh? I wouldn't trust you as far as I could throw you, Dermond. You or that red-haired bitch you work for."

"Dermond?" The Fae's body stiffened and he backed up, his smile gone in an instant. He stood with his hands behind his back like some soldier at parade rest. "I believe I understand our problem now. Permit me to introduce myself—"

"I already know who and what you are." She practically spit the words at him as she scrambled to her feet. "You're a kidnapping, bloodsucking, toady-assed . . ." she sputtered, struggling to find the appropriate curses for the fiend standing in front of her. "Faerie," she finished lamely. "I know all about you."

"I do not believe you do, my lady. You seem to have me confused with my brother. I am Devlin Al Tyrn, Guardian Lord to General Darnee Al Oryn." With a mock bow he continued, "At your service."

"Brother? But you're identical to . . ." She stopped, staring at the man.

Perhaps he was telling the truth. His eyes didn't seem to have that same hard, uncaring detachment she had seen when she looked into Dermond's eyes.

"Twins," he added with a raise of both his eyebrows. "Now that we have that settled, who is this Jesse you referred to earlier? More important at the moment, where is he?"

"I'm not sure where he is right now. I'm not even sure where I am."

She continued to study this man who claimed to be Dermond's brother. Now that she really looked, there were other differences. This man's hair was much longer than Dermond's, easily reaching the middle of his back. And when his lips curved in even the smallest semblance of a smile . . .

"You have a dimple!"

Devlin's neck colored a dull red. "I have the Mark of the Guardian as well, if you need to see that to prove what I say."

"You mean that snake tattoo thing?" As soon as she said the words, the connection clicked. "Like on the stone."

"If you saw the Mark on the stone, I suppose I have my answer as to how you got here, but where have you seen the Mark as a tattoo?"

"On Jesse's arm," she answered. The tattoo was the least of her concerns right now. "Since you seem to know how I got here, maybe you could tell me. And while we're at it, where is 'here' anyway?"

"A Guardian?" Devlin's forehead wrinkled in thought. "Does this Jesse of yours have a full name?"

"Of course he does." And she even knew it now. "Jesse Coryell."

"Coryell, Coryell," he murmured as if trying to place the name. After a moment his eyes lit with recognition. "Ah, yes. I have heard of him. Dallyn's newest man. You say you don't know where he is?"

Dallyn again. She'd heard that name when Jesse was discussing the Fae with Pol, but he'd never explained who the man was other than making some vague comment about his being a friend.

She shook her head. "He was roaming around the stones trying to figure out where we were. I found the Mark and fell against the stone and, well, here I am."

"Here you are." His smile was back, accompanied by an amused chuckle. "Lost in the Realm of Faerie with your Guardian trapped outside."

"Realm of Faerie?" she squeaked, not recognizing her own voice.

"And frantic he is by now, I'm guessing." Another chuckle as Devlin turned, leading his horse toward a vine-covered mound. "I find I have many questions for this Guardian of yours, my lady. What say we invite him in to join us?"

With that, he pushed his arm against the vines and Destiny watched in awe as a gap appeared.

Like a doorway cut in the scenery, vines and earth peeled back as the opening grew larger, revealing another place altogether. A place where it was dark and rain fell in a steady downpour.

A place where Jesse sat staring outside the opening, drenched. His hair was plastered to the sides of his head and water droplets ran down his face.

"Welcome, Guardian," Devlin boomed, reaching out an arm to invite Jesse to enter the Realm of Faerie.

Chapter 21

"So many centuries have passed since last I saw my brother, I sometimes find it hard to remember I ever had a twin."

Devlin sat on a small bench drawn back from the rustic fireplace, his head bowed. When he raised his head, Destiny could have sworn she saw tears glistening in his deep green eyes.

"I had hoped after all this time he would have made peace with himself and found a life of honor. Now I know the truth of it. He is lost to us. His soul will never rejoin those in the Fountain." He shook his head as if to reject the feelings he battled. "I can offer you little other than my apologies for what pain my brother has caused you."

"You're not responsible for his actions, Devlin."

Jesse's arm tightened around Destiny's shoulders as

he spoke and she realized he must have recognized their host's raw emotions, too.

Devlin had shared his food with them while they answered his questions about his brother and told him where they were headed and why.

The three of them sat together in front of an enormous fireplace that took up the better portion of one wall in this tiny shack. Devlin had explained it was an outpost shelter, one of many in Wyddecol. It served the Guardian Lords as a place to rest and take their meals while they patrolled.

The Fae stood abruptly, clearing his throat as if he'd shared more of himself than he cared to.

"With the knowledge that the Nuadians tread on the ancient grounds, I must be back to my rounds. They cannot be allowed entrance to the Realm. Rest well this night, my new friends. Though I have no power to help you on the other side, I will return in the morning to guide you to a door that will grant you exit in the Mortal world at a place called Achnatone. It is as close as possible to your destination of Fleenasmore."

Jesse rose to his feet, and the men went through what looked to Destiny like some kind of testosterone-driven, arm-grabbing, backslapping farewell ritual.

Men. Faeries, Mortal, some things were the same no matter where you were.

Jesse returned to his spot on the floor next to her after Devlin left, leaning back on his elbows and stretching out his long legs.

"So, what do you think of him?" he asked, his gaze fixed intently on her.

"Devlin? He scared me half to death when I first saw

him. But now that I've had a chance to talk to him, to get to know him, I can't believe I ever could have confused him with his brother."

"He seems like an okay guy," Jesse agreed.

There was one thing that bothered her about their conversation with Devlin, though.

"What did he mean about not having the power to help us on the other side?" That had seemed such an odd comment.

"Exactly what he said. You saw what happened when I tried to attack Pol. In our world, the other side of that door, their magic is useless and they can't fight in any way."

"But they can fight here? In their world?"

"Oh yeah. They're like regular flesh and blood here, the same as us. Well, except with magic." Jesse stretched out on his back, his arms folded under his head, his expression turning so serious it tugged at her heart. "It's hard to get your head around what it must have been like here when the Nuadians broke away and were kicked out. And because the Fae live so long, they've had centuries for that hurt to fester. It must suck to spend all that time worrying about what's happened to your brother only to find out—" He cut off his words midsentence, his eyes widening as they darted to hers.

He knew. She could see it in his guilty look.

"You think that sounds like my brother, don't you?"

It only made sense that Jesse would have done a background check and learned about Chase. And in spite of that, even knowing about her brother's having run away, he'd accepted her claims that Leah had been kidnapped. He'd believed her when none of the authorities would. That fact alone told her volumes about the man.

"I didn't mean to open up old wounds. I'm sorry. I wasn't even thinking when I spoke." Jesse looked away, focusing his gaze back on the ceiling.

"It's okay. I didn't take it personally."

In the silence that stretched out between them, Destiny hugged her arms around her legs and rested her chin on her knees.

Jesse's research staff might have given him the bare facts, but they didn't know her brother like she did. Of all the worries she might have had about Chase over the past six years, his going bad wasn't one of them.

She'd meant what she said about not taking his comment personally. The realization came as a shock.

It struck her as ironic, sitting here in a place she never would have admitted existed, that for the first time ever she was able to look at her brother's leaving in a whole new light.

Growing up, she'd coped with life by rationalizing everything. Denying those bits and pieces that didn't fit into her neat little worldview. Her ability to see the future wasn't a gift. It was nothing more than a coincidence when one of her visions came true. A curse more than anything. And Leah's gift for healing? Again, nothing more than coincidence when someone actually got well after Leah touched them. Faeries? Simply a by-product of her mother's drunken raving.

Her brother, on the other hand, dealt with it very differently from her. He had accepted it all. At eighteen, when their mother had died, he'd decided to go off on his own to find those missing Faeries.

Now, at last, she understood that he hadn't deserted her. His decision to leave had nothing to do with her at all. It was all about him and how he viewed life.

But this was the first time she'd ever been able to see it that way.

She owed that revelation to the time she'd spent with Jesse. Being with him had opened her eyes and directed them outward to the world.

"So, what do you think of this place?"

Jesse's question shattered the silence, jolting her from her thoughts.

The only things in the room other than the fireplace were two wooden benches and a couple of folded blankets.

"A little spare on decoration." She was being kind with that description.

"Trust you to be so literal." His eyes lit with his grin. "I was asking about Wyddecol, not this hole in the wall."

"Oh." What did she think of this Faerie world? Beautiful, but strange. "It's just like on our side, but not, you know? The forest, the colors, the sky—they're all the same, but more vivid somehow. More intense."

Jesse nodded slowly, his grin fading as he focused his gaze back on the ceiling. "I was just thinking, babe. Maybe tomorrow, when Devlin comes back, you should stay here while I go on to Fleenasmore."

No wonder he wouldn't meet her eyes. She'd wondered what had been on his mind. "Oh yeah? Well, *babe,*" she emphasized his little endearment as she turned it back on him. "I think you better think again. I haven't come this far to find my sister only to stay behind now."

"It's too dangerous, Destiny. You know they're just itching to get their hands on you, too. If you hadn't gotten away yesterday . . ." He stopped, as if he didn't want to finish the thought. "You'll be safe here."

"If I hadn't gotten away yesterday, you'd be wandering around some airport waiting to catch a plane to get to Scotland instead of already being here." Sort of here. At least when they walked through that door tomorrow they'd be in Scotland.

He was shaking his head as he stared at the ceiling, his mouth drawn in that stubborn line she recognized. "I'm not taking you anywhere near those Nuadians who have your sister. When I go tomorrow, you're staying here. End of discussion. As soon as I have Leah, I'll come back for you."

Oh yeah, right. Like she was going to settle for that.

"Nope. That plan's not working for me. We tried it that way once before, remember? This time I'm coming, too."

"You can't." His eyes cut to her and then away. "I'll make sure Devlin doesn't show you the doorway. You won't know how to get there."

He was deluding himself if he thought that threat would work. He and Devlin had explained earlier tonight how Faerie women could always see the openings between the two worlds. It's how she'd stumbled in here without him being able to find her in the first place.

"Fine. Do what you want. But once you leave, I'll go

through every doorway I can find until I get the right one. You can't keep me here. I won't stay."

He lay very still, his only movement the now familiar tightening of his jaw muscle that broadcast his irritation louder than words ever could.

She'd won this round and they both knew it. Still, it was hard to feel good about "winning" if it meant making him angry. And he was angry.

Maybe she could change that.

She lay down on her side next to him, one arm propping up her head so she could look down at him.

"Do you know many real Faeries?"

He didn't answer immediately. When he did, his words were clipped. "A few. Why?"

"No special reason." She waited a heartbeat before tossing out the next one. "I just wondered if they were all as gorgeous as Devlin."

That got his attention, just as she'd thought it might.

Eyes narrowed, he turned his head to stare at her. "You think he's attractive?"

Jealousy? She hadn't actually dared to hope for that much. The knowledge sent a thrill through her.

"Very," she responded, watching him closely.

The jaw muscle worked furiously as he fixed his glower back on the ceiling.

"But not half as attractive as I think you are," she murmured, tracing the tip of her finger over the lower portion of the tattoo exposed by his lifted sleeve.

The muscle flexed under her touch and he shifted his head to meet her gaze, reaching to trap her fingers between his arm and his opposite hand. A myriad of emotions seemed to dance through his eyes as she held them with her own: uncertainty, distrust, fear. Desire.

Emotions she recognized because they were the same ones she felt herself.

Jesse rolled to his side, lifting his hand to cup her cheek in his palm. "I don't want to screw this up by saying it wrong and making you angry, but I feel like it's too important not to say. If I let you go through that doorway with me tomorrow and something goes wrong, I honestly don't know how I'd deal with it."

She understood then, and the knowledge rolled over her like a hurricane, disorienting her and laying her bare.

He cared for her. Not just liked her, but seriously cared for her, as in long-term-relationship kind of caring.

He wouldn't admit it, though. She knew that in her heart because she knew she wouldn't be able to admit those feelings either.

Not yet.

Lifting her hand, she caressed the stress-tightened tendons of his neck, tangling her fingers up into his hair. Then, with the lightest touch, she pulled his head forward until their lips met.

Soft, warm, tender. The physical sensations of touching him sparked through her body, filling her with need.

The potential for them to have any life together after all this was over hung by a thread. A thin thread of trust. Though she had no idea what in his past was responsible for it, she understood now that his inability to trust anyone with his heart was as great as hers.

In a strange way, they were more alike than she could have imagined, as if they were two halves of the same whole.

He wrapped an arm around her, pulling her tightly up against him as he rolled, gently covering her body with his own. His lips set fire to her neck as he traced his mouth from collarbone to ear.

"Please, Des, don't put me through agony again," he whispered, pleading his case. "I can't handle the thought of those bastards getting their hands on you."

Her insistence on accompanying him caused him pain. She could see it in his eyes, feel it in his touch. It was in her power to remove that pain. All she had to do was agree to stay behind.

His hands were under her shirt and he shifted his weight off her body long enough for his fingers to make quick work of the hooks on her bra.

But how could she stay behind? She was supposed to be there to save her sister. Though she'd had no vision to confirm it, she was as sure of that fact as she'd ever been about any prediction she'd ever made.

She had to be there.

Her hands fisted in the soft cloth of his T-shirt as he palmed her breasts, running the rough pad of his thumbs back and forth across her nipples.

He made her feel so good, how could she do less for him?

A thought, the whisper of a plan, sprang into her mind. A way she could eliminate Jesse's pain.

But at what price?

He lifted her shirt and bra up and over her head, tossing them away as he rose to his knees over her, staring down at her like a pilgrim worshipping at a temple.

"So goddamned beautiful," he murmured before pulling his own shirt up and off.

Firelight glistened over the muscled contours of his chest and she reached up to skim her hands down the steely ripples, ending at the waistband of his jeans. It took no effort at all to slip the button through its little opening.

The zipper, with his erection already straining against it, took more care.

Wordlessly, infinitely still, he did nothing more than watch, his eyes dark with his own need, as she shaped her fingers around his shaft.

When she moved her hand, gliding slowly up and then down again, his eyes closed and his head fell back, the cords in his neck standing out in shadowed relief.

She loved the feel of his body, soft skin covering the raw power of the man.

Up and down. She tightened her hold and studied the effect, his body straining as his need built. Up and down. Up and down.

He grabbed her hand, his breathing heavy.

"Gotta stop, Des. Christ," he panted, holding her hands to his chest. "What is it with you? I can't ever seem to wait. My control is for shit."

"Then why are you waiting?"

She pulled out of his hold and began to unfasten her jeans, but he brushed her hands away. Finishing it himself, he pulled the pants down over her hips and she pushed them away with her feet.

One tug and she was kicking out of her panties.

And then he was on top of her, his skin burning wonderfully against her own as he fit himself between her legs and entered her.

The shock of it tingled through her body, joyfully igniting every nerve ending as he filled her.

"Yes," she rasped, almost against her own will, as he withdrew and filled her again, slowly, purposefully.

His eyes, still laced with his pain, blazed possessively, holding her captive, and she felt for that instant as if she could see into the depths of his soul. As if there was a place in there saved just for her.

Was that what her mother had meant about recognizing yourself in the eyes of your Soulmate? She wished she'd paid more attention to the things her mother had tried to tell her.

The thought shattered when her body exploded, the intensity of her orgasm equaling the need she'd felt for this man.

She gasped for breath like a marathon runner while he tensed above her, his head thrown back as he found his own release before collapsing on top of her.

If Soulmates did exist, as her mother had always claimed, Destiny knew she'd found hers. The one man she could see herself spending the rest of her life loving.

And here she was getting ready to risk losing everything.

"I'll stay here tomorrow when you go with Devlin," she whispered into his ear.

Not a lie, she rationalized to herself, even though she knew it might be no more than a half-truth at best.

The tension melted from his body in response to

her words even as she fought back the tears that threatened.

If she followed him tomorrow, she risked losing this, losing him, by destroying that delicate thread of trust that was only beginning to form between them.

She knew now what she could do.

She simply wasn't sure what she *would* do.

Chapter 22

~

"Where is Flynn?"

Adira stared into the emotionless eyes of a house-maid waiting for her response. It would be so nice to have these Mortals simply do as they were told without the necessity of removing every semblance of intelligence and personality with the compulsion. But that simply wasn't the way of it.

Mortals and their so-called morals. Such a bother.

"Master Flynn took a car into town, my queen," the woman answered tonelessly.

Of course, he would have. He was still angry with her.

She waved the useless woman away and stepped back into her sitting room to pour herself a cup of tea.

Flynn and his constant pouting were starting to get

on her nerves. It wasn't that she'd ever fully trusted the man. She'd learned early in life not to trust anyone. But he was comfortable. Familiar. Normally efficient.

In spite of that, she might have to consider replacing him if these obstinate little tantrums and hurt feelings continued.

Still, he did have his useful moments.

It had been Flynn, after all, who'd suggested the solution to her problems. Why she hadn't thought of it herself was beyond her. Too much on her mind, she supposed.

He'd stood at this very table this morning, eyes downcast, as she'd chastised him for having lost the Noble woman she'd wanted so badly.

Even now, even with her new plans under way, it still rankled her that she'd been so close to having the half-breed within her grasp. She'd wanted whatever powers the woman had for her own.

"What do you suggest I do now, Flynn?" she'd asked. "Now that you let that Mortal slip through your fingers? It's hardly as if I can look up 'Faerie descendants' in the ads or order one off the internet."

"You still have the girl." He'd looked up sullenly.

"Thanks to Dermond. He, at least, was able to hold on to his charge."

Flynn's face had colored at that remark. "I was shot."

She'd fluttered her hand to dismiss his excuse. "And you were healed by my own little pet. The one Dermond held on to. Who knows what the one you let get away might have been able to do for us?"

"My apologies, mistress."

"Tell me. How do you recommend I find others?" The longer she'd looked at him, his eyes not meeting hers, the angrier she'd become.

"Don't find them," he mumbled. "Breed your own women."

"What?"

Have her own daughters? Not bloody likely. Even without the Earth Mother's interference, which had destroyed the Nuadians' ability to bear female children, pregnancy was not something she would ever willingly choose for herself.

Adira Ré Alyn had sworn early on that she would never be one of those ugly, bloated, miserable breed cows.

Long ago in Wyddecol, she'd heard the contempt in the men's voices as they'd bemoaned their wives' swollen bodies. She'd seen them reject those fine ladies, coming instead to her bed for their pleasure.

In those days, she'd had no chance to think of the possibility of having her own children. Women like her weren't considered good enough for marriage outside their class. Their only use had been to warm the beds of the nobility and the wealthy.

She'd been good enough to entertain them, to bed them, but never to marry them. In her innocence, her naïveté, she'd dared to hope it would be different one day.

She'd quickly learned the harsh truth.

Those men of power and wealth who'd whispered sweet words of encouragement and false promises as they used her body for their own pleasures had no intention of raising her station in life. She'd been nothing to them, less important than the animals that ate from their scraps.

Reynard had saved her from that life, though she'd paid dearly for the rescue. Years of enduring every depraved indignity he could dream up, all to ensure her value to him. To guarantee he'd keep her at his side.

When the rebellion had gone badly, she'd been banished from Wyddecol along with Reynard and those like him who had fought against the Faerie High Council. But banishment had been no hardship for her.

The others, with their former lives of comfort and plenty, their rich families and splendid homes left behind, whined constantly about missing all they had given up for the rebellion.

But not her. Though she might miss the beauty of the Faerie Realm, life here in the Mortal World had been far better for her than anything she'd left behind.

She had used her body to buy her way here. Still used it when necessary. There was no way she'd ever consider ruining her greatest asset by filling it with a parasite. Growing inside her, feeding off her, distending her stomach, stretching and tearing her skin. The very idea made her shudder in revulsion.

A child was the one thing, the only thing, she'd ever denied Reynard. And supposedly his reason for bedding every Mortal he came across.

Perhaps even his reason for refusing her the one thing she had wanted—the legitimacy of marriage and the entitlement it would have given her to rule at his side.

She clenched her teeth at the memory of his refusal,

setting the fragile china cup on the table in front of her before she forgot herself and smashed it to the ground.

No matter now. She no longer needed Reynard or any male to give her anything. She'd learned to take what she wanted by her own hand.

Of course, she hadn't explained herself to Flynn this morning. Back in Wyddecol, his merchant-class family might have far outranked her own, but here things were different. Here, his subservient position didn't rate explanation of any kind from her.

"Don't be ridiculous, Flynn," she'd said, sneering. "You know very well the only child I'd be able to bear would be male. And another male to take care of is the last thing I need."

"I would never be so disrespectful, my mistress, as to suggest such a thing. I was recommending you should breed the girl. She's of an age and healthy. In this world, women younger than she already have children. Some more than one. And because the prohibitions of the Earth Mother obviously have no dominion over her, she is as likely to give you females as males. It will take time, of course, but if there's anything you have plenty of, it's time."

Oh yes, she had time.

Breeding her own stable of mixed-blood females, each with a gift of magic? Certainly it was no different from all those years ago when Reynard had bred his own stable of racing dogs.

Leah was, after all, her pet.

Certainly it would take a decade or two, slowing down her plans. But once begun, there was no telling what powers she'd have at her disposal. And if she were fortunate enough to find other females, other half-blood Fae mongrels, while she waited?

So much the better.

She could be patient. She could wait for the power just as she'd waited for revenge on all those she'd left behind.

And on some of those who'd come along with them.

Adira smiled, picking up her cup for another sip of the bitter herb tea she found particularly soothing.

Flynn had recognized the moment Adira accepted his suggestion. She'd seen it in his sly expression before he bowed his head in mock submissiveness.

"You'll need a loyal full-blood to impregnate the girl. I'm at your disposal in this, my mistress," he'd fawned.

"I think not, Flynn." She'd noted his looks of disdain when he thought she wasn't paying attention. "I believe we'll use Dermond for this task. Since I'm breeding the girl to obtain the purest forms of magic, a noble blood lineage is perhaps preferable to merchant class, don't you agree?"

Adira stifled a laugh at the memory of his shock. "Ah, yes, Flynn," she murmured aloud now. "The cutting edge of discrimination swings both ways, does it not?"

He was at her disposal? The unmitigated gall of the man. Of course he was at her disposal. Now that Reynard was gone, they were all at her disposal.

A light knock at her door and Dermond entered, bowing his head respectfully as he paused at the entrance.

"You sent for me, my queen?"

Adira smiled at the man. He truly was a beautiful specimen, with a physique more than one artist had attempted to capture for posterity. And a rare treasure at lovemaking. Her little pet was luckier than she knew.

"In light of Flynn's failure to bring the elder Ms. Noble along with us, I've decided to start my own breeding program."

Dermond's brow wrinkled.

Beautiful man, loyal beyond a fault, but not always the quickest thinker. That, perhaps, made him the perfect follower. Possibly even the perfect consort.

"What is it you wish of me, my queen?"

"I want you to mate with Leah. I want her impregnated so that she will produce daughters who, like herself, will have the honor of serving me. Serving our people. Do you understand my request, Dermond?"

"You want me to bed her."

The inviting smile that curved his lip as understanding dawned almost made her want to wait for tomorrow to put her plan in motion, keeping this delicious treat for her very own tonight.

"Yes, my darling. She's waiting for you in my bedchamber right now." Adira rose from her seat, heading for the door between her study and her bedroom.

The wrinkle of confusion returned to his lovely face. "She knows? And agrees to this?"

Adira laughed at his naïveté, shaking her head as she did so. Poor dear, darling man.

"No, my sweet. She has no idea what a wonderful experience awaits her. As for you, consider this your reward for loyal service."

His smile returned, along with a decadently wicked gleam in his eyes as he joined her at the door, which she pushed open.

"One caution, my darling. Be gentle with my little pet. She is my only one and I wouldn't want anything to happen to her. I simply want many, many more like her."

"What?" Leah slid off the bed as they entered, her eyes rounded, moving forward as far as the strap connecting her wrist to the headboard would allow. "What are you talking about?"

Adira stood back, allowing Dermond to swagger into the room, his confidence swelling. He was in his element here, sex and domination an integral part of his breeding.

He loosened the tie he wore before slowly unbuttoning his crisp white dress shirt, revealing the chiseled plane of muscles hidden beneath the fabric. His piercing gaze locked on the young woman in front of him, his expression of anticipation telegraphing his intent as clearly as any words ever could.

"What do you think you're doing?" Leah gasped, the scent of her fear rolling off her as she realized what was to happen in this room tonight. "No. You can't be serious."

Dermond chuckled, whipping the tie from his neck as he approached. "If you fight me, pet, I'll tie the other hand, too."

"No," Leah screamed, fighting uselessly against his superior strength as he captured her free hand. Her desperate eyes turned to Adira. "Don't. Please don't let him do this."

Heat pooled low in Adira's belly as Dermond ripped the satiny material of the nightgown Leah wore, exposing her firm, high breasts. The young woman's skin turned a pleasing shade of pink with her exertion. She fought, but it would do her no good.

Adira's breath came faster as she watched him slide his hand lower, coaxing the material down over the curves of Leah's hips. She knew the feel of those hands, but seeing them caress another woman's body, a woman struggling to avoid that touch, was more exciting than she could have imagined.

"Do you plan to join us?"

Dermond's silky voice pulled her back to her own awareness and she realized, to her surprise, she'd taken several steps into the room.

Join them? Not something she'd considered before, but almost too enticing an offer to turn down.

Adira licked her lips, stalling for time while she regained her composure. She hadn't gone to all the trouble to set up this little scenario simply for her own pleasure. There was a purpose to what happened in that bed tonight.

"I think not this time," she murmured, backing out of the room and shutting the door against Leah's screams.

There would be other nights. She would see to it now that she'd feel the thrill of such a liaison. She was a patient woman. Just as she'd waited for her revenge and would wait for the births of her own private stock of gifted females, so she would wait for the experience of joining Dermond as he enjoyed her pet.

The anticipation would make it that much sweeter when the time came.

She crossed to the door leading out to a balcony off

her study and quietly let herself out into the cool evening, wishing for a moment that Flynn were here at the castle rather than in town.

Yes, she was resolved to wait.

But not for too long.

"Begging yer pardon, mistress, but the neighborhood warden and a special constable are downstairs demanding to see you."

"What?" Adira turned to find one of the emotionless maids standing in her doorway.

"The neighborhood warden and . . ."

"I heard that part, you twit," she interrupted. "Send them away. I've no time for them right now."

Whatever the authorities in this little backwater village might want, this was certainly not the time to have them in her home. Especially considering what was going on in the room next door to where she stood.

Though she could hear Leah's muffled cries, she doubted the sound would carry to the lower level. All the same, if there was some sort of problem, she no longer had the ability to use a compulsion to diffuse the situation.

"I've already told them you dinna care to be interrupted, my queen, but I canna get them to go. They demand to speak to you or say they'll execute a search warrant of the manor."

Mortals. Inconvenient pests.

"Very well. Seat them in the library and tell them I'll be right down."

Adira waited until the maid had closed the door of her suite behind her before heading across to her bedroom. With Flynn away from the castle, there was only one other person who could control the minds of the men downstairs.

It certainly seemed as if all the Fates were conspiring against her plans tonight.

With an irritated sigh, she opened the door.

"Have you changed your mind you mind about joining us, my queen?" Dermond looked up from the bed where he lay across Leah, trying to hold her down.

Damn it all. Adira's irritation flared anew, at the men downstairs and at Flynn for not being here to take care of this problem.

"Unfortunately, no. As sorry as I am to interrupt you before you even get started, I'm afraid we'll have to call an end to this for the moment. I have need of you downstairs. Now."

"Thank God you changed your mind," Leah gasped, pushing away as Dermond stood up.

"But I haven't changed my mind at all, pet. This is merely a slight delay." Adira stared at the girl, her own satisfaction growing as the girl's eyes rounded with understanding. "Think of it as time to build some anticipation for what's to come."

As soon as Dermond could get rid of those imbeciles waiting in her library.

Chapter 23

⸺⸺

Was it another vision or only a horrible nightmare? Destiny couldn't tell anymore. The two had become so intertwined, so much alike, one might as well be the other.

Either that or she no longer had any dreams other than the visions.

"Don't go. Please, wait for me." Jesse's whispered pleas hovered around her, the words vibrating against her eardrums.

She was in a wide stone hallway, large and airy with small lights disguised as candles spaced along one side of the wall and large windows covering the other side. She moved soundlessly down the passageway, flowing without substance, more a fog of energy than an actual being. Her essence rippled through the air until she reached the place she somehow knew she was supposed to be.

She entered a fabulously feminine room, with chairs and a chaise lounge placed invitingly in front of a large fireplace. Against the opposite wall sat an ornate desk and chair surrounded on both sides by floor-to-ceiling windows, their gauzy coverings dancing on a light breeze.

Crossing to her right, she stopped at a door, knowing to the depths of her soul that whatever she might find behind the carved wooden portal would alter her world forever.

"Please. Don't go in there. Wait for me." Jesse's voice came from farther away, but even from this distance, it pained her to hear it.

She couldn't stop. She knew it now.

The door opened and she started to enter, pulling up short as she realized there were people in this room.

"Devlin?" She spoke aloud, but there was no sound coming from her—even her words were as the mist.

He stood, arrogantly naked, his side to her, his handsome profile in sharp relief. Only when he spoke did she realize her mistake.

"So sorry for this inconvenient interruption, sweetness. Will you miss me until I return?"

The cruel voice belonged to Dermond, not Devlin.

"I hate you."

Leah's voice? Destiny tried to move forward into the room, struggled to see around the large door to where her sister's voice seemed to come from.

"So you say now. But you'll change your mind." Dermond chuckled to himself as he stepped into his pants, pulling them up his long legs, staring straight ahead as he did so. "You'll learn to enjoy it, pet. Once I show you what I can do. I promise."

What was that animal doing in the same room with her sister, and without his clothes on? Again she tried to force herself forward and again she met resistance.

"Never!" Leah again, her voice stronger this time, dripping with venom. "You'll rot in hell first."

Dermond laughed at her sister's threat, advancing across Destiny's line of vision. Only as he swaggered beyond her sight was she able to move a little farther into the room.

Far enough to see around the open door.

Far enough that she wished she hadn't come inside the room.

Leah sat in the middle of a huge four-poster bed, bare but for the scrap of silk pooled at her hips and a pillow she clutched in front of her. A thin strap tied around one of the posters stretched across the corner of the bed to the girl, where it was attached to her wrist.

Destiny's heart broke looking into her sister's face, a splotchy pink, swollen from crying. But her eyes! Her eyes glowed with the intensity of her hatred, and in those eyes Destiny saw what her sister had endured.

What Dermond had tried to do to her.

And Leah's hatred became her own.

"No, pet. You won't see me dead." He reached out, grabbing the girl's arm with one hand as she swung at him. "But you will see me here again. And next time, we'll actually finish what we almost started." He tangled his other hand in her hair, pulling her face close to his, forcing his mouth over hers.

When he broke away, she spit at him, and again he laughed, wiping the side of his face. Still laughing, he turned toward the doorway, leaving Leah behind.

Rage such as Destiny had never known filled her as Dermond strode across the room toward her. She wanted nothing more at the moment than to attack the monster who had done this to her sister. To fling herself at him, hitting, biting, scratching, hurting him in any way she could.

Instead she floated there, helplessly, as he walked right through her and out the door, leaving her empty and shattered.

"Don't go there. For me."

Even as she watched her sister curled up on the bed, crying, even as she tried to move toward Leah, wanting to comfort her, she heard Jesse's voice again and felt herself torn apart, breaking into little pieces scattered on the wind.

She had no choice. She had never had any choice.

And if saving her sister meant losing Jesse, it was a price she'd have to pay.

Chapter 24

This feeling, this completely foreign emotion, filled his chest, almost painfully, causing his breath to shudder past the odd thickening in his throat.

Jesse studied the face of the woman sleeping in his arms, memorizing every little detail. He hesitated to wake her, fearing the tenuous bond formed between them last night would crumble and disappear, like dried leaves blown away in the wind.

He knew how strongly Destiny felt about going with him when he left here today to rescue her sister, how much she wanted to be physically present when he reached the people who held Leah. And yet, in spite of that, she agreed to remain behind.

For him.

With the possible exception of his sister, no woman

he'd ever known had put his feelings ahead of her own. None had given him a gift as precious as the gift of trust Destiny had handed him last night. Not ever.

It almost made him want to take her along with him, just to see her eyes glow with happiness.

Almost.

Not enough to take a risk with her safety, though. Not enough to risk her life.

His body betrayed him with another shuddering breath and he could have sworn his heart actually skipped a beat at the thought of losing her.

How had he allowed this to happen? Allowed her to crawl under his skin and burrow in so deep he couldn't imagine life without her.

A tiny moan escaped her barely parted lips. Her eyes moved rapidly under her closed lids and a single tear slowly slid down the side of her face, as if the dream she was lost in upset her.

He considered not waking her, wondering if what she experienced now was simply a normal nightmare or one of her visions. But the sun was already shining in through the cracks in the wall and there was little doubt that Devlin would arrive soon.

"Come on, babe. Time to wake up." He nuzzled against her neck, breathing her sweet scent deep into his lungs and holding it there for safekeeping.

Her eyes flickered open, a mixture of panic and sorrow skittering through them before she caught herself and shuttered away her emotions.

Guilt gnawed at the edges of his resolve. Though he might try to convince himself it was only the remnants of her dream reflected in her waking expression, he couldn't make himself believe it. He was responsible for those emotions.

Still, he'd rather have her sad and worried than falling into the hands of the Nuadians. If anything were to happen to her . . . No, he couldn't even think about that. He'd find a way to make it all up to her later, just as he'd find some way to keep her near him when all of this was over.

She was up and dressed, huddled on a bench against the wall by the time Devlin arrived, misery shining around her like a halo.

What a perfect pair they were, Jesse reflected. Her misery and his guilt.

"As soon as Devlin has shown me the portal, he'll be back to take you to his family's home. You'll be safe there until I come back for you." Jesse watched Destiny for any response.

She nodded, not meeting his eyes.

It was as they'd agreed when Devlin made the suggestion, an excellent plan. If only he could drive that haunted look from her expression. Even when she bravely tried for a smile, she still looked as if tears would follow shortly.

"Here." He reached into his pocket, pulling out the flat little flashlight he always carried. "Take this."

"How long do you think I'm going to be here?" she asked, the doubt in her eyes reflected in her voice as she clutched the tiny piece of metal in her fist.

"Not long enough to need that. But you have it." It was the only thing he had with him other than his phone. The only thing he had to leave with her.

This was so much easier with a typical client. He'd

never given their responses a second thought when it came to leaving them behind to wait.

But Destiny wasn't just a client. Somewhere in the last twenty-four hours, he'd finally given up pretending, even with himself, that their relationship was purely business. When the one you left behind was someone you cared deeply about, the logical action wasn't necessarily the easy one.

"Try to finish your breakfast, babe. Devlin will be back before you know it." He kissed the top of her head and walked away, out the door Devlin held open.

The thought of her sitting there in the murky light of that little shed alone for the next few hours hung heavy on his heart. So quiet. So miserable. So compliant.

So unlike Destiny.

He'd gone less than three yards from the cabin when his suspicions kicked in. It was the quiet, compliant part that had gotten to him.

If she were a woman like all the others he'd known, one who would willingly do anything to keep his checkbook open, those actions might have made sense.

But that wasn't Destiny. She'd already shown that neither his money nor his name impressed her.

No, when Destiny got quiet and compliant, things were not as they seemed. If his experience with her had taught him anything, those behaviors in her simply meant she was busy plotting.

"Wait a second." Spotting a long wooden bench in front of the cabin, Jesse made his decision.

He motioned for Devlin to come along as he backtracked to the shed, stopping to lift one end of the

A few worrisome moments staring down the different trails and Destiny slapped a hand over her mouth to
smother a chuckle.

To think she'd hoped the horse Devlin led along behind him would help her by being noisy. The animal
had done much better than that. He'd left physical evidence of the track they took.

Soft, smelly evidence, plopped right in the middle of
the trail.

Carefully stepping over the fresh pile of horse dung,
Destiny headed out, hurrying to catch sight of the men
who'd thought to leave her behind.

"I will see to her care, Guardian. She will be safe with
my family." Devlin spoke as he pushed aside a chunk of
shrubbery, revealing an opening into the world of man.

"Thank you." Jesse ducked his head as he stepped
through the portal, back into the Mortal World.

"No need to thank me. It is the least I can do. Until
your return, Guardian." Devlin bowed his head as he
backed away.

Jesse found himself staring at the face of the weathered, moss-covered stone where his friend had stood
only seconds before. It was easily as large as a normal-
sized woman. A carving stood out on the rock face,
clearly visible to him now that he'd passed through the
portal. A carving that matched the mark on his arm.

The stone was part of an abandoned circle, over-
grown and long forgotten. The circle still sat in a
mostly wooded area but through the trees Jesse could
a new home under construction, though no work-
n were around at the moment.

heavy bench. Devlin followed, and shortly they managed to block the doorway with the heavy slab of wood.

His concern might have been without merit, but
now he wouldn't have to worry. If she truly planned to
sit and wait for Devlin's return, it made no difference.

But if his gut was right on this one, and she tried to
come after him, he'd nipped that little problem in the
bud. There was no way Destiny would be able to open
that door and follow.

On her feet, pacing, Destiny scrubbed at her face.

How long was long enough to wait? She'd never tried
to trail after someone before and seriously doubted her
ability to find their tracks. Which meant she needed
to be close enough behind to hear them or see where
they'd gone without being so close they caught her following them.

They were on foot, though Devlin was taking his
horse so he could return more quickly. Maybe she'd get
lucky and the horse would be a noisy companion.

Her sense of time passing was off, thanks to a raging case of nerves. It already felt like the men had been
gone forever, though she knew it was only minutes.

Long enough.

Decision made, she strode to the door to peek out.
Just to make sure they were out of sight.

Quietly, stealthily, she turned the knob and pushed.

The door didn't budge.

"What the heck?" she muttered, shoving harder, putting her shoulder into it.

No movement at all.

Next to the door, she bent over, placing her eye to

one of the knotholes in the wood of the wall. Though her vision was obstructed, she could see what looked like half a tree trunk with legs blocking the doorway.

They'd locked her in?

"Aargh!" she yelled in frustration, straightening to stomp across the room. Turning, she crossed her arms under her breasts and stared at the offending door.

He hadn't trusted her. The nerve of that man! Here she'd been willing to give up what she wanted most for him and he hadn't trusted her. Granted, she had planned to follow him anyway, but he hadn't known that.

Or he shouldn't have.

"Dammit," she muttered, pacing again. Trapped like a rat in a box. Stuck in this Faerie world.

Her steps slowed. Faerie world. Just like her own world, Jesse had said, except with magic.

Magic?

Before she allowed herself time to scoff, she remembered Robert's advice to accept and move on.

It didn't have to be logical. It just was. She accepted that.

She was Faerie. Half, anyway. Enough that she had Faerie magic flowing in her veins. Magic strong enough to manifest itself in the Mortal World. Her dreams proved that.

So how could she use it here?

If her power lay in her sleeping thoughts at home, perhaps here, in a world filled with magic, it would inhabit her waking thoughts as well.

She stared at the door, concentrating. She imagined she could see through it, as if it were glass. Imagined the bench moving away from the door. Imagined she could

hear the scrape of its heavy wooden feet trenches into the dry earth as it slid along

Not allowing herself to think on the imp what she'd just imagined, not even for a m strode to the door, turned the knob, and pus ting her whole weight into the process.

The door swung open and Destiny fell landing with a thud on her hands and knees. Not ful, but effective.

Standing up, she brushed the dirt from her onto her pants and scanned the little clearing where cabin stood, refusing to let her eyes stray to the be by the door. She didn't want to spend much time thin ing about what she'd just done or even really want try to understand it.

If she could make things move in this world simply by thinking about it, with no knowledge or training, what kinds of things could the people who lived here their whole lives do?

It was too scary to let her mind wander down th path for long.

Instead she needed to put her energy into figu out how to find the men and the doorway she ne She might have threatened to try every door Realm of Faerie until she found the right one, would take time she didn't have. Besides, th headed to the exact door she needed.

How on earth was she going to follow t had no idea which way they'd gone. Trail three directions and they could have taken them. Tracking someone through the w hardly her forte.

He shook his head in sorrow at the loss of history. In time, man would unknowingly eliminate the majority of the remaining portals between the worlds.

He flipped open his cell phone as he made his way through the forest, hunting the nearest road. He punched in a speed dial code, and two rings later, Peter's greeting crackled across the line.

"Peter, I need your help."

"Jess? Good God, man! Your tracking signal freakin' disappeared. Where are you? We've been worried sick."

"Scotland. And before you even ask, it's a long story and now's not the time for it." His best bet was to keep Peter focused on the task at hand. "I'm near a stone circle called Achnatone. I'm going to need transportation and all the intel you gathered on any castles around Fleenasmore."

"Switch on your GPS so I can track you." Peter's voice slipped from concerned friend into professional backup without missing a beat. "Hold on. You're already there. I have you now. You're roughly a mile and a half out of Fleenasmore, give or take. Nearest town is Auldearn, but there's a village within about a mile of your location. Littlemill. Robert's due to land in Inverness within the hour and the airport is within ten miles of there. I'll send over coordinates for the two of you to meet up in Littlemill. You can plan your next move from there."

"Good. Thanks, buddy." Jesse ended the conversation to pick up the incoming message with directions to his rendezvous spot in Littlemill.

Leave it to Robert to stick to the plan to fly to Scotland, no matter what. His friend's much-appreciated tenacity meant he'd have the backup he needed when he confronted Dermond and the redhead, Adira.

Reaching the road, just as Peter's coordinates showed, Jesse headed for town. When Robert arrived, they'd head for Fleenasmore and check every possible location Peter had found. They'd go door to door if necessary, but he didn't plan to let another day pass without finding Destiny's sister.

After what she'd given up for him, it was the least he could do for the woman who meant everything to him.

Destiny crouched down behind the big tree, shimmying backward to hide under the ferns covering the forest floor. If there was anything down here under this foliage even remotely resembling a spider, she was going to be royally pissed.

Tracking hadn't been nearly as difficult as she'd expected, probably because the men made no effort to hide their trail. After all, they had no reason to suspect they would be followed.

Destiny tried to ignore the twinge of guilt she felt at that realization. She was too close to her destination to let a little thing like a guilty conscience get in her way.

The doorway she sought had to be very close. She'd ducked behind this tree, hiding herself in the heavy forest growth because ahead of her Devlin had emerged from a thickly wooded area.

Alone.

That meant Jesse must have gone through the doorway already.

She'd had plenty of time to plan her next step. No

more blundering blindly for her. After Devlin had passed by and she felt it safe, she'd search out the doorway. Then she'd wait, giving Jesse time to get far enough away from the portal that he wouldn't see her exit.

Nothing could bring her plans to a screeching halt faster than his standing there when she emerged from the doorway.

Since she had no idea how far from Fleenasmore she would be when she entered her world, her first step would be to find someone who could give her directions.

The next step was finding the castle and her sister. At that point, her plans dwindled away to nothing, but she'd determined not to worry about what she'd do when she made it that far. There was still time to work on those plans.

For now she had plenty of obstacles at hand to overcome.

The pounding of hooves thundered past her hiding place and Destiny held her breath, releasing it only as the sound faded in the distance.

She would wait after she located the doorway, but not too long. Devlin would no doubt come looking for her as soon as he found her missing. Having him catch her on this side of the door would be just as bad as bumping into Jesse standing on the other side.

Crawling out of her hiding place, she peeked around the tree, emerging onto the trail only after she'd assured herself the Fae was indeed gone.

The doorway itself was easy enough to find once she entered the thicket of trees. Its carvings stood out like a beacon.

She paced back and forth, nervously trying to decide

whether enough time had passed since Jesse had gone through. Finally, after what felt like hours, she pushed against the carving and stepped through the doorway to her own world, relieved to find herself alone.

The portal opened into a forest, but unlike the one in which she'd entered the doorway, this one was clearly in the Mortal World. Through the trees she saw a construction site and headed in that direction. If someone was building a house there might be people around doing the work.

The closer she got to the unfinished home, the more apparent it became that no one was working there today. None of the usual construction noise drifted her way.

"Okay, Ms. Strategy Queen," she muttered to herself, walking around the empty job site. "What now?"

This was no more than a minor setback. She wouldn't let it stop her. The dirt road from the house had to lead somewhere. The workers, when they did come, must use this way to get here from wherever they came from. All she needed to do was follow the road to a highway or street and she'd find people who could give her directions.

In spite of her best intentions, faith in her plan had begun to falter by the time she found herself near a paved road. Only when she spotted a figure on a bicycle headed her way did her spirits begin to lift.

She ran her fingers quickly through her hair, thinking for the first time that she must look as though she'd just rolled out of bed and gone for a hike.

"Hello," she called out, waving her arm as the boy approached, thankful he was young enough he probably wouldn't even notice how rumpled she looked. "Could you help me?"

The boy, who appeared to be in his early teens, pulled to a halt, balancing himself with one foot flat on the pavement as he surveyed the area around them.

"What are you doing out here all by yerself, miss?"

She'd been working on what to say to the first person she met ever since she left the construction site, but now that someone had arrived, she found her mouth suddenly dry as she stumbled into her story.

"I . . . I've gotten separated from my friends and I'm all turned around. Could you maybe give me directions to Fleenasmore?"

"Yer from the States, aren't you?" he asked, a big grin breaking over his face. "I can tell from yer lovely accent."

Her accent? He was more interested in her accent than in her story. Nerves still on edge, Destiny stifled the nervous giggle she felt bubbling to the surface and settled instead for returning the boy's infectious grin. "Yes. And I'm really lost."

"You've no a need to worry, miss. I live no too far from here and me mum should be home from the shop this time of day." The boy stuck his hand out, his grin growing even larger. "Edan Abernethy, at yer service."

She took the hand offered to her. "Thank you so much, Edan. I'm Destiny Noble."

Edan hopped off his bike to walk beside her along the road. "It's a little over two kilometers to Fleenasmore. I've ridden it many a time, but you look as though you've been walking about lost in the woods for quite some while, so it might be too far for you on foot."

She felt her face heat as she nodded her agreement. Obviously even very young men paid attention to how a woman looked. And though her feet were getting tired, she wasn't so tired that she'd miss an opportunity to learn what she could from Edan.

"So, you know the countryside around Fleenasmore pretty well?"

"Of course I do. Like the back of my hand," the boy returned, his shoulders straightening with pride. "I can find any spot you care to name."

Apparently the male ego was also firmly in place by early teens.

"Are there many old castles around?"

"Aye, there are a few, I suppose." Edan snorted a laugh, shaking his head. "You Americans and yer castles. Yer all the same."

In a short time, they turned off onto a smaller paved lane leading to a cluster of small whitewashed cottages.

"Here we are," Edan announced as he headed toward the door of one of the small houses. "You can have yerself a wee rest before we head out for Fleenasmore."

Destiny paused at the entrance, feeling suddenly unsure of herself. Facing an adult with her lies felt scarier than dealing with a kid.

"Wait. You don't think your mom will mind you dragging a perfect stranger into the house?"

"No at all," a feminine voice lilted from inside. "My Irish granny always told me I should never turn any stranger away. It could be an angel in disguise."

The owner of the voice appeared at the doorway, holding out her hand. "I'm Corinne Abernethy. Welcome to my home."

A pleasantly plump woman with light brown hair, Corinne had the most welcoming smile Destiny could remember having seen.

"This is Destiny Noble, mum. She got herself lost from her friends in the forest out near Achnatone and needs to get to Fleenasmore to find them."

Destiny followed the boy and his mother into the kitchen, allowing Edan to roll with his understanding of her story. It sounded much better coming from him anyway.

"Make yerself to home at the table," Corinne invited as she plopped a tea bag into a cup and filled it with steaming water before setting it in front of Destiny. "We'll have ourselves a lovely cup and some biscuits before we motor you over to Fleenasmore."

The aroma of the strong dark tea made Destiny's mouth water and she found herself eagerly reaching for the shortbreads Corinne placed on the table.

"Ms. Noble is looking for castles to visit around Fleenasmore," Edan added as he washed his hands before sitting down next to her.

"Castles, is it?" Corinne asked thoughtfully. "We've nothing nearby so grand as to compare to Cawdor or Brodie castles, of course, but we've a few small, private homes I could point out. Most locals would be more than happy to give you a tour if you asked."

"But no MacIntosh Hall, eh, Mum?" Edan laughed as he swept up another cookie.

"That's for certain, lad. I'd no even show that one to our guest. Especially not with herself in residence again." Corinne shook her head emphatically.

"The MacIntoshes don't like strangers dropping in?"

That sounded interesting. People holding a kidnapped girl prisoner probably wouldn't be too happy about having uninvited guests stop by for a visit.

"There's no a MacIntosh to be found in the hall these days. It's owned by an outsider who rarely comes to stay, but when she does, oh my!" Corinne shook her head again, her eyebrows arching up to touch the curled bangs she wore. "Her household staff is required to stay on the property when the lady is in residence. Their families say they canna even speak to them on the phone. Thank the saints she's so rarely here."

Destiny sipped at her tea, working up her courage. If she didn't ask, she'd never know.

"This woman, is she a tall, really pretty redhead?" She felt as if she should hold her breath after asking.

"That's her!" Edan blurted out around another cookie.

"If you can call someone with those hard eyes *pretty*," his mother added. "Do you know the woman?"

Sticking as close to the truth as possible seemed the best tack to Destiny. "Not really, but from the description, I think I bumped into her. Maybe you'd be willing to show me her place just so I know where to avoid."

Destiny took another sip of tea, keeping her eyes down, focused on anything but her hostess.

"She has a point, Mum. Best to know where not to go."

"So it is," his mother agreed, rising to refill her cup. "And a lovely home it is, in spite of the woman who owns it. We'll let you take a peek on our way into the village."

Destiny didn't doubt for one second she'd found the

place she hunted. As soon as she knew where the house was, and could manage to get away from the wonderful people who'd welcomed her into their home, she planned to go pay Adira a call.

And if she found that the nightmare she'd had last night was vision and not dream?

Then a visit wasn't the only thing Adira was getting from her. She'd personally see to it that red-haired bitch regretted the day she laid her hands on Leah.

Chapter 25

—◦◦—

"Mistress?" Flynn poked his head into the library as he called out, his eyes darting from one side of the room to the other.

"Over here, Flynn." Adira sighed and put aside the book she'd been trying to read. It wasn't holding her attention anyway. "I see you finally decided to return."

The man's jaw clenched, but he kept his tone respectful when he spoke. "I had a chance last evening to mull over the events of our escape from the desert and I have a concern. I felt I should bring it to your attention immediately, my lady."

He'd do well to have many concerns, as poorly as he'd performed recently. Letting Destiny escape after they'd only just managed to capture the woman was the tip of the iceberg.

It was his fault that she'd been forced to put her

plans on hold last night when the local authorities had arrived. If Flynn had been here as he should have been, he would have been the one to deal with them. It would have been him out at the pub until early this morning instead of Dermond.

Even now, thinking of the inconveniences Flynn had caused her, irritation sparked anew like kindling in a fire. She considered sending him away, ignoring him and his concerns, letting him stew in his incompetent misery a while longer. And yet, there was something smug in his demeanor today that didn't seem to belong. Something there, as if he actually did have knowledge that would benefit her.

As annoying as Flynn could be, he did possess an uncanny ability to dig up the most useful information, a trait that had continued to ensure his value. And his life, although she'd had second thoughts on that after the debacle last night.

Another sigh, this one designed to visibly express her irritation. "What? Out with it, Flynn. What is it?"

"May I sit, my lady?"

Sit? Oh, this had better be good.

She swept her hand out in an artfully careless invitation to join her on her sofa before turning to fix a stare on him.

His eyes, always so haughty, fluttered away from hers for a moment and she felt his unease. She understood his need to please her. Good. That was as it should be.

"Well? I'm waiting. Thanks to your incompetence, I've a busy day ahead of me."

"The woman, Destiny, is obviously working with

someone to locate her sister. Someone who proved a formidable obstacle in the desert."

"And?" she snapped. She was quite aware of the existence of new players in their little game. "I fail to see why this is of any importance to me right now."

Flynn arched an eyebrow in a smug expression she detested. It reminded her of too many men in her past. Too many who'd thought themselves so much better than she.

"As I sat alone last evening, mulling over the situation, it occurred to me that you had spoken of our destination in front of the woman. What's to stop them from coming here?"

His breath played across her face, setting the loose tendrils of hair brushing against her cheek as his words slammed into her like a physical assault.

She had never even considered the possibility, had barely remembered the conversation with Dermond about coming to the castle. It had meant nothing more to her at the time than soothing words intended to placate her distressed lover.

How stupid of her to have missed such an important slipup. How careless. Already they had been here long enough that those working for Ms. Noble could be on their way to this very spot. Could be closing in at this very moment.

"It shouldn't prove much of a challenge to find our location. There can't be too many places in the world named Fleenasmore." Flynn put words to her own fears as he edged closer, the heat of his skin burning against her arm.

Damn the Fates. She needed to come up with an

alternative—and quickly—or she risked losing everything.

Too late, she realized her panic must have been reflected on her face. Flynn had moved closer still, leaning in toward her, his hand resting over hers on the sofa.

"Can we travel in the same way we did from the desert? We could build a circle of stones here." This time Flynn's gaze didn't falter or move away.

Though she didn't like to share any more information than necessary with Flynn, this might be one of those necessary times.

"No. A circle won't work here." It wasn't stones, it was the energy lines she needed, and she didn't know of any travel points near this castle. It would take time to do more research to find other such locations. The only one she could remember offhand, other than through the stone circle on Lewis, was at Avebury.

The ancient text she'd found in Reynard's library would certainly be useful now. Unfortunately she'd left it with her other possessions at the estate in France when she'd traveled to the States.

With no readily available options of her own, this might be a good time to test Flynn's resourcefulness.

"Do you have any ideas, Flynn?"

"Perhaps. There is a company Reynard used in Scotland once before. Helicopter transport. It's the fastest route to get away from here. Shall I arrange to have one sent to pick us up?"

That would have to do. Get them safely away from here and far enough south to send for a car. Then they could drive to Avebury. From there she'd figure out how to get home to France.

She nodded her agreement, reaching out to run one finger down the side of Flynn's face. She'd seriously underestimated the man. Perhaps she should be making better use of his intelligence than she had up to this point. Better use of him.

"And when we reach our new destination, Flynn"—she trailed her hand down his chest to his leg, allowing her fingertips to tighten against the inside of his thigh as she leaned in closer—"would you join me in my bedchamber?"

A smile played about the corners of his lips, and from the calculating gleam in his eyes, she knew he'd accept her offer.

"Of course." He paused, holding her gaze. "Whatever you ask, my queen."

Adira watched Flynn's sure stride from the room, too pleased with his long-overdue acceptance of her rightful position to waste time chafing over this minor setback. She'd dropped her guard and gotten sloppy, but she was nothing if not a quick learner. She would be more careful in the future.

For now, she'd find a way to get the girl back to her estate in France. Once there, they'd be safe and she could continue with her plans.

One day soon, everything would be hers to command.

Chapter 26

~⁓~

Destiny stood in a thicket of trees across the road from the driveway entrance to MacIntosh Hall, studying the layout, desperate for anything even remotely resembling a plan to pop into her head.

The house was massive, and though it might not qualify as a true castle, it was three stories of old stone, with an iron-railing-enclosed widow's walk at the top. To Destiny, it looked like something creepy and haunted, right out of the 1800s.

A huge stone walkway snaked around the perimeter of the house, and the whole thing sat in what looked from the road like a park, with flowers and trees and huge bushes everywhere.

She *could* wait for Jesse to show up. In fact, that was probably the smart thing to do. Smart for her safety, maybe, but not smart for her sister's well-being.

While she'd been watching, a car had pulled into the drive and a man had gotten out. Not just any man, but the one who'd taken her captive at the Farmers' Market in Sedona.

He certainly didn't seem any worse off for the gunshot wound in his arm.

Her stomach tightened as she realized why he wouldn't. They had Leah. They would have forced her to heal his wounds.

Dammit! The idea that these creeps would put her sister through that kind of pain stoked her anger all over again.

No, she wasn't waiting. She was going in there.

Walking up the drive and knocking on the front door to announce that she had come to rescue Leah was hardly the way to go. She needed something better than that.

The stone fence that surrounded the property was only a little more than waist high. Surely she could climb over and slip around back unnoticed, using the trees and foliage for cover. They obviously didn't have guard dogs, since there was no gate at the driveway to keep them inside.

That was it, then. That was her plan. Maybe Jesse would show up in time to help and maybe not. But whatever happened, she wasn't waiting any longer. She didn't intend to give those monsters one more second with her sister.

She made her way back down the road, keeping to the cover of the trees, coming out into the open and crossing the road only after she'd gotten far enough away from the house she couldn't see it clearly through the foliage.

Hoisting herself up to sit on the fence, she swung her feet over the top and dropped down to the other side, slipping behind the nearest tree, waiting for her clamoring heart to slow down.

She could do this. She could. There was no way she was letting the fear hold her back again. Not now. Not this close.

Again, staying to the cover of trees and bushes, she made her way to the back of the house, where she hit her first major snag.

While the front of the property reminded her of a park with its wealth of trees, bushes, and flowers, the back was more like a golf course or a football field. The open green space seemed to go on forever.

Again her heart began to pound, her lungs constricting as if a fat man sat on her chest.

"No." She spoke aloud to assure herself this was real. "It doesn't matter." She simply needed to be more careful. More watchful.

Only one door in sight along the back, but lots of windows. Given time, and cover, perhaps she could find one unlocked.

Three tall, thin juniper-like trees stood clustered at each corner of the house, their branches perfectly shaped, joining to form a point reaching well above the first story. If she could make it to one of those, it would give her cover to decide on her next move.

Two deep breaths to prepare herself and she raced across the open lawn, squeezing behind the evergreens.

Eyes closed, she fought to catch her breath. When all this was over, she really needed to get on a regular exercise plan.

Opening her eyes, she found herself inches from one of the largest spiders she'd ever seen. Paralyzed, she watched as the beast sat there in its massive web, staring at her like she was lunch.

Stop it!

It's just a bug. Okay, not really a bug, but a buglike thing. Squashable, like a bug. But she'd have to touch it, and there's no way in hell she could bring herself to touch it. It would be better to have every one of the evil Faeries in that house come out and catch her than have that creature touch her skin.

Stop it!

Near hysteria over a spider? Focus. Leah was what was important, not this almost-insect.

But if she'd already found one spider in these trees . . .

"No!" she whispered under her breath. Keep going. Don't think about it. Don't think about anything but Leah.

Pressing her back against the wall, she bent her knees and slid down until she reached all fours, intending to crawl around the corner behind the cover of the trees. As she started forward, her knee scraped against a piece of metal protruding from the ground.

Examining it closely, she realized it wasn't just a piece of metal. It was a handle. She brushed the layers of pine needles away to discover it was a handle attached to a wooden door in the earth.

Fully expecting it to be locked on the inside, she pulled up, shocked when the wood gave way and lifted, puffing a smell of musty air in its wake.

Although the branches of the trees prevented her

from fully opening the door, the space was already wide enough for her to slip inside.

Once again her heart pounded, and she fought the urge to retch as she used her sleeve to wipe the spiderwebs from the opening. The black hole yawned before her like a wickedly toothless mouth, and she made her decision before she had time to scare herself out of going. Turning, she stuck her legs into the hole and slipped feetfirst down into the inky darkness.

Chapter 27

❧

"*H*old on." Robert put a hand on Jesse's forearm to get his attention. "The Gordon woman is headed in this direction."

Jesse shoved the car into PARK and bit back his irritation. They'd just wasted the last hour "touring" this woman's home, pretending to take photos for a book they were writing about castle homes in Scotland. By the time Mrs. Gordon, her white curls bouncing with every step, toddled herself down the drive, there was no telling how much more time they'd lose.

"Patience is a virtue," Robert murmured under his breath, though whether his reminder was aimed at himself or his companion, Jesse wasn't sure. He pasted a smile on his face all the same.

Peter's research had left them with four possibilities of homes around Fleenasmore likely to fit the description of the one they sought. This was the second on their list.

They'd quickly ruled out the first when they learned a family with young children lived there. The mother had reluctantly offered to let them inside, but from her harried look and the screaming toddler in her arms, Jesse had felt certain it would be a waste of time.

They'd offered to come back later and the woman had seemed genuinely grateful not to have to be a gracious hostess at the moment.

Mrs. Gordon, on the other hand, was thrilled with the idea of having photos of her home appear in their book, in any book. Jesse had quickly realized their visit was the social highlight of the woman's week. Week, hell. What was he thinking? More like the highlight of her year. She'd talked their ears off as she'd led them through the winding hallways of her home, her metal-tipped cane tapping in time to her halting steps, her yapping dust ball of a dog winding around everyone's feet.

Robert rolled down his window as the elderly woman reached them.

"Oh, lads, I almost let you get away without the biscuits I promised. I know how young lads love the shortbread." She chuckled as she handed over her napkin-wrapped bundle.

"You shouldn't have troubled yerself, Mrs. Gordon, though we certainly do appreciate yer thoughtfulness."

Jesse's fake smile grudgingly turned into a real one as he watched his friend in action. Robert was always the model of proper behavior with women, whether they were eighteen or eighty.

"Will you be headed to the MacGuivers' home next? Poor Lucy with all those babies, she's run ragged, that's a fact. You may want to come back inside and give her a ring first."

Robert reached out the window and patted Mrs. Gordon's hand. "Thank you, dear lady, but we've already been and set an appointment to go back at a better time. As you say, the lady has her hands full."

"Do you have the Butlers on yer list?" She peered into the car as if she could actually see the list of which she spoke. "Geraldine will be thrilled to have you. We used to get together for tea once a week, but the poor dear has trouble getting out and about now. Company will make her ever so happy, though you may have to wait until her son gets home from work to lead you round through the house for yer photos. Young Arthur's a special constable, you know. A busy man, he is."

Jesse drew a mental line through their visit to the Butler home.

"And MacIntosh Hall?" Jesse leaned across toward the open window as he spoke. "Do you know the owners there very well?"

Mrs. Gordon's lips tightened as he spoke. She leaned farther in, her eyes darting to each side as if she wanted to make sure no one else would hear what she had to say.

"I'd avoid that place if I were you. Oh, they've a lovely garden there, they do. But they dinna deserve to be in yer book. Not at all." She shook her head for emphasis.

"Really?"

Robert's one-word question was all it took to set the

woman off again, her eyes sparkling with her excitement to share a little local gossip.

"The woman who owns the property is only there now and again, and a tyrant she is, too. Hateful to her staff—all locals, you know? Geraldine was telling me on the phone just before you came that her lad had been called out to MacIntosh Hall just last evening to accompany the neighborhood warden. They went to speak to that awful woman about reports of her security people openly carrying weapons on the property." She shook her head, setting her white curls bobbing. "Imagine that. Security. Like she thinks she's one of those stars on the telly or something. No. You'll no want to be going there, I assure you."

"Thanks again for all yer help, Mrs. Gordon. And for the tea and crackers," Robert called out as they pulled away, turning a solemn face to Jesse. "We'll be headed to MacIntosh Hall next, I assume?"

"That we will," Jesse answered.

Mrs. Gordon might have wasted their time showing them every room in her great house, but he felt sure she'd set them on the right track at last.

Chapter 28

The drop down into the hole was farther than Destiny had expected. She hit the uneven ground with a thud, her legs buckling under her and her elbow smacking into the sharp edge of a wooden stair as she fell backward.

Too bad she hadn't known those were there earlier.

She stood, feeling every inch of the fall she'd just taken as she tried to get her bearings. The newly discovered stairs were behind her, the outside wall to her left. Straight ahead, close enough for her to reach out and touch: another wall. Any door or stairs leading into the house would have to be to her right.

Trouble was, in the pitch-blackness of the cellar where she stood, one wrong step and she'd easily lose her sense of direction.

Her purse, its shoulder strap slung across her chest,

had worked its way around behind her, bouncing against her butt with each step. She pulled it back around, digging inside for Jesse's flashlight. Considering the small size of her purse and its meager contents, she didn't have any trouble finding the light. It lay right next to the small kitchen knife she'd "borrowed" from the Abernethy's home when she'd helped clean up after their tea time.

One more thing her conscience would require her to return when this was over. Assuming she got the opportunity to do so.

No. No more negative thinking.

Using the tiny beam of light, she made her way across what turned out to be a rather small room to a set of stone stairs, obviously installed back in a day when safety railings weren't considered a building-code necessity.

At the top of the stairs she found a door, long unused if the webs covering it were any gauge. She might have escaped a barricaded room once today, but this was the real world. Any Faerie magic she might have wouldn't do diddly for her here if she found herself locked in. She held her breath and turned the knob, thankful the door opened a crack.

A stealthy peek out the tiny opening reassured her no one was waiting for her, and she pushed the door just far enough to allow her to squeeze out.

The hallway she found herself in was dark, but nothing like the little cellar room below. She pocketed the light, fearing someone might see its reflection.

She had to make a quick choice. To her left down the long hallway stood a closed door. The other direction offered another set of stairs, this one winding its way up. Chances were they would be holding her sister upstairs, not on ground level, so she headed for the stairs.

By the time she reached the door at the top, she felt certain she'd gone more than one floor level. The door at the top was old and narrow, with a keyhole so large Destiny could imagine an ancient iron key being used for it. She hoped against hope that she wouldn't need one of those massive keys, and, as with the others, this door opened easily.

As she started to step into another long, dingy hallway, she heard steps approaching from the other end and quickly ducked back inside. Squatting down, she peered through the keyhole, watching as a woman in a black-and-white maid's uniform entered the hallway from a staircase at the other end and made her way to one of the doors lining the hall. As soon as the woman disappeared inside the room, Destiny stood and slipped through the door.

Should she stay low like in the movies or creep down the hall on tiptoe? After only seconds of indecision, she tossed out all the Hollywood stereotypes and bolted toward the other end, hoping her soft-soled sneakers would cushion any noise.

She passed another, smaller set of stairs going up, deciding to ignore them for now, and headed instead for the end of the hallway where the maid had entered.

The stairs here led down. It was only when she reached the bottom and cracked open the door that she realized the floor she'd just come from must have been the servants' quarters.

This level looked entirely different. The hallway was

wide and airy with rooms leading off only one side. The other side had large windows looking out over the parklike property surrounding the mansion.

Two steps into the hallway, an eerie feeling of déjà vu swept over Destiny—so strong it stopped her in her tracks.

She'd been here before.

Panic bubbled up in her chest and she slapped a hand over her mouth, not trusting herself to keep her horror silent.

The nightmare hadn't been a dream at all. It had been a vision. Everything she'd seen, everything her sister had suffered—it had all been real.

Anger seethed and bubbled, replacing all her fear.

They were going to pay for what they'd put Leah through. Once she had her sister safely out of this place, she was coming back. And when she did, all the Faeries in Wyddecol wouldn't be able to stop her from hunting down that pig, Dermond Tyren, and making his sorry ass so much sorrier than he ever could have imagined.

Images of pulling the trigger on a really lethal-looking weapon danced through her mind, energizing her. Focusing her. She might not know how right now, but she was going to make that man pay.

But first she had to find Leah and get her out of this hell before it was too late.

She stopped at the door she recognized from her vision, straightening her shoulders and taking a deep breath before she entered.

As in the vision, the room was beautifully decorated, but unlike what she'd seen before, suitcases stood by the door as if someone had packed them and they were waiting to be taken away.

She hurried across the room to the door she remembered. The door that had led to Leah in her vision.

The knob turned easily in her hand. She opened the door and slipped inside, instantly greeted by her sister's angry yell to get out.

Destiny ducked as something whooshed past her head, smashing against the door behind her.

"Oh my God, Destiny!" Leah stood beside her bed, one hand covering her mouth. "What are you doing here? They'll be back any minute. They'll find you."

One quick glance down at the remains of the lamp her sister had thrown and Destiny ran to Leah, throwing her arms around the girl. "What do you think I'm doing? I'm getting you out of here." She brushed back the silken strands from Leah's face, noting with renewed anger the dark circles under her sister's eyes.

Dermond would pay for those, too, she silently promised herself.

"You can't." Leah lifted her arm, jangling a small metal chain, one end attached to a band at her wrist, the other fastened to the large post on the headboard. "We'd need the key."

Damn. There had been only a strap of some sort in her vision.

"Okay. Just give me time to think." Destiny scanned the room for something, anything that could help them, finding absolutely nothing.

"It's no good, Desi. We're out of time," her sister whispered. "Hear that? She's coming."

Outside the door, the sound of heels clipped across the tile floor, headed their way.

"Over there." Leah pointed to a tall wardrobe centered on the far wall. "Get inside and stay quiet."

Destiny raced across the room, shoving the clothing out of her way as she climbed inside and turned to pull the double doors closed. Through the gap of the closing, she watched as Leah's bedroom door swung open.

"Time to go, pet."

Adira entered, dressed in white from head to toe, like some sick parody of angelic innocence. Destiny hated every inch of the woman, from her white stilettos to the tacky see-through blouse that left nothing to the imagination.

The woman stopped inside the doorway, obviously inspecting the broken lamp on the floor.

"Having another temper tantrum, were we?" She made a tsking noise and shook her head as she approached Leah. "What did I tell you about that? Lucky for you, pet, our ride's due any minute. No time for punishment right now."

She twirled a little chain around her finger as she walked. Round and round it swung, with a tiny key hanging from the chain like a small silver charm.

That was all Destiny needed to see.

While she waited for Adira to unlock her sister, she pulled her purse around to her front and reached inside, her fingers closing over the knife.

Her hand shook as she pulled the weapon from her purse. Could she use it on the woman? Could she cross the room and actually stab the knife into a living person?

"We'll take up the matter of your behavior later. In fact, I've just decided on a surprise for you, pet." Adira unlocked the band from the bed and wrapped it around her hand, dragging Leah forward and shoving the girl toward the door in front of her. "When Dermond comes to you tonight, I'm going to send along a second playmate. After satisfying both Dermond and Flynn, we'll see if you still have enough energy to break my things tomorrow."

Destiny had her answer. Yes. Oh, hell yes.

Quietly she opened the doors of the wardrobe and crossed the room. Slipping behind Adira as the two women reached the doorway, Destiny held the knife with both hands, her arms raised above her head. Her mind filled with the hateful things this monster planned to do to her little sister as she plunged the knife down into the woman's back.

Adira screamed and fell to her knees.

"Go!" Destiny shouted at her sister, who stood, eyes wide with shock, staring at her tormentor on the floor.

"I told you to go!" she ordered again, more quietly than before, stopping only to snatch the tiny key and chain from the floor where Adira had dropped it.

The bedroom door she slammed did little to muffle the woman's furious screams and threats, all of which she blocked from her mind.

Destiny grabbed her sister's hand, leading her back the way she had entered, down the hallway and up the stairs. Halfway down the hall, the door ahead of them opened and Destiny dove for the small staircase she'd bypassed earlier, shoving Leah up ahead of her.

The staircase was dark and narrow, ending at a door

so low she was forced to duck her head as they passed through, out onto the open widow's walk.

She leaned against the door, catching her breath, only now realizing her mistake. There was no cover up here, no place to hide. She didn't see any way down, either.

Her blunder had them trapped like animals, waiting for the hunters to pick them off.

Chapter 29

The throb in her back was like nothing Adira had ever experienced, but it paled in comparison to the fury she felt.

She pushed up to her knees, gasping for breath against the pain as she tried to reach whatever that bitch had stabbed her with. She could just touch it with her fingertips, but couldn't get a grip.

In her agony, her outrage, she screamed again, stopping only when the door burst open.

"By the Mother, Adira! What's happened to you?" Dermond dropped to one knee at her side, clutching uselessly at her arm, one hand sliding down her back.

"I've been stabbed, you idiot! What does it look like?"

"It looks like a kitchen knife," Flynn stated quietly, entering and dropping to her side.

He pulled the utensil from her back, eliciting another scream of agony she couldn't hold back.

"Who's done this to you? The girl?" Flynn pressed his hand tightly against her back, leaning her body against his. "Get me a towel, Dermond. Can't you see she's bleeding?"

Adira rested her forehead on Flynn's shoulder, grateful to have him here to deal with Dermond.

"Not the girl. Her sister. She's here. As you warned." The pain made it hard to speak. The white-hot fury made it difficult to think. "Get them. Get them both."

She'd have them hold that troublesome bitch down when they caught her. Make her watch her sister's agony as Leah healed what she had done. See how she liked watching her own sister writhe on the floor as she felt the burn of a knife blade sink into her back.

"You go after them," Flynn ordered when Dermond handed him a towel. "I'll get Adira to the helicopter. I hear it coming in now. If you think you can handle both of them, that is."

Dermond growled his rage, hesitating only a moment before he started for the door, his face grim with his intent.

"Alive, Dermond!" Adira forced the words through gritted teeth. "I want them alive. Both of them."

"But . . . but, she hurt you," he stammered, staring down at his blood-covered hand.

"You heard your queen." Flynn stood, lifting her in his arms. "You have your orders. She wants the women alive. We didn't pass them on the way here so they must have gone up to the servant's floor. Start there."

Dermond pulled a weapon from his shoulder harness

as he ran from the room ahead of them. She would have to depend on him to catch her valuable prey while Flynn carried her downstairs and out to the back of the mansion.

"When Dermond brings them to you, they'll need to be taught they can't get away with attacking you again."

"Yes," she whispered, allowing her cheek to rest against Flynn's broad shoulder. She'd made the right decision earlier. Dermond might be the more beautiful of the two, but Flynn was more intelligent. More cunning. More of what she needed at her side.

She was their queen now, as she always should have been, though Reynard had denied her that honor. He'd held it over her head, out of her reach, to keep her in her place. To remind her of her status. To excuse his abuse of her.

All that was changed now. Reynard was gone and she'd never serve as anyone's underling again. She'd be the one to mete out humiliation and punishment. She'd be the one to deny favors. Or to grant them when she chose.

"Perhaps I'll leave their punishment to you, Flynn. So long as they're undamaged for my purposes." Undamaged and able to produce litter after litter of magically gifted mongrels, all for her use.

All to add to her power.

She felt better already.

Chapter 30

—◦—

"*H*oly Mother of God. Look up there!" Robert pointed toward the roof of the house as Jesse slammed on his brakes.

No. It couldn't be. Jesse's breath caught in his throat.

But it was. Destiny and her sister on the widow's walk of MacIntosh Hall.

Robert was out the door the second they stopped, banging his fist on the back of the car. "Open the damned trunk."

Jesse met him at the back, in time to have a Glock shoved into his hands. The weapon was old and not the model he preferred, but it would have to do. Peter had done a thorough job in having weapons waiting for Robbie when he arrived.

He slapped the bullet cartridge into place and grabbed a spare before he started forward.

"You'll cover them from here," he barked, knowing the order was unnecessary. Even with a strange rifle, Robbie was their best chance of protecting the women on the roof until he could reach them.

He jumped the fence without breaking his stride, staying low, using the trees for cover. Halfway to the house, he felt the wind pick up, along with the noise level, as a helicopter flew in low over the property, sounding like it landed somewhere behind.

He took advantage of the distraction and sprinted for the front door, waiting only for a count of one before kicking it open.

Weapon at the ready, he headed straight for the stairs, his back to the wall as he climbed.

He wasn't even going to think about how she'd managed to end up on the goddamned roof when she was supposed to be safe and sound at Devlin's home in Wyddecol.

A bloody handprint splayed on the doorsill of the second door he reached stopped him cold. Droplets that had splashed on the tile at his feet led to a bedroom beyond and a dark red puddle on the floor. The metallic smell would have identified it as blood even to a blind man.

He raced from the room, to the end of the hallway. Starting up the stairs, he found another, larger handprint on the wall, assurance he headed in the right direction if nothing else.

His mind raced ahead, his nerves strung tight.

Whose blood? Please, not hers.

Why hadn't she stayed put as she'd promised?

Because she hadn't promised, he realized with a start. She'd only agreed to stay behind. And she'd only done that for him.

Goddammit!

A third, fainter print marked the corner up to another set of stairs, narrower and darker, ending at the top with a small doorway.

When he caught up with her, he was going to wring her silly neck. Shake her until her teeth rattled. Hold her in his arms and never let her away from his side again.

And if they'd harmed her in any way, he'd kill every single one of them with his bare hands if it took the rest of his life to hunt them down.

Chapter 31

"Take this." Destiny tossed the tiny silver key to Leah. "Get down to the far end of this balcony and scrunch yourself into a corner."

"You think they'll come up here after us?" Leah's fingers shook, setting the key clinking against the metal band around her wrist.

"Don't you? Now get down there." Destiny braced her back against the door, knowing she had no real chance of keeping anyone from coming through.

A loud thrumming noise sounded above her, accompanied by a fierce wind whipping at her hair and clothing. A helicopter passed low overhead—so close she could see the two figures in its glass bubble. Wild thoughts of grabbing on to one of its legs and making a spectacular escape flashed through her mind but not for more than an instant. James Bond she was not.

The doorknob pressed against her back and she braced her legs for the onslaught, but it did no good. In one massive push, the door burst open, throwing her forward and to the rough floor of the widow's walk.

From her hands and knees she looked up to find a very angry Dermond Tyren glaring down at her. He grabbed a handful of her hair and jerked up. Forcing her to her feet, he hauled her close to him.

"That you'll get to take your next breath, bitch, is a gift from my queen," he hissed, a fine shower of spittle spraying over her face with his words. "If it were up to me, you'd be dead."

"Funny, I feel the same way about you, asshole."

His eyes narrowed and he tightened his grip on her hair, dragging her at his side as he walked forward. She looked up at him through the prism of tears that formed in response to the pain.

"What have you done with . . . there she is." Satisfaction evident in his voice, Dermond strode forward, wearing the evil smile Destiny remembered from the night she'd first met him.

"Run!" she shouted, throwing her whole weight against Dermond, hoping to give her sister a chance to get away.

The force of her weight didn't faze the man in the least. He threw her to the ground like tossing aside a rag doll before he turned to her sister. Leah crouched in her corner as if frozen to her spot against the wall. He hoisted her to her feet with a grip around her arm.

Silent tears streaked Leah's face and her whole body shook in his grasp.

"Let her go, you bastard!" Destiny screamed, scrambling to her feet and hurling herself at him again.

He met her charge with a vicious backhand, sending her reeling backward and knocking her from her feet. Her body hit the stone wall of the house and slid down. She could feel the stone scraping into her skin as she fell.

She lay still, her face to the cold, rough surface of the walkway, waiting for the pain to stop, or at least to dull enough to allow her to catch her breath. Everything hurt.

Turning her head, she opened her eyes to find Dermond still had his hands on her sister, leering down at Leah, pulling her closer.

She had to do something to stop him. But first she'd have to get up.

Jesse climbed the stairs cautiously, his weapon at the ready. If only his emotions were at the ready, too. He seriously needed to pull it together. Usually the adrenaline kicked in at this point on a mission, the point of imminent confrontation, but what he felt now wasn't anything like his normal experience.

He'd been in similar situations too many times to count, so why couldn't he slip into his calm, efficient, business-as-usual mode now, when he needed it most? Why couldn't he detach himself from the bloody handprints on the wall?

Because none of those other times had ever put the woman he loved at risk.

His foot faltered on the next step as the realization drove home.

The woman he loved.

When had that happened?

His heart pounded in his chest as he tried to accept the idea. Tried to deal with it.

It didn't matter when it had happened. It just had. And when all of this was over, he'd make sure Destiny knew it.

He understood for the first time how his sister must have felt all those years ago when they'd gone to rescue her husband. The driving determination. The crippling fear.

It was like nothing he'd experienced before. These unfamiliar, raw emotions tore at him, scattering his thoughts, robbing him of his focus.

Until he heard Destiny's scream.

In four long strides, he was at the door. Shoulder down, he burst through, expecting the worst.

And finding it.

Two steps ahead of him, Destiny appeared to hold herself upright against the wall by sheer force of will. Blood striped the side of her face nearest him. Farther down the walkway, Tyren held a terrified Leah.

Jesse realized instantly that the way Tyren had positioned himself with the girl gave Robert precious little chance to pick him off. With his own rifle, Robert could have made such a shot, but he'd undoubtedly be reluctant to take that kind of chance with an unfamiliar weapon unless he believed he had no alternative.

Jesse knew because it was the same problem he faced.

Still, given the scene in front of him, it seemed uncharacteristic of Robert not to have taken some action by now.

Ahead of him, Dermond raised his gun, pointing

straight at Destiny, who had begun to inch her way toward the man and her sister.

"Stop where you are. My queen might want you alive, but I certainly don't. I'd love to have an excuse to end your miserable life."

"Exactly how I feel about you," Destiny responded, her voice trembling.

Jesse knew what was coming next as well as if he were the one with visions of the future. He read the deadly intent in Tyren's eyes.

When Destiny pushed away from the wall, his world moved into slow motion. Quickly calculating the risk, he aimed and pulled the trigger on his weapon.

The silence that greeted him was a sure sign of misfire. In the precious seconds it took to slam the butt of the gun against his palm and rack another bullet, he did the only thing he believed would be fast enough to save her.

He threw himself in front of her, knocking her to the ground. As they fell, he heard the expected crack and felt the burn of the bullet as it tore into his back.

"Looks like your hired help is too late, Ms. Noble. I certainly hope you didn't pay this fellow too much."

Dermond's cruel laughter came closer as Destiny scrambled to climb out from under the weight of Jesse's body.

On hands and knees, she stroked the cheek she knew so well, the day's growth of whiskers rough against her fingertips.

This couldn't be happening. Not to him. Not to the one man in all the world she loved.

She placed a hand on his back, the stain growing on his shirt, wet and sticky under her palm.

"No." The denial escaped her on a breath. "No!" she screamed, crouching over him, pulling her body close to his.

She couldn't lose him like this.

Leah swung her fist at Dermond's face, but he grabbed her wrist with his free hand, blocking her intended blow.

"Oh, what's this, pet? You finally get your wits about you? Aren't you happy to see to me? Surely you didn't think I'd let you get away. Not after having been robbed of the chance to break you in properly." He mashed his mouth to Leah's in a grotesque parody of a kiss, crushing her body to his.

Destiny watched from the ground, a red haze of hatred washing over her, filling her mind, urging her forward.

After all that monster had done to Leah, and now to Jesse, she couldn't stand the thought of his winning.

With a scream of rage she didn't recognize as her own, she launched herself at the man, fastening one hand in his hair as she clawed at his eyes with her other.

Her only thoughts were of hurting him, of forcing his hands off her sister. She kicked wildly, scraping at his skin with her fingernails, as he tried to fend her off. His arm brushed past her face and she fastened her teeth onto his bicep, biting down as hard as she could, taking pleasure in his yelp of pain.

"Run!" she ordered through clenched teeth, wanting her sister away from this place. Away from this man.

Dermond laughed at her desperation. "Running will do her no good. Adira will hunt her to ground wherever she goes. She'll never be free of us."

And then Destiny's feet lifted from the ground, Dermond's fingers digging into her throat, squeezing tighter as he swung her around and slammed her body against the metal railing.

Her vision sparkled with bright bursts of light and she clawed at Dermond's fingers, desperate for air as he increased the pressure of his hold. From a great distance, she heard Leah's screams for him to let go, but her ears felt too full to allow her to fully understand the words.

She didn't matter anymore. At least she'd managed to give Leah a chance to get away. No price was too great to pay for that. Hadn't she already lost her future?

Her arm dropped to her side; she was too weak to fight any longer. She focused her gaze on Jesse, his body somehow now slumped against the door, a pool of his own blood forming beside him.

Just as she'd been willing to give her life to save Leah, he had offered up his to save her. As her vision tunneled to darkness, she wanted him to be the last thing she saw.

Perhaps she wouldn't lose him. Perhaps they'd spend their eternity together in a better place.

Adira felt Flynn's arms tighten around her as they neared the slowly beating rotors of the big machine. He lifted her up and other hands pulled her out of his arms and into the craft, lowering her into a small leather seat.

Flynn and the others could handle the details of their

escape. The only matter of any importance to her was having her pet on board before they took off.

She allowed her head to rest against the back of her seat, her eyes too heavy to hold them open. Someone stretched a harness across her shoulder and lap but she ignored their touch.

"She's taken enough of the girls' blood. Even with this wound, she should heal well enough in time."

Adira had only seconds to wonder at Flynn's audacity in discussing her so intimately with a stranger before he spoke again.

"Any sign of Dermond and the women?"

"No. But we spotted a shooter in place outside the gates when we flew over. We radioed down. The danger should be neutralized by now."

Adira didn't recognize the voice and wasn't sure she had the energy or interest to open her eyes to look his way. Surely this was all something Flynn could manage.

"Gunshots!" the strange voice yelled, and suddenly the rotors sounded as if they beat faster.

"Flynn?" Her own voice sounded weak and far away amid the obvious clamor of activity in the confines of the helicopter. "We can't leave yet. Not without my Leah. I must have my pet."

"Too late! We have to go now!"

The stranger, no doubt the pilot, clearly didn't understand who was in charge.

"Flynn! We wait. You must do as your queen orders." The effort of forcefully issuing the command had drained the last of her energy. Apparently Flynn still lacked the necessary discipline after all.

"Queen?" A voice from her past, so very close to her

ear his breath danced across her face. "I don't think so, *ma belle*. Flynn wisely takes his orders from me, as he always has."

Adira's body trembled against her will as she forced her eyes open to stare into the emotionless gaze of the man who'd made her life a living hell for centuries.

"Reynard." She struggled unsuccessfully to mask the horror she felt. "You're alive."

Reynard Servans stroked one long finger across her cheek, smiling his promise of pain to come as the helicopter lifted off the ground.

"That I am, *ma belle intelligente*. We must go now, but never fear. Since you've discovered for me what the girl can do, I will tear the world apart to locate your little pet again. I will find her, I promise. There is no country in which she will be able to hide from me. The days of freedom are short."

With a sinking heart, Adira realized his threat was directed as much at her as at Leah.

She'd come so close and now it was all in vain.

A shot rang out and the steel grip on Destiny's throat loosened as Dermond jerked back from the railing. A second shot sounded almost simultaneously, this one very near. Dermond pitched forward again, pinning Destiny between the metal railing and his body.

She coughed, her throat in spasms as she gasped in great lungfuls of fresh, renewing oxygen. But when she lifted her gaze, his eyes, pinched with pain and hatred, captured hers and he tightened his hold, threatening to once again cut off her air.

Grappling at his fingers, she fought to be free of

him as his full body weight pressed into her, bending her backward over the railing three stories above the ground.

"She'll never be free of my queen," he hissed, spraying spittle over her face.

Leah screamed from somewhere behind him, and a great force hit Dermond's body, pressing the metal rail into the small of Destiny's back until her feet lifted off the ground and she thought her bones would break. And then the pressure was gone.

Dermond, already off balance, pitched over the rail, his arms and legs flailing wildly through the air in the moments it took him to hit the stone walkway below.

"Rot in hell, Faerie, where you belong." Leah stared down at the broken body three stories below, her arms wrapped around her middle.

Unable to stand on her own, Destiny fell to her knees and crawled the few feet separating her from where Jesse had propped himself against the wall, his gun lying across one knee.

"You're safe now, babe," he murmured, lifting a hand to her hair as she wrapped her arms around him.

She pulled away, brushing her fingers across his face, and he closed his eyes. His breathing was shallow and his skin so cold, it terrified her. When his hand fell back to his side, she found herself sobbing.

So much blood. His blood. Everywhere.

"Hold on, Jesse. Talk to me, please. Don't give up. I love you. Do you hear me? Don't you dare die on me. I love you!"

"Love you, too, babe." His eyes flickered open and he tried for a smile but failed. "Bad timing. Us."

"No, don't say that!" she pleaded. Her mind whirled with her panic. "Help me!" she screamed, not knowing who she begged for assistance, but only that she needed it.

"Get out of my way." Leah shoved her roughly to the side as she kneeled down in her place. "You should have told me sooner he was important to you." With one deep breath, she lowered her head and laid her hands on Jesse's chest.

Leah's body convulsed and stiffened, but she held on until at last she threw back her head and screamed, a shriek so primal and animal, Destiny knew she would remember the sound for the rest of her life.

Her sister's eyes rolled back in her head and her body went limp, falling on top of Jesse.

Destiny crawled back to them, the two people she loved most in the world, in a heap before her. Fear nearly paralyzed her, but she fought it, reaching out to place one hand on her sister's back, the other on Jesse's chest.

The door behind them burst open and Robert stood over her, his eyes wild, blood dripping from a gash on his head.

"They're alive!" was all she managed before dissolving into tears.

Chapter 32

"We'll find a way to keep your sister safe. You have to trust me on this. I meant every word I said back there. We'll find a way to work things out."

Destiny stared up into Jesse's eyes, wanting more than anything in the world to believe his words. In the garden just now, he'd told her again that he loved her. He'd told her he wanted to spend the rest of his life with her.

Everything she'd ever dreamed of, all standing right here in front of her, was almost more than she could believe.

She nodded her agreement and he gave her shoulder a reassuring squeeze.

"Come on, Des. Let's do this thing," he encouraged, leading her into the massive living room at Sithean Fardach where his entire family had gathered.

"You don't know them like I do," Leah said earnestly as they entered. "They'll find me." She looked small and frightened huddled into the big chair in the corner of the room.

They'd come here, to the home of Jesse's sister and brother-in-law two days ago. Since then, it seemed to Destiny as if his entire family had descended on them, all of them in this room right now.

She reached out a hand and Jesse captured it, squeezing lightly as he pulled her to sit on the arm of the chair where he sat down.

"We'll no let that happen, lass. Dinna you worry yerself about it." Connor, Jesse's brother-in-law, leaned against the doorjamb next to Robert, both of them looking like guards on either side of the main entrance to the room.

Destiny didn't miss the look of concern that passed between Connor and Jesse.

Leah apparently saw it as well. She shook her head, her serious brown eyes haunted in her fear. "You don't understand. You have no idea what they're like. They're Faeries, for God's sake. I'll never be safe from them."

"No all Fae are evil, Leah." Mairi, Connor's sister, spoke from her spot on the sofa next to her husband, Ramos. "But we do know what you fear. We've dealt with these renegades ourselves."

Leah shook her head but didn't answer, tears dripping down her cheeks.

Destiny crossed the room to kneel at her sister's side. "We'll think of something. I promise. That's why we're all here."

"There's nowhere I'll be safe," Leah whispered, clutching at Destiny's hand. "I can't go back to them, Desi. I can't."

"You'll stay here." Connor spoke again, authoritatively, as if his decision ended the conversation.

"That won't be enough to keep her safe," Ramos countered. "She's right. Adira won't give up. We need a more secure spot."

"I believe I may have a solution." Pol, who'd sat quietly throughout the conversation, rose to his feet. He glanced sadly toward Leah, as if well aware of her fear of him. "If our young guest is agreeable to my plan."

Leah sat up straighter, her mouth drawn tight. In spite of her show of bravery, the hand Destiny held trembled. "What is it?"

"If the Nuadians' new strength prevents Leah from living out her life without fear, perhaps we err in looking for a *where* to take her. Perhaps we should consider a *when*."

That sounded insane. But she must have missed something in what he said because everyone else in the room went deathly quiet, exchanging looks with one another as if they completely understood.

"It could be done," Jesse's sister said thoughtfully. "We'd need to choose the spot carefully. Send her to someone we can trust."

"And we couldn't send her alone," Mairi added as if she had warmed to the idea.

"Send her where?" Destiny asked, staring straight at Jesse. "What's going on here that I'm not getting?"

"Not where," Jesse explained. "When. They're talking about sending Leah back in time."

"That's crazy." She looked around the room at all the serious faces, settling on Pol's at last, only to realize she was fighting windmills again. After all she'd been through, all she'd seen and experienced, she should know better.

Still, Leah would never agree to leave. . . .

"You could really do that?" Her sister's voice sounded hopeful for the first time since they'd arrived here.

"Yes," Jesse answered. "They can. But you'd need to understand, once you're there, there's no guarantee they could ever get you back."

"Like you think I'd ever want to come back?" Leah scooted forward in her chair. "I'd spend my life in the Stone Age if it meant I could be safe from . . . from them."

Destiny's throat tightened as she listened to the excited chatter around her, horrified that they discussed sending her sister away forever as if it were no more than a spring-break vacation.

"I promise it's not the Stone Age we're considering." Cate smiled. "But it would be a very, very different life for you."

"Anywhere." Leah tightened her grip on Destiny's hand. "How soon can I go?"

"As quickly as we can make a few preparations," Cate answered.

"And decide who's to accompany you," Mairi added.

"I'll go."

Jesse rose from his chair and crossed to where

Destiny kneeled next to Leah's chair. His words set Destiny's heart pounding. If they couldn't guarantee getting Leah back, how would they get Jesse home? What about the life together they'd discussed over the last two days?

But she didn't get the chance to ask.

"Not you." Leah shook her head, rejecting his offer. "I didn't go through all that agony to save your life just so you could abandon my sister. You need to take care of her."

Heat bloomed up Destiny's neck to her face, but her embarrassment fled when she looked up into Jesse's gaze.

"She already knows that I have every intention of doing exactly that," he said.

He reached for her hand and she gave it, forgetting everyone around them for the moment as he gently pulled her to her feet and into his arms.

"I'll do it. I'm the one to go with the lass."

Robert's statement broke into her thoughts, bringing her back to the moment.

"Yer sure about this?" Connor questioned.

"Even knowing we can't guarantee getting you back here?" Cate added.

Robert shrugged. "I've a small matter left undone by my unplanned departure. It would be good to get it off my conscience after all this time."

Destiny looked down at her sister, feeling as if her heart were being torn from her chest. Leah was all the family she had in the world. Letting her go would be the most painful thing she'd ever done.

But she had to think of Leah's feelings, not her own.

Her sister's beautiful face shone with hope for the first time in days.

Destiny took a deep breath, choking back her fear, doing her best to disguise her own pain. "Are you sure about this, baby?"

"I am. I feel like they're offering me a chance to actually live my life now." Leah took her hand, squeezing tightly. "I don't want to leave you alone, with no family at all. I know how this hurts you, but I can't stay here. Please understand, Desi. I can't. I'm so afraid, all the time. I feel like I'm losing my mind."

"You don't have to worry about Destiny. She won't be alone." Jesse pulled her back against him, wrapping his arms around her protectively. "I'll always be there for her."

Destiny turned in his embrace, gazing up into the beautiful eyes of the man she loved with all her heart.

"And as for family, she'll have plenty." He gently framed her face with his palms, speaking directly to her. "After all, everyone in this room will be her family once we're married. If she'll still have me, now that I've announced it to the world."

If she'd still have him? Hadn't she already told him there was nothing in the world she wanted more than to spend the rest of her life with him? She just hadn't expected him to tell everyone so soon.

"I don't care who you tell. I love you," she managed before giving in to the bittersweet tears she could no longer hold back.

Jesse kissed her then and the room erupted around them. Congratulations, questions, planning—it was all a blur of chatter and details to Destiny, the individual voices and words drowned out by Jesse's whispered, "I meant it when I said I'll love you forever."

Gazing into the loving eyes of her Soulmate, Destiny knew she'd been wrong before. Faerie-tale happy-ever-afters truly did exist in her world.

And she was looking at hers.

Epilogue

Destiny climbed down off the little stool and stepped back to have a proper look at her handiwork.

That was the perfect spot to hang her picture.

Jesse had carved the frame for her and she'd picked out her favorite wedding photos to place in the little ovals behind the brightly colored matting.

Photographs from both of her weddings.

The first had been an unofficial, hurried, informal affair, thrown together quickly in Cate and Connor's living room so that she could have her sister as her maid of honor, before Leah left.

The second, a full three months later, had been a hugely lavish family celebration, overflowing with Jesse's relatives and friends—so many she still couldn't keep all of them straight.

To someone who'd grown up with such a small circle

of family, Jesse and his extended clan, both Mortal and Faerie, continued to be a source of happy amazement.

She certainly had no more worries about being alone. In fact, she was learning that sometimes the problem with such a large family was in carving out enough alone time.

She took another step back and bumped into Jesse's large leather recliner. She sat down and tucked one foot under her, admiring her little home, remembering the first time Jesse had brought her to this wonderful house in the Highlands of Scotland.

"See?" he'd pointed out proudly, that infectious grin of his covering his face. "It's all ours. I told you once before I was a real Highlander. And now you're one, too."

Their home was no rival to the huge manor house his sister and her family lived in, but Destiny loved this place, and steadfastly ignored Jesse's efforts to talk her into building a larger house on the property.

"Hey, babe." Jesse hurried in the door, a wicked grin on his beautiful face. "Finally got rid of Dallyn. That is one Faerie who just does not know how to take a hint."

Destiny smiled up at him, her heart doing a little happy dance as he crossed the room to her.

Dallyn, Jesse's friend and mentor, showed up at their home regularly. Interestingly enough, usually at mealtime.

After moving here she'd learned that the property housed a Portal to the Faerie Realm. It was the reason Jesse had bought the land in the first place. He was a Guardian and the sanctity of the Portal was his responsibility.

She'd been surprised to learn that until recently Guardians weren't allowed to marry. Apparently the Faerie Realm was modernizing itself, though. Either that or they were hard up for a few good Guardians, so the rules had changed.

Jesse grabbed her hands and hoisted her from his chair, dropping down in her place and pulling her to sit in his lap.

"Now where were we before that pesky Faerie boss of mine showed up?" He grinned at her and wiggled his eyebrows in a most attractively suggestive manner. "Ah yes, I remember."

He slipped a hand under her heavy sweater and in one quick move popped open the hooks on her bra.

"We were just getting ready for some baby-making practice."

It was his standard line. They'd agreed from the first that they both wanted children. Someday. But for now they were enjoying each other. Their "practice sessions" were very much a part of that enjoyment.

"No, Jess," she giggled as she playfully slapped away his fingers tickling along her sides, "we can't yet. Mairi's supposed to call with an update tonight."

As it had turned out, her sister-in-law, Mairi, was a professor of medieval studies and an amazing expert at research documentation. The woman had been hunting for clues for her on Leah's life.

Destiny preferred to think of anything they might find as news from her sister living far away rather than something that had happened in the past. She knew it was little more than a mind game she played with herself, but it made Leah's being gone easier for her.

She shook her head as she did every time she considered what they'd done. The whole time-travel thing was still hard to wrap her mind around and any tidbits Mairi might find would only serve to make her feel better about her sister's decision. She just wanted to know that Leah ended up with her own happy-ever-after.

"So?" Jesse drew her attention back to him, nibbling at her earlobe in the way he knew drove her wild. "We can hear the phone from the bedroom."

"Yeah, right," she laughed. "Like we'd stop to come answer it?"

"Fair enough." He stood up, forcing her to her feet as well. "Never let it be said that Jesse Coryell can't compromise."

"What are you doing?" She watched in amusement as he picked up their coffee table and carried it out of the room.

When he returned, he left little doubt as to his intent as he tossed throw pillows from the sofa to the rug in front of the fireplace just before he pulled his shirt up and over his head.

"Well, that's not fair," she complained, trying without success to hide her own grin.

He always knew how to get to her. She could never resist that man's chest, with its solid wall of rippling muscles. It was like having her own private pinup guy at her beck and call, and even after all these months, she sometimes wanted to pinch herself to believe he was really hers.

"Come on, babe." He plopped down on the rug and wiggled his fingers at her. "Don't keep me waiting."

She dropped to her knees beside him, reaching out

to run her hand down his chest, but he stopped her, grabbing her wrist before she could touch him.

"Sweater first," he encouraged.

She happily lifted her top up and over her head and then allowed him to pull her down to lie next to him.

He tangled his fingers into her hair and moved in close for the kiss she wanted.

When he drew away, she opened her eyes to find him smiling down at her.

"You're the best thing that ever happened to me, Des."

She returned his smile and reached for him. "I know I am, you big Highlander."

She was, after all, his Destiny.

POCKET BOOKS
PROUDLY PRESENTS

A Highlander's Homecoming

Melissa Mayhue

Coming soon from Pocket Books

Turn the page for a sneak peek of
A Highlander's Homecoming . . .

Prologue

---

*T*hundering hooves echoed through the dark, misty Scottish night.

Robert MacQuarrie leaned into his massive black destrier, urging his mount to give him all the speed the animal could muster.

He rode like a madman, without care or caution, his only thought to reach Merlegh Hall before it was too late.

Before his friend Thomas MacGahan took his last gasping breath.

Thomas was more than a mere friend. If not for him, Robert would have died in battle on the point of a Saracen spear. A spear Thomas had taken in his stead and lived to tell about it.

He owed his life to Thomas.

Robert kicked the sides of the wild beast he rode, demanding more.

Faster.

"He calls for you, MacQuarrie. To be at his side when his spirit departs his poor broken body. To carry out his last request."

The watery blue eyes of the old shepherd who'd brought Robert the message haunted his memory now.

"I dinna believe he'll last through the night. You maun ride hard, lad, if yer to fulfill his final wishes."

Robert had just left an audience with his king, Alexander, when the messenger had arrived. In two days' time, he was to accompany Alexander to the wedding of a fellow King's Guard, Connor MacKiernan. Learning his friend Connor had found a woman to settle his wandering ways, Robert had left the king's chambers with a full heart. Though there was the little matter of the rumored threats against Connor's safety that concerned Alexander, it should be nothing too serious. Certainly nothing that he and Connor couldn't handle together. They were, after all, two of Alexander's finest.

Robert had been on his way to find a celebratory libation or two when the exhausted shepherd had entered his life, sending him on this urgent mission.

For Thomas to die in such a fashion simply wasn't fair.

Not that Robbie considered himself a man to waste undue thoughts as to the fairness of life. The things he'd seen, the places he'd been had taught him well the lesson that there was little in the way of fairness in this world.

But this, the loss of a warrior like Thomas to such a cruel twist of fate, brought a cry of foul to Robert's lips.

Thomas, who'd survived more battles than most men ever fought, laid low by a sharp turn in a muddy track at mountain's edge.

The warrior and his horse had tumbled over the precipice, the great beast landing on top of Thomas on a ledge below. Now, instead of a quick death on a glorious battlefield, Thomas faced the slow agony of drowning in his own fluids.

Ahead of him, the flicker of light caught Robert's attention.

Torches. He'd reached his destination at last.

The faces surrounding him as he made his way into the hall were a blur, his thoughts focused on one man only.

A woman—a redhead, of all the foul luck—approached, the keys dangling from her waist announcing her position as Merlegh's chatelaine.

"Come with me. He awaits you."

Following the woman's steps, he hurried through the dark hallways. If the shepherd's warning hadn't been enough to convince him of the seriousness of Thomas's condition, the grim faces he saw here certainly did. The expressions of those he passed and that of the chatelaine. A redhead. Always a bad sign for him.

After what seemed an eternity, he entered his friend's room.

"Robbie? Is that you?" Thomas lay in the center of a great bed, his voice weak as he asked the question.

Shock coursed through Robert. Though his friend was little more than a decade his senior, the man lying in that bed looked to be ancient, his face ashen and drawn with his pain. Only his piercing blue gaze remained the same. A cough wracked his body, sending small flecks of blood to decorate his lips and the linen bedding where he lay.

Robert shook himself to action, crossing to Thomas's side. "Aye, my friend. I've come as fast as I could."

"I've a boon to ask of you." Thomas paused, a strange gurgling sound coming from his chest as he strained to fill his lungs with air.

"Anything you ask. My debt to you is without bounds."

Robert fought the urge to take his friend's hand. He recognized the signs of Thomas's coming end all too well.

"I've a daughter," Thomas rasped. "You must give me yer oath to protect her. When you carry word of my death, my father will be—" His words dissolved in another struggle to breathe.

"You need say no more, my friend. I will go to yer family and see to yer daughter."

Thomas reached out, his hand wavering unsteadily in the space between them until his fingers clutched at Robert's wrist. "It's no that my father is an evil man. It's just that Isabella is . . ." He struggled as if trying to find the words he wanted. "She is different, as was her mother. She's but an innocent child, and with me gone she will need protection and guidance. It willna be easy. Your oath, Robbie. I must hear yer oath."

"I'll see to yer daughter's safety. I swear it. On my honor. On my life."

"Then it is done." Thomas's fingers slipped from Robert's wrist. "Go now. Leave me in peace to meet my saints."

A strange tightening of Robert's throat prevented his speaking. He bowed his head respectfully and turned, leaving his friend for the last time.

Fighting for the emotional distance he regularly wore as part of his persona, he mounted his barely rested horse and set out for his return to Alexander's court.

As close as they'd been, he'd never known that Thomas had a child. And what had he meant by saying she was different? What would he do with a girl child? He was a warrior. A good one, too. A knight to King Alexander III of Scotland. A family had no part in his plans. Someday, certainly, but not now.

Apparently his plans would have to change.

MacQuarrie Keep had been a fine place for him growing up and though he would not return to his family home to live, he felt certain the child would be welcomed there.

With something of a plan formed, he pushed all thoughts from his mind. None of them mattered for the moment. When he finished the task his king had assigned him, nothing save death would keep him from his oath to see to the safety of Isabella MacGahan.

Chapter One

As it turned out, death was exactly what had kept Robert from fulfilling his oath to protect Isabella MacGahan. Or more precisely, the death he would have suffered had Connor MacKiernan's bride not whisked him more than seven hundred years into the future through the use of her Faerie Magic.

The battle they'd fought to overpower those who had sought to murder Connor and Cate had been hard won. Robert had paid with a sword to his rib cage that would have ended his life had he not had the expert medical care afforded him in this new time.

That had been almost ten years ago, and though he found this new world to be very much to his liking, his failure to carry out his oath to Thomas had haunted him since that day.

Leaning against the doorjamb next to his friend Connor, Robert pushed away the memories of his past as he scanned the people in this room. His new clan surrounded him here. MacKiernan, Coryell, Navarro—all as much a part of him now as if the blood of the MacQuarries ran through their veins. A good thing since he'd likely never have the family he'd imagined in his youth.

A fierce loyalty to each and every one of the people in the room surged up in his breast as he forced himself to concentrate on the urgent matters at hand.

"You don't know them like I do. They'll find me." Leah Noble spoke up from the corner of the massive living room in Connor's home. The teenager sank back into her chair, arms crossed defensively in front of her, almost as if she hoped to make herself invisible.

As a Faerie descendant, Leah carried the gift of the Fae Magic. That gift had made her the target of the evil Nuadians, renegade Fae exiled to the Mortal World. They'd held her prisoner for over a month, subjecting her to things no young woman should endure. She and her older sister, Destiny, had gone through hell before Jesse Coryell, with Robert's help, had rescued them.

Now they were both here in Connor's living room, surrounded by those who would do everything in their power to change the women's lives for the better. And considering how many of those present were also of Fae heritage, that *power* was considerable.

Destiny reached out a hand and Jesse captured it, pulling her to sit on the arm of his chair, close to him.

Robert smiled to himself at the seemingly unconscious action. Anyone with eyes could see that his friend Jesse had found his Soulmate.

"We'll no let that happen, lass. Dinna you worry yerself about it." Though Connor spoke with absolute confidence, his expression betrayed the concern they all felt.

Leah shook her head, her serious brown eyes haunted in her fear. "You don't understand. You have no idea what they're like. They're Faeries, for God's sake. I'll never be safe from them."

"No all Fae are evil, Leah." Mairi, Connor's sister, spoke from her spot on the sofa next to her husband, Ramos Navarro. "And we do know what you fear. We've dealt with these renegades ourselves."

Leah rejected their comments with a shake of her head but didn't answer, tears dripping down her cheeks.

Destiny dropped Jesse's hand and crossed to kneel at her sister's side. "We'll think of something, I promise. That's why we're all here."

"There's nowhere I'll be safe," Leah whispered, clutching at Destiny's hand. "I can't go back to them, Desi. I can't."

"You'll stay here." Connor spoke again, taking charge as he was wont to do. As if by the power of his sheer will he could eliminate the young woman's fear.

"That won't be enough to keep her safe." Ramos turned to look up at his brother-in-law. "She's right. Adira won't give up. They'll find her and then every female in this family will be at risk. We have to find a more secure spot."

Robert silently agreed. If anyone in this room should know what the Nuadians were capable of, it would be Ramos. After all, he'd been raised by the devil's spawn.

"I believe I may have a solution." Pol, High Prince of Fae, long-distant ancestor of many in this room, rose to his feet. He turned his gaze toward Leah, his eyes sad. "If our young guest is agreeable to my suggestion, that is."

Leah straightened in her seat, her face a mask of false bravado. "I'll do anything that keeps me away from that woman. What's your plan?"

"If the Nuadians' new strength prevents Leah from living out her life without fear, perhaps we err in looking for a *where* to take her. Perhaps we should consider a *when*."

Of course! Leave it to the Prince to point out the obvious. The solution that none of them would have ever considered on their own.

"I suppose it could be done," Cate said thoughtfully. "We'd need to choose the spot carefully. Send her to someone we could trust."

"But we couldn't send her alone," Mairi added her voice, betraying her growing excitement to anyone who knew her as well as Robert did.

"Send her where?" Destiny's face had taken on an ashen look of panicked suspicion that spilled over into her voice. "What's going on here that I'm not getting?"

"Not where," Jesse explained. "When. They're talking about sending Leah back in time."

"That's crazy."

Robert fought the urge to shake his head. After all the woman had been through, how could she still doubt?

How could she not, he reminded himself. The knowledge that Faeries and magic existed was difficult to work your mind around in the beginning. He'd had his own time to get used to the idea. Destiny would need hers as well.

"You could really do that?" Leah sat up straight, interest lighting her eyes.

"Yes," Jesse answered. "They can. But you'd need to understand, once you're there, there's no guarantee they could ever get you back."

"Like you think I'd ever want to come back?" Leah scooted forward in her chair. "I'd spend my life in the Stone Age if it meant I could be safe from . . . from them."

"I promise it's not the Stone Age we're considering." Cate smiled at the young woman. "But it would be a very, very different life for you."

"Anywhere." Determination radiated around Leah. "How soon can I go?"

"As quickly as we can make a few preparations," Cate answered.

"And decide who's to accompany you," Mairi added.

"I'll go." Jesse rose from his chair and crossed to where Destiny knelt next to Leah's chair.

Robert's spine stiffened. Jesse felt as much brother as friend to Robert after all these years. There was no way he could allow Jesse to take this kind of risk. Not now that he'd discovered the one woman fate had intended for him.

Before he could voice his opinion, Leah rejected the offer herself.

"Not you." She shook her head, her hand fisted on the arms of the chair. "I didn't go through all that agony to save your life just so you could abandon my sister. You need to take care of her."

"She already knows that I have every intention of doing exactly that," his friend responded indignantly.

This time Robert made no attempt to school his expression. If there was a single soul in the room who couldn't see how Jesse felt about Destiny by now, they were too far beyond blind for help. They were lost in the land of stupid.

Those two might need a lot of things going forward, but time apart wasn't one of them. In fact, there was no one sitting in this room who could afford to take the risk of being left behind in time.

Except him. Were he to go, there would be no one left behind to worry over his return. No loving wife. No passel of children.

He pushed the thought away. His was a good life, filled with trusted friends and blessed opportunity. That he seemed destined to live out this lifetime without finding his own Soulmate was out of his control. Had these people not become a part of his life, he would never even have known that he was supposed to have a Soulmate. He would have simply traveled his life's journey alone, accepting what came to him.

He wouldn't waste his days filled with envy for what his friends had found. Perhaps in another lifetime he would cross paths with the one meant for him. For this life, he would simply have to content himself with filling that empty spot in his heart by being the friend, the uncle. He was a warrior. Certainly he could be strong enough to face life alone.

Besides, this could well be his one and only opportunity to redeem himself. A last chance to keep his promise to a dying friend.

As far as the risk was concerned? He scoffed at the idea. He lived on the thrills that came from risk. This situation was a gift, pure and simple.

Taking a step forward, he broke the silence that had fallen in the room.

"I'll do it. I'm the one to go with the lass."

"Yer sure about this?" Connor questioned, his ice blue eyes intent as they turned in Robert's direction.

"Even knowing we can't guarantee getting you back here?" Cate added, her pretty brow wrinkled with concern.

Robert shrugged. His going only made sense. He'd sworn an oath. What happened to him was of little consequence as long as he was able to keep his word. "I've a small matter left undone by my abrupt departure. It would be good to get it off my conscience after all this time."

The one nagging failure of his life. Bad enough to have failed a friend. Inexcusable to have failed a helpless child. Though he would never have children of his own, there was one small girl waiting for him to rescue her, seven hundred years in his past. At long last he'd keep that vow.

Across the room, Jesse chose this moment to announce his intention to marry the woman who gazed adoringly up into his eyes. Right there in front of all of them.

About time the man publicly acknowledged what they all could see.

Robert smiled and shook his head, turning from the celebration erupting around him and heading out toward the silence of the well-shaded grounds surrounding the renovated Scottish castle.

Though he shared his friend's joy, he needed to step

away from it for a moment. Not that he envied his friend. Not that the couple's happiness highlighted the empty place by his own side. The empty place in his heart. He was too strong for such womanly feelings as that. No, it was simply that he needed the quiet and solitude to think. He needed time alone. Time to carefully plan.

There actually were any number of details to take care of before he left. Charlie, his bright-eyed Boston terrier came to mind. He knew Connor would see to picking the dog up from boarding and take it to his home where Charlie would be cared for and well loved. That was no worry. Though the idea he might never see his adoring pup again—that was a bit harder to stomach.

There were other arrangements to make as well. Legal paperwork of some sort would be required. He should set up a power of attorney, turning all his property over to someone.

Just in case.

If all went well, he'd do what needed to be done and then the magic would bring him home. The problem with using Faerie Magic was that it didn't always do the expected, and Robert knew going into this he could well be giving up the life he'd come to love.

When a woman with Cate's considerable Faerie Magic told you she might not be able to get you back home, you'd be well advised to take her seriously. If this was going to end up being a one-way trip, he'd best make sure someone here would have access to his belongings. None of his wonderful toys, not the vehicles or the machinery he'd collected—none of it would do him any good where he was going.

When he was going, he corrected himself. The Highlands of Scotland in 1272. The exact same time he'd left behind all those years ago. As long as they'd determined to hide Leah in the past, he could think of no better time than the one he'd left. It would suit both their needs. He'd be able to fulfill his vow to Thomas, and there were many people in that time they could trust to keep Leah safe.

The Nuadians had vowed to hunt her down, no matter where she went. No one in the room he'd just left doubted for a moment they would do exactly that. But as everyone sitting in that living room had reasoned, while the Nuadians might well track Leah down wherever she hid in this world, they'd have no chance at all of finding her in a completely different time.

He would accompany Leah on her unimaginable journey to thirteenth-century Scotland. He'd see her safely settled.

And then?

Then he'd be free to fulfill the oath he'd made over seven hundred years ago. He'd find Thomas's daughter, Isabella, and take her to his own family's home, where she would be cared for properly.

"Mr. MacQuarrie?"

Robert looked over his shoulder to find Leah picking her way across the damp lawn toward him. Though the young woman herself was almost hidden in the baggy jeans and heavy sweater she wore, she couldn't hide what she most wanted to remove from her identity. Whether it was the long golden hair tossed by the breeze or simply the way she carried herself, there was no denying her Faerie heritage.

If he ever had been blessed with a daughter, he would have wished for one as brave as this girl.

"Robert, lass. Call me Robert. Is there something you need of me?"

She nodded, her eyes fixed on her feet even as the color rose in her cheeks.

"Everyone back there's pretty excited about planning a wedding. I didn't want to interrupt them." She lifted her gaze to meet his steadily. "But I have so many questions. Can you tell me where we'll go? What it will be like?"

"I can try," he answered as he led the way to two garden benches separated by a small table.

When he reached toward her, she flinched, a haunted expression fleeting across her face.

How could he have been so thoughtless? Considering what the lass had been through, he shouldn't be surprised she could bear no man's touch. The filthy Nuadian bastards had kidnapped Leah and held her captive, poked her with needles as they drained her blood to increase their own powers, and all but raped her.

Stepping back a respectful pace, he waited for her to choose one seat before he took the other.

"You've no changed yer mind about going, have you?" Was that the root of her questions?

Her eyes rounded and she shook her head vehemently, her fingers playing over the stone hanging from her neck. "Oh no, not at all. I want to go. We can't leave soon enough as far as I'm concerned." She shrugged and looked out over the expanse of garden. "I just . . . I just want to have some idea of what I'll be facing when I get there. I mean, it's not like we're talking about a trip across the country. I remember from my literature class last year that the language used in medieval Britain was entirely different from what's spoken today. How are we even going to communicate with people?"

Robert nodded thoughtfully. That one had concerned him, too, when he'd first come forward in time. "You'll have no problem, lass. I canna explain how, but the Faerie Magic takes it all into account. What you'll speak, what you'll understand when you arrive in that time—it will all be the same to yer ears and to those around you. The only difference you'll note is that some of yer words are unknown to them, so they'll likely find yer speech patterns to be strange."

"What kinds of words?" Leah leaned toward him, her thirst for knowledge lighting a fire in her eyes.

"Words for those things they've no understanding of. Cars, for example. Or airplanes. Do you get my meaning?"

She nodded thoughtfully, wisps of gold hair falling over her shoulder. "So I don't need to worry about learning a new language. Do you have any idea where we'll go?"

It was Robert's turn to nod slowly. He'd been giving this some thought since the moment he'd volunteered to accompany Leah. "We'll head for the MacQuarrie Keep. I'm thinking you'd be safe there, with my own family."

His parents would welcome her into their home even though he wouldn't be able to stay there himself. Not under the same roof with that redheaded bitch his brother had married. MacQuarrie Keep stopped being his home the day Elizabeth moved in.

When Leah's brow furrowed, he held up a hand to forestall the questions he saw running through her mind. "It's where I came from, lass. *When* I came from, to be more accurate. Just over nine years ago, Jesse's sister, Cate, used her powers to bring me forward in time to save my life. It's too long a story for now, but I'm sure you'll hear the whole of it as we prepare for our journey."

Too long and too painful for him to recount to the lass. Likely the women of the house would fill her in later.

Leah chewed on her bottom lip for a moment before making eye contact again. "Is that why you said you'd go back with me? Because you feel like you have a debt to them? I'd hate to think you're disrupting your whole life because you feel like you have to."

He shook his head. It was a debt that was driving him, all right, but not the one the girl feared.

"Dinna you fret yerself over this, lass. Accompanying you is but a piece of my reason for returning. I've my own purposes to be met in going back."

Purposes long past due.